Sweet Luck

Arizona Heat, Book Two

Hilary Dartt

Also by Hilary Dartt

Arizona Heat Series

Pure Luck

Terrific Luck

Christmas Luck

Love Under the Arizona Sky Series

All the Stars

The Whole Sky

To the Moon

The Mint Creek Ranch Series

My Favorite Story

My Favorite View

My Favorite Place

The Seedling Homestead Series

A Summer of Wonder

A Dream of Home

A Promise of Forever

The Intervention Series

The Dating Intervention

The Marriage Intervention

The Motherhood Intervention

The Garden Club Series

Jasmine's Pact

Studying Sequoia

Just Holly

Sweet Luck

Arizona Heat, Book Two

Hilary Dartt

To friends that become family.

Chapter One

Just her luck. Lila Sullivan had *finally* made it big, and everything she'd worked for was about to implode. She stared at the latest anonymous message in her inbox: *Let me take you to dinner. I'll be at your apartment at 7.*

Those words seemed innocent enough, but they followed a spate of similar messages she'd received over the past several weeks: *You're so beautiful. Can I have your address? I'd like to send you something. It looks like you live near the library. Can we meet?*

Then, flowers on her doorstep ... from *An Admirer*. And not just any flowers. Daffodils, for unrequited love.

Just as she was deciding how freaked out to be as a result of this latest message, her laptop dinged with another: *I'm outside your apartment.*

Chills rushed from her scalp down to her shoulders. She jumped at a movement in her peripheral vision before realizing it was her dining room mirror reflecting the dancing leaves on the tree outside her window.

She could piece together his process for figuring out where she lived; the videos and photos she posted often showed her working out or posing next to the window in her living room, which overlooked the library with its distinctive, angular architecture.

Yes, she'd dreamed of receiving positive attention for years as she built her online fitness brand ... but the creep factor with this particular follower officially reached alarming.

A knock sounded at Lila's door. She jumped and looked around her second-floor apartment as if she could figure out who it was without moving from her seat at the table. Heart hammering, hands shaking, she got up and walked to the front door. Her legs felt weak and shaky. Black swirls overtook the edges of her vision.

Even if he sees my shadow pass over the peephole, he can't come in.

Still, she checked the deadbolt before she got close enough to look out. Relief flooded her veins, bringing tears to her eyes, when she saw her visitor wasn't a creepy stranger but her best friend, Rebecca Brown.

Lila unchained and unbolted the door and yanked it open, then grabbed Rebecca by the arm and pulled her in before shutting the door and chaining and bolting it again.

"I'm so glad it's you."

Rebecca's eyes were huge. "What do you mean? Who else would it be?"

"Come here." Lila grabbed her arm again and towed her into the hallway where they wouldn't be visible from outside any window.

"Lila! What's going on?"

"Shh. Wait here."

Lila ran to the big window and slammed the drapes shut, then crept to the kitchen and closed the blinds there before motioning for Rebecca to join her.

She retrieved a bottle of vodka from the cabinet above the fridge. "I know it's a little early for this, but—" she took a long swig and wiped the her mouth with the back of her hand. "I need something to take the edge off."

"What—"

"Wait. One more." Another swig down the hatch and she was ready to tell Rebecca everything that had happened.

As she spoke, her friend's eyes got even bigger and her mouth dropped open. "How long has this been going on?"

Forlorn, Lila shrugged. "I don't know. A few weeks. At first, it seemed sweet. But obviously it's devolved."

"Obviously. Why haven't you said anything?" Rebecca took the vodka bottle and took a swig, herself.

"I didn't want to worry you. But then you happened to knock on my door literally the minute I got this latest, creepiest message."

"You thought I was him."

"I did."

Rebecca took another drink and passed the bottle to Lila. "You need to call the police, Lila."

"The police? You think it's that serious?"

"Absolutely. Where's your phone?"

"Right here." She pulled it out of her leggings pocket. "I mean, do I call 9-1-1?"

"They have a non-emergency number. I'd call that."

She did, and the operator told her an officer would head over soon.

Ten minutes later, he knocked on the door and Lila went through her check-the-peephole-and-unlock-both-locks routine. Officer Mauricio Gomez introduced himself and Lila admired his thick handlebar mustache and offered him a seat at her dining room table.

"So tell me what's going on."

Rebecca pulled her chair close and Lila went over the details.

Gomez ran a hand over his face. His eyes looked tired. "I mean, this could just be a super fan." It appeared he didn't believe that himself, and dread filled Lila's torso so she couldn't breathe.

"Why would a super fan say he's outside my apartment? I mean, why not just ask to meet up in a public place? Asking for my address is *weird*. Irrational. Stalker behavior."

"You can't think of anyone who'd have a beef with you?" Gomez looked over the top of his glasses at her.

"No," she said. "In the past few months, I've grown my fan base and a few of my posts have gone viral. I get a handful of hateful comments on almost every post."

"Any repeat offenders?"

"A few."

Someone with the username Ronzoni often asked if she photo-shopped her pictures, and GymBabe had wondered about her bra size. But those things weren't totally outside the scope of normal … or were they?

Gomez nodded and she realized she had given him almost nothing to go on.

He confirmed her suspicions. "While I can say that what you're telling me definitely crosses the line into the creep zone—that's an official police term, by the way (he chortled at his own humor)—right now, this person hasn't done anything illegal. I didn't see anyone outside when I got here, otherwise I could have questioned him or her."

"So what should I do?" Lila fidgeted with the ends of her sleeves.

"Well, I'll take a report and that way we'll have something in the system. I'm going to give you my card so you can email me if anything else happens." He slid it across the table. "Meanwhile, be aware of your surroundings. Let someone know where you're going and when you expect to get there."

Lila nodded while Officer Gomez opened his notebook. "Can you provide me with the dates and times you received the messages and flowers?"

She pulled up her social media account and read off the information, nerves creeping in again.

"And you didn't see anyone outside your apartment today?" Gomez looked up at Lila, his pen poised above his paper.

She shook her head. "No. I've been home all day."

He nodded, closed the notebook, capped his pen, and put it in a little pocket on his vest. "Like I said, be extra cautious. Call me if anything new happens, okay?"

"Okay," Lila said. "Thank you."

"Sure thing."

"Great," Rebecca said when he was gone. "That wasn't much help, was it?"

"It wasn't." Lila sighed. "I'm scared, Becca."

"Want me to stay the night?"

Lila did—desperately. But she was afraid Rebecca staying there would only put her in the guy's crosshairs.

"No, thanks. I appreciate the offer, but I'd hate for him to see you here. Besides, I'm sure you have something better to do than babysit me. I just realized I was in such a panic earlier, I didn't ask why you came over."

"*I* forgot why I came over. But look." She walked over to where she'd left her messenger bag on the entryway bench and opened it to pull out a folded-up magazine. "I don't know if this is going to make you happy right now, in this very moment, but when I saw it, I was so proud."

She turned the magazine around to face Lila, who read the masthead out loud. "City Fitness."

"Open it to page thirty-six."

Lila did, and gasped. There she was, in full color on a two-page spread. *Local Influencer Changes Lives, One Colorful Post at a Time.*

"I'd forgotten all about this article," Lila whispered. "The reporter interviewed me a couple months ago."

"I know," Rebecca said. "Which is why I figured it would be a nice surprise. If you weren't dealing with everything else."

"It is." Lila hugged her. "Thank you for bringing it over."

"You're welcome. And now I'd better get going. I'm supposed to meet Alex for dinner. Are you sure you're going to be okay here by yourself?"

With more confidence than she felt, Lila waved her off. "I'm fine. How's it going with Alex, anyway?"

"It's going. He said he wants to take things to the next level." Rebecca shrugged one shoulder.

"Your enthusiasm is underwhelming."

"I don't know," Rebecca said. "I mean, we've been together for five years. What does the next level mean, if it doesn't mean getting married? But he hasn't proposed, so ... I guess I imagined we'd be married with a kid on the way by now."

"I thought so, too." Lila smiled. "But things have a way of working themselves out, don't they?"

"They do. Okay, I'm going to be late. But call me if you need anything, okay? I'll leave my phone on and I'm only a few minutes away."

"Okay. Thank you."

They hugged again and after Rebecca left, Lila got out her salt and poured it in a line just inside the door to her apartment. Restless, she returned to the living room and pulled the curtains apart just far enough to peek down onto the street. Rebecca's slim form was already several blocks away and Lila experienced a rush of gratitude for her friend as she watched her familiar, quick walk.

Alarm replaced gratitude in a split second when she noticed a man standing on the sidewalk in front of her apartment, arms crossed. He was, without a doubt, looking at her window. Sure enough, as soon as she spotted him—and flinched—he smiled. Eyes cold, he lifted a hand in greeting. Lila didn't waste any time before snapping the curtains closed again, spinning around, and leaning against the window.

I have to get out of here.

The thought, as irrational as it may be, gave her what she needed: focus. She had to pack a bag, call for a police escort, and leave.

Only, where would she go?

Her computer dinged, notifying her of another message.

Body vibrating, she rushed back to the dining room table to read it. *Come out and play.*

Even though the day was warm and her thermostat was set to a comfortable seventy-three degrees, she started shivering like she was out in the snow wearing nothing but shorts and a t-shirt. Rebecca had said to call if she needed her, but if Lila called now and Rebecca came back, she'd be a sitting duck for the man standing outside.

I need a plan.

She would leave town and shut down her social media account. Those were the only reasonable steps to take. She had enough money in her account to pay the rent on her apartment for three months and could just find another regular, anonymous job to pay for a hotel in a different city.

Although it pained her to do, she sat back down and deactivated her social media accounts. Each time she clicked "Deactivate," she could swear she felt physical pain in her chest. *It's only temporary.* "Amazing how something you worked months to build can be undone with a few clicks." Her throat felt tight.

Then she reminded herself it wasn't *undone* undone; just paused. Hopefully, temporarily. But she knew that when she stopped posting at least twice a day, her stats would go down ... and so would her income. Still, she'd built her following once, and she could do it again.

Inspiration hit: she should take a photo of the man on the street.

She picked up her phone, put it on speaker, and dialed Officer Gomez's number. While it rang, she opened her camera app and moved back to her window. Again, she opened the curtains just the tiniest bit.

The sidewalk was empty.

Where could he be?

All the possible answers rushed through her brain, and then, "Officer Gomez."

Her words tumbling out on top of each other, Lila explained what had happened, and he said he'd send someone over right away.

While she waited, she adjusted her plan. She couldn't just leave. If the stalker was watching, he'd know the second she left and could follow her. For most of her life, she'd considered her natural, almost-orange hair a curse, and now she knew it was. She'd have to dye it. Disguise herself. Find somewhere to go. And *then* leave.

Chapter Two

Travis Wilder wasn't the type to get mad. His brothers always referred to him as the easygoing, even-tempered one. The level-headed one who never got his back up.

That was before he'd learned his dad had nearly gambled away their family home before dying and leaving them with a huge back payment due just to avoid foreclosure. Now, as Levi Wilder would say, they didn't have a tail feather left. And Travis was pissed.

It was noon, and he sat at his dining room table with his head in his hands after coming to a frightening conclusion: it was going to take a miracle to make the place profitable again.

Yes, the four Wilder brothers had put on a fundraiser and earned just more than enough to cover those back payments and avoid foreclosure, but now they were treading water.

And Travis, damn fool that he was, had taken on the task of figuring out how to get Sweet Springs Ranch up and running again. Not just on solid financial footing but also back to being a viable cattle-growing business.

Sterling, the oldest and the one in charge of remodeling the big house—where they'd all grown up—had moved their dad's antique desk into Travis's house, just fifty yards over, and Travis had spent seventy-two hours there going through box after box of bills, invoices, and paperwork. He'd caught a few cat naps, but otherwise he'd kept his butt in the chair.

Sterling's new pickup truck, its diesel engine's growl like a fingerprint, one-of-a-kind, pulled up outside, interrupting Travis's thoughts (which he welcomed).

Grateful for the distraction and the reason to stand up, stretch his legs, and give his eyes a break, he opened the front door before his brother even knocked.

"Whoa, man." Sterling took a step back. "That's a sight."

Travis grunted in response. He rubbed his jaw. "Yeah. I forgot what I must look like. Haven't shaved or slept in a couple of days."

"That bad?"

"Worse."

Sterling swore. "Got any coffee? I'm coming in."

Travis stepped back and Sterling went through to the kitchen, where he began filling the coffee pot with water. Just three months before, this scene would have been inconceivable. Sterling, the first to discover their dad's gambling, had left and started his own company ... without telling his younger brothers what he'd learned.

He came back only to help with the fundraiser—and ended up staying when he fell in love with the event planner they hired, June Cartwright.

"I'm so glad you're here, man," Travis said.

Sterling shut off the water and turned around. "Don't think I'm going through that paperwork, though. I've got the roofers coming today."

"That's not what I meant," Travis said. "I meant, I'm glad you're home."

"Aw, man." Sterling turned away and started scooping coffee grounds into a filter. "You're getting all mushy on me. But I'm glad I'm home, too. Tell me what's got you looking like you've been trampled by a herd of cattle."

Travis sighed and Sterling pressed the brew button. They both leaned against the kitchen counter and crossed their arms.

"Where do I start? There's just so much paperwork and it's hard to make heads or tails of it, much less imagine being in a place where we can talk about rebuilding."

"I saw all the file boxes and my first instinct was to light them up. Imagine the bonfire we could have."

Despite the tension in his shoulders and neck making its way to his head, Travis chuckled. "A big one, for sure."

The coffee maker beeped, finished with its half-pot. "Have you thought about hiring someone?" Sterling got a couple of mugs out of the cabinet and poured.

"Never crossed my mind. *My* first instinct is to keep anyone that isn't family a thousand yards from this mess."

"Same. But look what happened with June."

"True." Travis took a mug when Sterling offered it. "Okay, let's say I decide to hire someone. How do I find a person?"

Sterling shrugged, the movement drawing attention to his massive arm and hand, which dwarfed the coffee mug. "I guess you put out an ad. Do people still do that? Ooh. Or what about one of those websites? But I guess I've heard tons of people apply and sorting through them can be time consuming. They call it a cattle call."

"How do you find guys for your crew?"

"Word of mouth, mostly." He held up a finger. "Callie's a lawyer. She might know someone. Surely the kind of person you're looking for travels in the same circles as attorneys."

Travis considered. "Okay. If I *do* decide to hire someone, I'll text Callie first."

Sterling nodded and touched his fist to Travis's shoulder. "Good man."

"Why did you stop by, anyway?"

"Oh, nothing big. It can wait." Sterling's eyes darted around the kitchen.

Was he uncomfortable? Travis's curiosity sparked to life, pushing aside his stress. "No, I'm not going to let you leave without telling me why you came."

Sterling turned toward the coffee maker again, pulled out the pot, and froze before he started pouring. "I wish we had something stronger than coffee."

"What's going on, man?"

He replaced the coffee pot. Turned around. Took a deep breath that moved through his chest. "You know, I proposed to June."

Panic flooded Travis's veins. Sterling looked so serious. He wasn't considering breaking things off with June, was he? He couldn't. She was perfect for him. *Don't be an idiot.* Travis couldn't be sure whether that admonition was directed at himself or Sterling.

"Yeah. We were all there, weren't we?"

"Right." He fidgeted with his mug. "Anyway. We decided to get married in a month."

Travis blew out a breath. "A month?"

"Yeah. But don't worry, we—"

"No, no, no. My sigh was relief. I thought you were going to say you were breaking things off."

His brother's face split into a wide grin. "No, you idiot. I'd never break things off."

"Good. So, let me guess. You decided to get married here."

Humor sparkled in Sterling's eyes. "You catch on fast."

"But the big house—"

Sterling held up a hand. "It's a disaster. I know. But we're not going to get married at the big house."

Travis sighed then, and felt his own chest move as another wave of relief washed over him. The last thing they needed was a bunch of people hanging out at the big house before he got everything organized.

"You don't have to freak out," Sterling said. "We're only inviting a handful of people. We're going to build a little archway, throw up some chairs, hire a couple of food trucks."

Travis nodded. "Sounds like you have it under control. So what do you need me for?"

Again, Sterling's eyes darted around the kitchen. "You can say no. I didn't realize how stressed you were."

Travis shook his head. "Just say it, man."

"June says I need a best man. I was wondering if it could be you."

Travis's heart leapt. Despite everything they'd been through, or maybe because of it, Sterling was his favorite brother. The fact that he wanted Travis as his best man made Travis's heart sing. He launched himself at his brother and wrapped his arms around him. "Of course I will. I'd be pissed if you asked anyone else."

Sterling hugged him back and he could hear the relief in his voice. "Thanks, bro."

"You bet. And I'm going to throw you the best damn bachelor party anybody ever had."

"No pressure though, okay? This is supposed to be fun. Low-key. I keep asking June if she's sure she wants to keep it small. She insists that she does. 'This is about our commitment, Sterling,' she keeps saying. 'Not about how big of a party we can throw.'"

Travis laughed. "Kind of ironic, coming from an event planner. But I guess she's seen her fair share of couples whose extravagant weddings don't match up to the strength of their relationship."

Sterling touched his finger to his nose. "You're right on."

"Well, it seems I'm going to get a whole lot busier. I think you just made my hiring-someone decision for me. There's no way I can be a kick-ass best man if I'm doing everything else on my own."

"Only if you're sure. I don't want to pressure you into anything. And if the best man duties get to be too much, just tell me. Hey, maybe I can have June plan my bachelor party."

Travis held up a hand. "Absolutely not. I know June is the best event planner we know, but there's no way she's planning your bachelor party."

"I figured that would seal the deal."

Travis grinned, surprised that his new responsibilities actually seemed to lessen the weight he'd been carrying around. "It'll be my honor."

Suddenly serious, Sterling said, "Thank you. I really appreciate it."

"You're welcome, bro."

"I'll be happy to plan your bachelor party when the time comes."

Travis shook his head. "That time is never going to come. I plan on being a lifelong bachelor."

Sterling was halfway down the walkway. "You never know. The right lady could come along."

Travis didn't respond. He just shut the door, refilled his coffee cup, and returned to his desk. What Sterling didn't understand was that in Travis's experience, a person couldn't count on love. Hadn't he been the loyal one, the one who stuck around and cared for their dad, tried to care for the property? And yet, his dad had deceived him until he died. No, he wasn't dumb enough to fall for the lie that was true love. But he would go ahead and enjoy his brothers' romances vicariously.

Enough of that.

First things first. He opened his texting app and sent Callie a message: *I'm considering hiring someone to help me sort out all the ranch paperwork. Do you know anyone?*

While he waited for her response, Travis pulled up a popular employment listing website. To get a feel for the process, he signed up for a free account and started entering his business information. He kept the details vague. He didn't want anyone local to come across the ad and know how much help he needed—everyone had been so generous at the fundraiser, and he didn't want them to think that generosity was for naught. In the *Location* field he typed *Arizona* and under *Business Name*, he typed *Defunct Ranching Operation*, then replaced *Defunct* with *Small*, then *Small* with *Growing*. That should do it. Callie texted back and Travis's heart sank when he read her message. *Not off the top my head. I know some great legal secretaries, but those skill sets don't match up with what you need. I'll keep an ear open for sure. In the meantime, why don't you make some job listings?*

Travis swore. He'd much rather hire a friend of the family than trust a complete stranger with this mess the ranch had morphed into. But he needed help *now*.

His focus back on the website, he clicked *Post a Job Opening*. In the job title field, he typed, *Primary Damage Controller*. He deleted it.

Giant Mess Cleaner Upper. He deleted that, too.

After a few more attempts, which included words like *chaotic* and *impossible*, he settled on *Bookkeeper, Accountant, and Assistant*. He'd be asking for a lot more than bookkeeping and accounting, but he would deal with that during the interview.

Next, he had to fill out the box for *Job Description*. Looking around at the mess of papers—he'd brought in a whole separate table just for Sweet Springs Ranch correspondence—Travis grimaced. He wanted to write, *Get this damn business organized and figure out how to make it profitable*. Instead, he typed, *Organize paperwork and create bookkeeping and accounting systems for long-standing business*. Seeing the words on the screen, Travis groaned. That sounded so simple. Whoever got this job might see the actual piles of paperwork and head for the hills.

"How can I sweeten this terrible deal?"

On a whim, he added, *Live and work onsite*.

The old bunkhouses were sitting there unused. All he had to do was clean one up and throw some sheets on the bed. *Cross your fingers, bro*.

Another wave of hesitation hit him. He should be able to manage the task himself. Only, as Sterling had pointed out, he had other things to do.

Foremost, he had to find some cattle. Before he could do that, he had to make sure the fences were in good working order. The persistent headache threatened, again. One thing at a time.

Next up: *Salary*.

He was surprised to see an option to require applicants to upload a photo. His first thought was that someone's looks didn't matter, but then he realized the benefit of seeing someone before scheduling an interview: he'd know if anyone local applied, so he could turn them down. He selected yes. Before clicking *Post Job*, Travis went over his listing one more time. Satisfied that he'd never be one hundred percent satisfied, he shrugged and posted the job.

Then, because the task was infinitely more interesting than paperwork and job listings, he searched the Internet for upcoming cattle auctions. He may not be ready to buy just yet, but it didn't hurt to dream.

Chapter Three

Lila wasn't going to leave her apartment until she changed her look. She decided to order disguise supplies from the big-box store around the corner and hire a delivery service to bring it to her.

After making herself a cup of tea, she sat down at the computer. Perusing the selection of at-home hair dyes, Lila marveled at how much she'd changed. The thing she once hated most about herself—her bright orange hair—had become not just a trademark of her brand but also a huge, positive part of who she was. And now she was going to erase it with a few clicks and one delivery order.

The images on her laptop screen blurred and she dashed away her tears with the heel of her hand.

"It's just temporary." The words had become a mantra. She couldn't believe that after all this time, after years and years of working to feel strong and confident in her own skin, she was going into hiding.

The moment she decided to disguise herself, she knew she'd go with black hair. Black blended in, unlike the coppery mane she'd grown up with. People didn't give black hair a second glance, and they didn't call it names.

Echoes of her schoolmates' voices as they shouted, "Ginger!"

through the hallways made her feel sick to her stomach and she forced herself to focus on the present moment. They couldn't hurt her anymore.

After what felt like hours deliberating the differences between the hundreds of shades of black—jet black versus coal black versus blackbird versus little black dress—Lila finally settled on obsidian. The stone had grounding properties that cultivated confidence. Exactly what she needed. She added it to her cart.

In addition to new hair, she was going to need new clothes. For the past two years, she'd lived in workout gear. Leggings and crop tops paired with hoodies or zip-up jackets. For now, she was going to have to change things up. She spent another hour shopping for fall clothes: jeans, sweaters, and boots, grateful the cool-weather clothes would hide her physique. She grimaced when she viewed her cart and saw that her items totaled nearly four digits.

It's worth it.

In her instructions for the delivery, Lila instructed the driver to knock three times and ring the bell twice, then leave the bags on the doorstep. That way, she'd know it wasn't a crazy stranger at her door. The driver would probably think she was crazy, but she didn't care.

The delivery website promised the items would arrive later that day and for the first time since she'd seen the guy outside on the sidewalk, she felt her body relax, just a little. Bolstered by her shopping success, she opened a new tab and searched for job-hunting websites. A list of available jobs popped up and she blew out a breath.

"I'll bet a million people apply for each job." She groaned. "Not like I have another option at the moment."

After filling out a questionnaire about her skills, job preferences, work experience, and underwear size (not really, but they may as well have asked), she clicked through to see relevant job listings.

She sorted them so she could see those posted most recently, and quickly nixed the food service jobs. Standing at a host station just inside a restaurant or serving food to hundreds of people per night seemed risky.

Her stomach churned at the idea of applying for jobs like accountant, assistant, bookkeeper ... she was great at the work, but found it about as mundane as watching paint dry. Escaping that sort of position was a main driver of her success as a fitness influencer. But it was *safe*.

One such listing caught her eye. *Live and work onsite.*

"I would never have to leave the place." Her whisper sounded wondrous in the silence of her apartment.

For luck, she touched the amethyst she wore around her neck. Then she proceeded to fill out the application for the job, which required strong organizational skills, self-directed work, and experience with creating systems.

Just when she thought she was done, the website prompted her to upload a picture of herself. She panicked and the tang of adrenaline hit the back of her throat. "What kind of maniac asks job applicants to upload a picture?"

Uploading a current picture was too risky. One of her fifty thousand followers might see her and if word got out ...

She considered. She could wait until her hair dye arrived and upload a picture post-makeover. But who knew how many others would apply for the position during that time? Or, she could upload a completely different picture. A caricature, maybe, or some kind of icon or avatar.

Inspiration struck.

Within a couple of minutes, courtesy of a quick search, she'd found and uploaded a picture of another Lila Sullivan—a slightly older woman who looked exactly like an accountant. Glasses, oversized nose, and all.

Whoever posted the job probably wouldn't even look at the picture that carefully. And by the time they met in person, the job poster would have seen so many photos, he or she wouldn't even realize *this* Lila Sullivan wasn't *that* Lila Sullivan.

She clicked *Submit* and closed her computer.

Realistically, she should apply for more than one job, but the live-and-work-onsite element was just too great to pass up and she didn't want to spread her energy too thin. If she hadn't heard back by the next day, she decided, she'd find more postings.

Three knocks sounded at the door and Lila jumped even though she'd been expecting the delivery driver. Two rings of the doorbell followed, and Lila waited a full three minutes, stock still, before tiptoeing to the door, looking through the peephole, and then opening the door and snatching the bags, carefully lifting them over the salt barrier. She then shut the door, locked it, and leaned against it, breathless.

After several minutes of deep breathing, she felt calm enough to carry the bags into the apartment and set them on the dining room table. She quickly found the box of dye and opened it. She felt fairly confident until she unfolded the instructions, which were printed on a poster-sized piece of paper in teeny tiny, nearly illegible print.

"Maybe you should have dyed your hair back in junior high. At least then you'd have some practice."

Junior-high Lila would have given her right arm to dye her hair, but her parents forbade it. "You're beautiful just the way you are" was their mantra ... and it took her years to believe it.

She froze when her phone rang, but then snatched it up when she saw who was calling. "Rebecca. This is divine timing. I'm about to dye my hair and I have no idea what to do."

"Didn't the dye come with instructions?"

"Yeah, but it's like reading a novel. In four-point font."

"Want me to come over and help you?"

Lila sighed. "Are you done with Alex already?"

Over the sound of traffic, Rebecca's sigh came through. "Yeah. That's a whole separate story."

"Want to fill me in?"

"Not right now. You've got enough going on."

"I could use the distraction." Lila made her voice singsongy, and Rebecca laughed. "Wait. Why are you dyeing your hair?"

"It's a disguise."

"Are we living in a spy novel?"

Lila shared her plan, from going incognito to finding a new, faraway job.

Silence.

"Rebecca?"

"Are you sure it's a good idea to run away? I mean, you're kind of ... I don't want to say—"

"Just say it."

Her friend huffed out a sigh. "You're kind of letting this jerk win."

"I know, I know. I had the same thought. But right after you left, I saw someone standing on the sidewalk, looking up at my window."

Rebecca gasped. "You're right. You do need to get out of here. I'd want to leave, too. You think it was the same person who's been sending you messages?"

Again, a panicky feeling made Lila's body feel like an untethered hot air balloon. "I think so. He'd just written that he was outside my apartment."

"Did you call the police?"

"No. What would I say? A guy was standing on the sidewalk? People can stand on sidewalks, right? Like Officer Gomez said, he wasn't breaking any laws."

"I guess. But Lila, even if you leave, it's not like he's going to leave. When you come back, he'll still be here."

The words made Lila feel even sicker. "I'm hoping he'll forget about me."

"And what? Move on to his next victim?"

"That's not what I meant." *God, was it?*

"Are you sure you don't want me to come over? Not just to help you with the dye, but so you're not alone."

"No." Lila swallowed. She *did* want Rebecca to come over, more than anything. But she didn't want to put her best friend in danger. "Thank you. I'll be fine. I'll read the directions, take it one step at a time, and before we know it, I'll have obsidian hair."

"Obsidian?"

Lila gulped. "It'll change up my look, right?"

"It will, but Lila, your red hair is so beautiful. So *you*. It breaks my heart to imagine it covered up."

"It's only temporary." *At least, that's what I keep telling myself.*

They talked for a few more minutes, with Lila promising to keep Rebecca posted and Rebecca promising to come over at a moment's notice.

Then Lila spread the hair-dye instructions on the table and started fresh.

"Step one. Comb or brush your hair and section it into four pieces (or more if you have long or thick hair)." There was even a diagram. "Simple enough."

Apply the Color to Your Hairline.

She could do that. The dye bottle resembled a ketchup bottle, and she squirted the dye into her hairline like the picture showed. Next, she colored her part and the back of her hair, and then the rest of it.

"Easy peasy."

After setting the timer, she cleaned up her supplies and then checked the employment website again. No response from the job poster. Not that she'd expected one this quickly, but she did feel a prickle of disappointment.

She navigated to the home page for her now-defunct social media account, and scrolled through the posts she'd made. Every one featured bright, cheerful colors, and especially her signature color, aqua. When it came to branding, she'd worked to instill fun, so her followers could feel how fun strength and confidence could be. How amazing it felt to put in the work to be the best version of yourself.

Her throat tightened as she remembered the *#MondayVibes* post she'd made a few weeks before. There she was, smiling, her eyes dazzling as she held up her coffee cup. That morning she'd felt particularly grateful for the life she'd created ... and now she was putting it on hold.

The timer went off, bringing her out of what she knew could easily turn into a downward spiral.

In the shower, she watched as the blackened water swirled down the drain. The hair-dye instructions said to rinse until the water was clear, and that seemed to take a literal eternity. A little scared, she didn't look at herself in the mirror until she toweled off and put on clothes. When she braved a glance at her reflection, she realized the effect was stunning.

Red hair and green eyes with pale skin had always made her look like a classic Irish person. Or a leprechaun, as some of her classmates were fond of saying.

But this?

The onyx-colored hair brought out the emerald green of her eyes and made her pale skin look luminous. The effect wasn't her, but it was striking. *And, it's only temporary.* She took the time to blow-dry and style her hair, then, bolstered by renewed confidence in her look, took a selfie and sent it to Rebecca.

Her response came back right away: A starry-eyed emoji and *Wow! I never would have thought it, but you look absolutely gorgeous. And I guess you figured out the instructions.*

Lila wrote back: *Thanks. And yes, I did. Easier than I thought.*

Easier than she thought to erase years' worth of work and become someone else.

Chapter Four

Eight hours after Travis posted the job opening, he was back at his computer—completely overwhelmed. Sterling was right about one thing: once Travis posted his ad, people applied. Dozens of them. The number of applicants was astounding and overwhelming. Upon seeing the list, which apparently went on for *three pages*, Travis dropped his head into his hands. "I'm going to need a beer for this."

He got up, grabbed one from the fridge, and leaned against the counter, giving himself permission to daydream. Earlier that day, he'd found a few cattle auctions he'd love to check out. He pictured himself, bidder number in hand, vying for the cows and bulls that would populate Sweet Springs Ranch.

His phone dinged and a text came up from Cash, the brother just before him in birth order: *We're going to A Cold One. Want to come?*

Sighing because he *did* want to go, and because he *should* stay home and wade through the applications, Travis responded, *Sure.*

And then, knowing he'd kick himself if he didn't do something right away to move the process forward, he cursed and took his beer back to his desk. He needed a system. First, he'd eliminate applicants who didn't have experience. Whoever walked into this was going to need their own system, which was born of having done the work before.

That narrowed the field to thirty-seven.

Next, he'd nix all but those who listed accounting, bookkeeping, *and* administrative assistant experience.

"Bingo."

Just seven applicants remained. They were all women. Mostly middle-aged, judging from the pictures, and a couple of older women. Two of them were from Arizona and he eliminated those with a couple of clicks. The others were from all over: Utah, Minnesota, Washington state, Texas, and Alabama. *Perfect.*

He invited the five remaining applicants to interview, then closed his laptop, poured the rest of his mostly full beer into the sink, then stepped into his boots and out the door.

As Travis approached the bar at A Cold One, Sterling held out a beer. He accepted it, taking pleasure in the cool glass against his palm. Before he could even take a sip, June stood up from her spot at the stool next to Sterling's and hugged Travis. He raised an eyebrow at his brother. "How'd a guy as prickly as you end up with such a devastatingly beautiful and overwhelmingly charming woman?"

Releasing him, June swatted his arm. "Hey, he's been less prickly lately, hasn't he?"

Her eyes glinted with humor and Travis wanted to squeeze her again as a thank-you for bringing Sterling back. Literally and figuratively.

"Any luck today?" Sterling wanted to know.

Travis shook his head, took a drink. "Some, I guess. I did finish setting up a job post and received several dozen applications. Then I spent about three hours daydreaming, at which point I got Cash's text. I then spent about three minutes narrowing the applicants down to five and inviting them to interview."

"Impressive." Sterling offered a fist bump. "That's a lot of interviews."

"Yeah. Well, I would have weeded them out even more, but Cash texted and said we were going for beers."

"Speak of the devil."

Cash came through the old-fashioned saloon doors and Travis couldn't help but smile. As their mama used to say—before she left—the Wilder boys were a good-looking bunch. In his boots and jeans and cowboy hat, Cash was the epitome of Western sex symbol ... and he knew it.

He flashed his grin at a group of women sitting in a booth along the wall and they giggled.

"Always turning heads, that one," Sterling said.

"And then there's our other two love birds," Travis said as Hayes and Callie came in, arm in arm, laughing together while she gazed up at him with hearts in her eyes.

Jerry, the bar's owner and resident bartender, materialized behind the bar. "One for all the newcomers?"

And just like that, Travis was surrounded by his family and his troubles were forgotten, at least momentarily.

"Is there a special occasion for tonight?" Travis asked Cash.

"What?"

Hayes punched Cash on the shoulder. "Stop making eyes at those girls and listen to your brother."

"You're not the boss of me."

Callie and June exchanged a look and rolled their eyes.

"I know," Hayes said, and Travis pricked his ears. "Let's take a drink every time Cash flirts with a woman tonight, even if it's from across the room."

"No way." Travis held up his hands. "Every time we play this game, I end up drunk as a skunk."

"Oh, we're playing."

Immediately, Cash got up to his antics, ordering a round of sex on the beach for the group of women, who, Travis noticed, had already started to show more cleavage.

"Drink up, fellas." Hayes grinned at Sterling and Travis in turn, and then directed his smile at June and Callie. "You, too, ladies, if you're up for it."

"I think we'll get ourselves a table." Callie grabbed June's arm, and June nodded. "A nice, quiet table. In the corner."

They walked off together while Sterling and Travis took matching swigs.

Travis leaned over to stage whisper in Sterling's ear. "How does he do that?"

"He's always had that shit-eating grin," Sterling said, and Hayes said, "Remember how it always got him out of trouble?"

"And now it's about to get him *into* trouble." Travis lifted his chin toward the table full of women, and the others shifted their gazes accordingly.

Sterling laughed out loud. One of the women, dressed in shorter-than-short shorts with such a low-cut waistline, he could see the lace edge of her underwear above it, strutted toward them, her breasts nearly falling out of her plaid-and-paisley halter top, her eyes focused on Cash.

"Wow, Cash." Travis was human, and did feel a hot surge of jealousy. But, he reminded himself, he didn't want a relationship, serious or otherwise. Life had shown him that even the people who claimed to love you would leave you—and they didn't always come back.

"What, bro?"

Before Travis could say anything, Cash extended his hand toward the woman. "Cash Wilder. You must be Gorgeous."

"Drink," Hayes said, his voice nearly cracking with glee as the woman tittered. He, Sterling, and Travis drank again.

"What?" Cash was all innocence. "Wait. Don't tell me. It's Coca-Cola. Because you're so-da-licious."

This time, disappointment infused Hayes's voice when he said, "Drink."

"I'm gonna have to pace myself, bro." Travis drank anyway.

"Where does he come up with this stuff?" Sterling wiped his mouth with the back of his hand, and they all quieted to listen to Cash's conversation.

"You're cute." The woman giggled. Again. "I'm Daphne. And why don't we order some tequila shots, and you can find out just how delicious I am?"

Cash turned away from Daphne to give his brothers a can-you-believe-this look, his eyebrows in his hairline and his mouth in a wide-open grin.

"And drink, drink, drink." Hayes guzzled his beer, set the empty on the counter, and said, "We're going to have to stop this. I'm not carrying my fully grown brother out of here in a bucket."

"Agreed. We'll give them ten minutes." Sterling's eyes danced with laughter as he watched.

"Isn't this something like what happened when you met June?"

Sterling's elbow connected with Travis's ribcage, and he was grateful he hadn't taken a drink when Hayes instructed them to— the beer would have sprayed right out of his mouth.

"This is *nothing* like what happened when I met June." He looked across the bar at his fiancée, whose gaze was already on him. They exchanged a glance so intimate, Travis wanted to look away. At the same time, he was mesmerized by what the two of them shared.

"Sorry, bro. I was just kidding."

Sterling tore his eyes off June and smiled at Travis. "I know you were."

"Drink."

Cash was leading Daphne onto the dance floor, holding her hand high like a gentleman might do for a lady at a fancy ball.

Travis shook his head and he and Sterling drank.

"Her friends are all looking this way." Sterling was right. Travis didn't let himself look for too long. He didn't want them to think he was considering asking one of them to dance, too. "Why don't you go ask one of them to dance?"

"Absolutely not," Travis said. "I'm not fixin' to get myself caught up in any kind of romance, dancing or otherwise. Just leads to trouble, if you ask me."

"What if you ask us?" Hayes stood, feet planted far apart, arms crossed.

This was a conversation Travis did not want to have. "Oh, but I'm *not* asking you."

"Maybe you should."

"Nah." Travis took a drink even though Hayes hadn't told him to.

On the dance floor, Cash dipped Daphne, who practically swooned. And *then* Hayes told them to drink.

Sterling punched Travis. "What do you mean, 'Nah'?"

"I mean," Travis said, punching him back, "I'm perfectly fine being single. In fact, I am more than fine being single. I am married to the ranch, and I'm committed to it. I'm going to get it up and running again, fill the place with cattle, and contribute to this community. And I'm going to do it all without the distraction of a relationship. Don't you think the ranch is messy enough without love?" He felt his upper lip curl into a sneer on love and immediately felt guilty. The same mean tone still in his voice, he said, "Drink."

Hayes and Sterling looked at each other, shrugged, and drank.

And, a few minutes later, Travis tasked himself with getting Cash out of A Cold One before he got too amorous with Daphne. She waved at them from the door before they got into the ride share.

"I can't believe you're tearing me away from Daphne." Cash flopped into the backseat, proving that he was losing control of his faculties.

"You're welcome," Travis said. "Want to sleep at my place or yours?"

"Save the money. I'll crash on your couch."

A few minutes later, Travis spread a blanket over his brother. "Sleep tight, man."

"Thanks, bro. And, Trav?"

"Yeah?"

"You know I'm just foolin' around with the girls, right? I'm not out sowing my seeds or anything, and I don't really think one night in a bar is going to lead to true love. I'm just having a good time."

Travis wanted to ask him why he did it, then. Why he flirted so shamelessly for nothing. Why he didn't want more for himself. Maybe it was for the same reason Travis avoided women all together. "Yeah, I know. Get some rest."

"You, too."

He should go straight to bed, but he felt restless with all these topics swirling around in his head, buzzing like bees in a hive. Cattle. An assistant. Sterling and June's wedding. Love.

Checking an item off his to-do list would help, so he filled a glass with water and returned to his desk, which at that point, felt like a torture chamber.

He opened the employment website, where a bubble popped up to let him know he had notifications. He clicked on it. "Well, I'll be."

There, staring back at him, were three green checkmarks: *Interview Request Accepted.*

Below the checkmarks, another button invited him to *Schedule Interviews Now.*

He clicked the button and selected the first applicant. He scheduled all three interviews for the next day and went to bed. For the first time in weeks, he slept hard, all night long.

Chapter Five

Lila gave herself quite a fright when she caught a glimpse of her newly dyed hair in the mirror the next morning. She recovered fairly quickly, her heart rate returning to normal as she checked the salt barrier in front of her door before pulling on a pair of sweatpants and a sweatshirt. Her lips twitched as she remembered the representative from the company that sent them to her calling the outfit a lounge suit. It was a good, old-fashioned sweatsuit.

Even if she was going to dye her hair and change her wardrobe, she would still go through her morning rituals. After all, she attributed the majority of her success to them. They centered her and grounded her so she started each day calm and focused. The very fact that she felt like her life was falling apart made those rituals more important now than ever, didn't it?

First up: opening the drapes and the blinds.

One arm extended, she froze. She could open the drapes but not the blinds. If that guy from the night before was lurking around, he'd be able to see her. Letting her arm drop, she decided against even opening the drapes. What was the point? When the blinds were closed they didn't let in any light, anyway. Bolstering herself, she turned on all the lights.

After filling the teakettle with fresh water, she set it on the stove and turned on the flame. Then she retrieved her lucky teacup from its spot in the cabinet and filled the tea infuser with the special tea she'd bought to promote good fortune. Once she set that in the cup, she put away the tin tea box. While the water came to a boil, she recited her daily affirmations twelve times: "I am strong. I am courageous. I am Lila Sullivan."

For good measure she added, "This is just temporary," at the end.

The kettle whistled. Steam rose when she poured the water over the infuser, and closing her eyes, she inhaled it and let it kiss her face. The tea steeped and she leaned against the counter and ran through her daily visualizations. Typically, she envisioned herself as strong and confident during each part of her day, especially as she created her social media posts. But today was going to be different. She wasn't going to record any posts ... which made her heart ache.

The tea was done, so she brought it to the table and did her gratitude practice, which also looked a little different from the norm.

I am grateful for my health.

I am grateful for new opportunities.

I am grateful for the courage to seize those opportunities.

I am grateful for my friendships.

I am grateful for my skills.

She sipped her tea and envisioned it infusing her body with good fortune. Next, she wrote down her intentions for the day:

Participate in a successful job interview.

Deactivate social accounts (it's only temporary).

Pack items to take with me.

Plan road trip to Arizona.

Exercise.

Complete evening rituals.

Finally, morning rituals complete, she took twelve deep, cleansing breaths and opened her laptop.

You've been invited to an interview.

"Yes." She accepted right away, and was surprised when the next webpage loaded, asking her to schedule one.

The next available time slot was later that morning and without thinking, she clicked *Schedule*. Another page came up, asking her to select the interview type (phone or video), and she groaned. She should choose video. Her mouse cursor hovered over that selection. No, she'd rather be safe than sorry. She chose phone and the site confirmed her appointment.

That's when she panicked.

Shouldn't she do something to prepare for this? What kinds of questions would the job poster ask her? Hands shaking, she typed into her search bar, What will an employer ask me on a job interview for accounting or bookkeeping?

The search results were varied, ranging in topics from software experience to regulation knowledge to specific examples of helping previous employers save money or organize their finances.

Shit.

It had been a few years (which felt like forever) since Lila thought about regulations or software. She'd hired an accountant, herself, as soon as she started earning enough money through her online fitness channels.

Breathe, Lila. You can do this. She closed her eyes and took twelve deep breaths. Then she opened her eyes, closed her Internet app, and opened the accounting software she'd once used. After about ten minutes, she'd re-familiarized herself with the software itself and also with the terms and phrases and regulations she hadn't used in ages. "That's going to have to be good enough."

If she started right away, she'd have exactly enough time to complete a weights workout and shower before the interview. If there was a silver lining to not recording her workouts and having to edit the videos before posting them, it was that she'd have a ton of time on her hands.

Five minutes before the time she'd chosen for the interview, Lila returned to her dining table, made sure her ringer was on, and waited. In the silence, she closed her eyes and visualized herself answering questions with confidence. She repeated her mantras. She breathed.

The phone ringing startled her, and she fumbled her phone as she picked it up to answer.

"Lila?" The voice at the other end literally melted her insides while simultaneously giving her chills. Was this guy for real? He couldn't possibly be a rancher. Surely he was a phone sex operator. Did they even still have those? "Hello?"

Shit. "Yes. This is Lila. Sorry about that."

She thought she detected a smile in his voice. "That's all right." A long pause followed. He cleared his throat and she wondered if he was as nervous as she was. "My name is Travis Wilder, and I'm looking for help." Something almost like desperation came through.

"I guessed that, based on the fact that you posted a job listing." She bit her lip, hoping that comment had come across as she intended—a little funny—and not snarky.

He chuckled and suddenly she was picturing herself in bed with a very sexy rancher, her cheek on his bare chest while he laughed, all deep and rumbly. Heat rushed to her cheeks and her lady parts and she willed him to say something else.

"You're right. Sorry. I've never done this before."

"You should probably start by asking me about my qualifications."

"Right. What *are* your qualifications?"

Oh, my God. Out of nowhere she was a sex goddess who wanted to tell him how she was qualified to pleasure him in bed and she'd never even met the guy. *Get yourself under control right this very minute.* For all she knew, he could be twice her age and married with grown children and grandkids.

"I've been a business owner for several years now. Although my recent venture has nothing to do with money, I had my own accounting and bookkeeping business for four years. It was very successful."

"What kinds of businesses did you work with?"

"Oh, all kinds. A coffee shop, a gym, a daycare center, a bookstore." Was that enough? Should she list more?

"So why did you switch gears?"

What to say? "I've always had a passion for fitness and I wanted to use that to help people." She cleared her throat. Was that enough? Too much? She'd been purposefully vague and hoped he didn't ask for more details.

"Why are you looking for a job, then?"

Oh, boy. She couldn't let her answer make it sound like she'd *failed.* "I, ah, suffered an injury." An injury to her sense of safety, but still.

"That's too bad."

And now she was picturing him cradling her, protective, trying to make her feel better. She screamed at herself, internally.

"Yeah. But the silver lining is that I have these skills. I'm really good at what I do. I'm organized and efficient and I have an eye for detail." She sounded desperate. *I am confident.*

A sigh came through her earpiece. "Well, that's good, because I've got a real mess here."

At once intrigued and nervous, Lila laughed. "What do you mean, a real mess?"

He didn't speak right away and she wondered if she shouldn't have asked. "Let's just say I recently discovered no one's been keeping the books for a while. Things are ... a bit overwhelming. I'd do it myself, but it wouldn't leave time for my, ah, other ventures."

To Lila, this sounded like the perfect distraction. Also, something about his voice—tired, defeated, sexy as hell—made her want to reach through the phone and hug him. *Please don't be an eighty-year-old rancher with bowed legs.* "So you just need someone to go through the books, get you organized, set up a system."

"Yeah, basically. It'll be pretty full-time at first, but after you wade through the initial wreckage, it could be part-time. You could work remotely if you wanted to. Once you, ah, get back to your fitness job. I mean, if you wanted to."

Perfect. She could stay onsite until she sorted out the books and then she could come back home. *Play it cool.* "That sounds good."

"But I think, with the nature of the mess I have here, you should come for a trial period. Say, a week? That way you can get the lay of the land and decide whether this job is something you're interested in."

She said, "Sure," but in her mind, she'd already committed to a longer-term arrangement.

"So what else should I ask you?"

Laughter bubbled up from Lila's center, releasing some of the pressure that had been building for the past couple of days. She thought back to the research she'd done to prepare for the interview. "You could ask me what software I use. Or when I could start."

He laughed, too. "Okay. When can you start?"

"Tomorrow?"

"Aren't you in Alabama? Don't you have loose ends you need to tie up? And that's at least a twenty-hour drive. Or did you plan on flying? I just assumed you'd want a car while you were here."

Lila's stomach lurched at the thought of driving that far, alone, when someone was following her every move. Maybe flying would be better. She could get a long-term car rental. Which would eat up her savings even faster.

"I'll probably fly." She did her best to convey that flying was no big deal.

"All right. Are you sure—I mean, would you really want to come tomorrow? You can come whenever you want, but if you come tomorrow, you can take the day to settle in and I can give you an orientation the next day."

Something about the idea of Travis Wilder giving Lila an orientation made her heart pound. "That works."

"Before you come three-quarters of the way across the country, don't you want to know what kind of company I'm running, here?"

Did that even matter? "Oh! Of course."

"It's a hundred-year-old family ranch in Prescott, Arizona. Sweet Springs Ranch. My dad was the most recent proprietor, but he had a bit of a gambling problem and fell behind on bills. We're all caught up now, but I'm looking to restore the place as an active cattle ranch. Once the books are in order, of course."

A ranch? *Well, that's unexpected.* She pictured a corral teeming with cattle and her nose wrinkled involuntarily as she remembered the smell of cattle ranches she'd driven past on the interstate. Lila had no knowledge of ranches and how they worked. Was she making a mistake? No, she'd figure it out. Books were books, right? "Great!"

"Okay. Great. Then I'd like to offer you the position. I'll send you an email with information about the two best airports to use, with driving directions from both."

They hung up and Lila set down her phone. She'd imagined all her nerves would dissolve once she accepted a job offer ... but now they felt like ants crawling around her body.

She woke up her computer and typed into the search bar, *Sweet Springs Ranch, Arizona.*

The result that caught her eye first was a news article about the success of a recent fundraiser for the ranch. She clicked on it, and her eyes widened when she saw the photo that accompanied the article. The caption read, *The four Wilder brothers (from left to right) Sterling, Hayes, Travis, and Cash, pose during the recent fundraiser, the success of which they attribute to the generosity of the Prescott community.*

"Wow." Her voice was breathy, awestruck. "There must be something in the water in Prescott." The Wilder brothers looked like actual movie stars. She dropped her head into her hands. "What have I done?"

Chapter Six

"What in creation just happened?" Travis stared at his phone screen.

Using only the powers of her voice, Lila, who was apparently a world-class seductress, had managed to get him to offer her the job despite the fact that she was the first applicant he'd interviewed. "This must be some kind of witchcraft."

On his computer, he navigated back to the employment website and to the applicants page. He hadn't paid too much attention to the pictures before, but he should have looked at hers before the interview. He clicked to enlarge it. "Huh." She could be anyone; she looked *average*.

But her voice.

In desperate need of someone to tell him he hadn't lost his mind completely, he left his house in search of Sterling, who was likely on the property somewhere. As Travis expected, his brother was at the big house, tools in hand, cutting wood.

When Sterling saw him, Travis raised an arm.

"Good morning," Sterling called. "Are you here to help?"

"I definitely could. It would take my mind off whatever the hell just happened."

Sterling set down his saw and turned to face Travis, one hand on his hip and one on the work table. "What do you mean?"

Sensing he might be unintentionally freaking Sterling out—hadn't they had enough surprises over the past year?—he shook his head. "Nothing bad. Only the fact that I just hired the very first person I interviewed."

"Well that's good, isn't it?"

Travis threw up his hands. "I have no idea. I mean, I didn't even hire her based on her qualifications or experience. I hired her because there was just something about her voice."

Sterling tilted his head. His eyes twinkled. "Is that right?"

"I know." Travis huffed out a sigh. "It's crazy."

"It couldn't have anything to do with this person's picture, could it?"

Travis's laugh came out as a strangled sound. "That's the thing. I didn't pay that much attention to the pictures before I called her, and when I looked at hers afterwards, I realized she just looked ..." He shrugged. "Normal. I can't tell how old she is or anything. For all I know, she could be somebody's grandma."

"This should be interesting. When does she start?"

Again, Travis threw up his hands. "She's coming *tomorrow!*"

This time, Sterling laughed, and the sound was anything but strangled. It was a full, head-thrown-back belly laugh. "This just keeps getting better, man."

Despite his panic, Travis felt the corners of his mouth tugging upward. "Yeah."

Suddenly serious, Sterling said, "You'd better get that bunkhouse set up."

Shit. Travis had completely forgotten about that. "I need help."

Sterling's gaze slid over to the big house, and the words tumbled out of Travis's mouth. "It doesn't have to be from you. Do you think I could sweet-talk June into putting a feminine touch on the place? I mean, nothing fancy, just, you know, livable."

"I'm sure she'd be willing to help. She has a few things going on today, but I know if you ask, she'll give you a hand."

Travis nodded. *Stupid, stupid, stupid.* He'd let the woman's voice get to him, mesmerize him, turn his brain into complete mush. But who could blame him? Her voice was literally captivating. Swearing again, he dialed June.

"Well, good morning,." She sounded so genuinely happy to hear from him. Gratitude rushed through his veins. He hoped she would still be happy to talk to him after he told her why he was calling.

"Good morning, yourself. Just to be up front about things, I'm calling to ask you a favor."

"Then let's get down to business. What do you need?" God, he couldn't believe Sterling had found such a completely wonderful woman.

He paced the length of the work table, turned around, and paced back the other way. "I'm sure Sterling told you I was planning to hire someone to help with the books."

"He did."

Sterling gave Travis a thumbs up and then hefted a stack of two-by-fours onto his shoulder and carried them into the house.

Travis cleared his throat. "I hired someone today. She's coming tomorrow. Can you help me get the bunkhouse ready? I can clean it and everything, but I could use some help with all the feminine touches."

He could picture his future sister-in-law, lips twitching. "You mean, stuff guys wouldn't think of? Like bedsheets, a duvet, stocking the fridge?"

Travis nodded, pivoted, paced. "Exactly. Is there even a fridge in there?"

"You should find out and let me know."

"Right." He stopped pacing. "What the hell is a duvet?"

"You know, like a comforter. The blanket you put on the bed."

"Of course." He resumed pacing. "Do you have time to help me with this before midday tomorrow?"

"Of course I do. Let me move some things around and I can go shopping this afternoon. Can you have the place cleaned by, say, three p.m.?"

Travis exhaled. "Yes. Absolutely. I'll get started on it now. And June?"

"Yeah?"

"Thank you." If she were standing in front of him, he'd grab her shoulders and give her a big, loud smacker. "You're the best. I owe you, big time."

"Anytime, Travis. And if we're being totally honest, I'm doing it for myself, too. Because poor Sterling has been agonizing over your stress level. I think this will make us all feel better."

"Aw, has he? That warms my little heart."

"Very funny. I'll see you around three."

Although Travis had made his that-warms-my-heart comment sound like a joke, his eyes actually prickled with tears at the thought that Sterling worried about him. For so long, Sterling had eliminated himself from the family, and knowing he was back, not just physically, but emotionally, really did warm Travis's heart.

With a renewed sense of purpose, he returned to his house and gathered up his cleaning supplies. The bunkhouse door creaked when he opened it, which seemed pretty spine-chilling for a woman on her own (he'd seen plenty of horror movies). So he jogged to the shed on the side of the barn and grabbed a can of lubricant to oil the hinges before going all the way in. Once inside, he realized quite some time had passed since anyone set foot beyond the threshold.

Cobwebs hung from the corners of the ceiling and the curtain rods, and a thick layer of dust had settled on every flat surface. Why hadn't he thought to cover the furniture?

"I'm going to need a lot more than cleaning spray and paper towels."

He returned a few minutes later armed with his vacuum cleaner and broom, laundry detergent, and furniture polish.

The first thing he did was to take the curtains off the rods and put them in the washer. Then he set to work with the vacuum, focusing first on the cobwebs and then the couch. Before he did the floor, he dusted all the countertops and furniture, then shined their surfaces.

The windows were dingy with grime and dust, so he found a container of the heavy-duty ammonia-rich window cleaner and went to work on those before throwing them open to let in the clean fall breeze.

By the time June knocked on the door jamb at three, Travis had lost track of time, discarded his flannel, and worked up a good sweat. And, he was happy to notice when he stood back to admire his work that the place looked great. The countertops gleamed and the air smelled like lemon. Sunlight streamed through the windows, everything shined, and there was no sign of dust or grime.

"Come in," he told June, who was saying, "Wow, Travis! This looks great!"

He took some of the bags she carried. "Thanks. I've been working since we talked."

Setting the bags on the counter, she grimaced. "Yeah, the place was pretty grimy, wasn't it?"

"Yeah. I don't know why I said she could come tomorrow."

"Sterling said something about her voice?" Her forehead wrinkled. "Come on, I've got a whole nother load in the car."

Travis followed her out, hoping their trek to the car would distract June from her line of questioning. It didn't.

"So. Her voice."

"Right." From the trunk of June's car, Travis picked up a laundry basket full of towels, sheets, laundry detergent, dish soap, and a set of dishes. "I don't know how to describe it. It was almost like she had magical powers. Before I even knew what was happening, I'd offered her the job."

"Huh." June hefted a cardboard box from the backseat and used her hip to shut the door. "I cannot wait to see this unfold."

"What is that supposed to mean?"

"Oh, I don't know. Just seems like you're normally a lot more ... pragmatic than that."

He'd followed her into the house and she was already unloading the cardboard box, zipping around the bunkhouse putting things away. Bereft, he stood inside the door holding the laundry basket until she came to take it from him and set it on the counter.

"Pragmatic?"

"Yeah. Practical. Logical. Commonsensical. Hiring someone based on her voice is almost mystical or something."

"Is that bad?"

June paused as she reached to put away the dishes. "No. At least, *I* don't think so. It's going with your gut, right? I'm a big believer in that. I'm just saying I think it's going to be interesting when this mystery person arrives."

All this talk was making Travis nervous, and he told June so.

She stopped moving, shrugged at him, and grinned. "I mean, what's the worst thing that could happen?"

That question sent adrenaline shooting through his veins. "She's actually not an accountant and is just looking for a place to stay, and we end up with a squatter we can't get rid of."

June laughed out loud.

"I never should have hired her without meeting her in person. I'm an idiot."

"You're not an idiot." She came around the end of the kitchen counter and held out a stack of towels. "Go put these in the bathroom." He started walking. "Not just on the counter. Put them in the cabinet."

After June left, Travis closed up the bunkhouse and headed for the barn. He should box up the paperwork for Lila to sort, but he felt restless and taking a ride was the only thing that would quiet the inner voice that was now yelling at him for being the opposite of pragmatic, whatever that was.

Plus, he needed to check the fences. It didn't have to be done now, but still. Chewy and Leia knickered and bobbed their heads when he slid open the barn doors, and leaned into his touch when he reached up to rub their necks.

He saddled up Chewy and put a bridle on Leia so she could come, too. He led them into the sunshine and mounted Chewy, who danced around like he couldn't wait to run. And then they were off, sprinting for the far corner of the property. For his whole life, being on horseback and tearing across the land, the wind rushing past his body, had brought Travis a certain peace, a sense of calm.

It did that now.

Yes, the whole hiring-a-stranger-based-on-her-voice thing was still there, but it shrank and faded from the forefront of his mind as his body fell into a rhythm matching that of Chewy's strides.

The fall sunshine felt warm on his shoulders and the breeze smelled like the changing leaves. The horses' hooves beat the ground, and Travis's heart beat in time with them. In what felt like seconds, they'd reached the corner of the property.

Travis brought Chewy to a walk, and Leia slowed down, too. As breathless as the horses were, Travis let them move at a slower pace for a while. He'd brought a small notebook with him and jotted down fence-related items that needed attention: an oak shrub needed trimming, a panel needed repairing, and a leaning fence post needed straightening.

After he got Lila settled the next day, he'd grab a brother or two, load up the Ranger with tools and supplies, and come back out to tend to all of it.

A couple of hours had passed by the time Travis had ridden one section, and he'd managed to expel most of his nervous energy and work up a good sweat. By the time he put up the horses and fed them, and then showered and fed himself, the day would be practically over.

Chapter Seven

As a child, Lila had always been a big reader. She remembered so many stories where people left under the cover of darkness, and now she could see the appeal. Her flight didn't leave until eight a.m., which meant she didn't have to leave her apartment until six.

But knowing someone was lurking around, she decided to leave at four when the sky was still an inky pitch black aside from the glow of the city lights.

Even though she'd chosen that time because she figured no one would be crazy enough to sit outside then, she found herself stepping quietly, peering into the dark spaces, and hurrying along the sidewalk until she made it to her car, where she shined her phone flashlight into the backseat before getting in.

As she drove, too, she found herself looking into the rearview and sideview mirrors to make sure no one followed her. The airport's long-term parking lot was nearly empty. Nobody would hear her scream if someone attacked her.

The short-term garage suddenly seemed like a significantly safer option; it was attached to the airport terminal and people were always coming and going. But the cost to park there was almost twice as much, and she didn't know how long she'd be gone.

She'd researched the timing for the airport shuttle and exactly as she'd planned, it pulled up just as she made her way to the stop. Inside, the airport was quiet, sleepy travelers going through the motions. Lila joined them, checking her bag and getting in line for the security checkpoint. Her eyes felt gritty with exhaustion, but she found she couldn't relax enough to sleep while she waited. Instead, she pulled her baseball cap low and put her head down while she read a magazine, willing time to pass more quickly.

Naturally, her mind wandered, straight over to Prescott, Arizona and the Sweet Springs Ranch. From there, of course, she thought about the Wilder men. She couldn't stop envisioning the picture she'd seen with that newspaper article. *From left to right. Sterling, Hayes, Travis, and Cash.* They were all handsome, but her focus zeroed in on Travis. He was taller than the others, with broader shoulders. If she'd seen the photo in an actual newspaper, she wouldn't have been able to see the blue-green of his eyes or the way those eyes looked serious despite the smile.

At long last, it was time to board. Lila had booked a window seat so she could feign a deep interest in the scenery and avoid talking to anyone. The plan worked. She kept her face turned toward the window and her fellow passengers left her alone.

Finally, *finally*, the plane touched down in Phoenix, and Lila rushed to the car rental counter. A few minutes later she was on the road to Prescott. The relief she felt made her breathing easier. The farther she got from Phoenix's city center, the more her lungs expanded. She was safe. For now. She'd get to Sweet Springs Ranch, settle in, do the job she was hired to do, and then figure out her next steps.

Yes, she'd have to go back to Huntsville eventually, but she didn't want to think about that at the moment.

Her navigation app took her through downtown Prescott, which appeared to be an adorably old-fashioned city center. A grassy quad surrounded a stately old courthouse with wide staircases leading up to ornate wooden doors. Tall shade trees bordered the quad, and people milled around chatting, walking their dogs, and sipping on drinks. It all looked so *simple*.

Next, she drove out of the town and ended up on a wide-open road that wound through pastures and fields. Horses grazed and the clouds looked light and fluffy and Lila could swear she'd found a kind of paradise.

Within a few minutes, her phone told her to turn off that main road and there it was: Sweet Springs Ranch, Established in 1924. The journey felt so long and now, suddenly, she'd reached the ranch.

Lila gasped.

A canopy of trees shaded the long driveway and when she emerged from under it, a large arena and barn came into view. Those seemed empty, so she drove further onto the property. Ah, *there* was a house. It was under construction, but she could tell that in its heyday, it had been something to look at. A couple of trucks and a large camping trailer were parked outside, and Lila saw the first signs of life: a man was carrying a pile of boards on one shoulder as he walked toward the house.

He must have heard her car because he turned around, squinting. Sterling. Again, Lila thought about how good-looking Prescott grew its men, and wondered what in the world she'd gotten herself into. While she pulled up to park alongside the trucks, he jogged into the house. By the time she'd parked, he re-emerged, empty-handed and smiling.

So that's where the term lady killer comes from.

She parked and got out and he was standing in front of her, a hand extended, his grin practically splitting his face open. "You must be Lila. I'm Sterling." Before she could answer, he grabbed her hand and pumped it. "You'll be wanting Travis. Let me just give him a call."

Still grinning like the cat that ate the canary, he pulled his phone out of a holster on his belt. Lila clasped her hands behind her back and waited, unsure of where to focus her attention. She didn't want to stare at Sterling and she didn't want to let her gaze roam aimlessly around the place, so she decided to look at the house. It was old, for sure, and definitely hadn't been kept up. The paint was peeling and faded, and the front porch sagged. If she had a level, it'd probably show the whole thing leaned to one side. That explained the boards Sterling was carrying.

The muffled sound of someone answering came through Sterling's earpiece and it was obvious he could barely contain his laughter when he said, "Trav, Lila's here."

Travis must have asked what was so funny because Sterling gave one bark of laughter and said, "Nothing, man. Come on over to the big house."

He put his phone back on the clip and looked at Lila. "He's on his way. My fiancée should be around here somewhere. June!"

Lila jumped at the volume of his holler. He noticed, and his expression turned apologetic. He reached out as if he wanted to take her arm, but then apparently thought better of it, as if she looked like a frightened animal (she was sure she did), and dropped his hand. "Sorry. It's a bit chaotic around here. We've found it's easier to find each other if we just bellow. Like a bunch of country folks."

The humor hadn't left his eyes, but there was something else there now, too ... a softness. Pity, maybe? Curiosity? She couldn't be sure and she didn't have time to think on it any more because the breeze carried another holler to them on the breeze. "Coming!"

And then June appeared, bright as a summer day and twice as pretty. For a split second, her expression was warm, friendly. Then she took in Lila's appearance and she, too, seemed to find something about it humorous.

Suddenly Lila worried she might have food on her chin or something in her teeth. Or, worse, what if the dye was coming out and she had black smudges on her cheeks?

"Be right back." Sterling pointed to the house. "Just gotta go stack that wood where it's supposed to be."

As soon as he was gone, Lila seized the opportunity. "Do I have something on my face?"

"What?" June looked surprised. "No. You're fine. Clean as a whistle. Why do you ask?"

Relieved and newly unnerved, Lila inhaled. "Because you and Sterling both look amused."

June didn't deny it, but the sound of footsteps coming around the side of the house robbed her of the opportunity to say anything.

And there he was in person: Travis Wilder. When he saw her, he froze. Their eyes met. For the briefest span of time, an eyebrow quirked up in confusion. *The picture.* Lila panicked. She'd forgotten all about that. How was he going to feel about her uploading a picture of someone else?

Then he smiled. And God, was he gorgeous. Angels were singing. Golden sunlight shined down from the heavens. Glorious music filled the air. All her thoughts, all her worry, dropped away.

Then the music screeched to a halt as something shifted. His smile faded and the friendly lines around his eyes relaxed and he strode forward and stuck out his hand. "I'm Travis."

"Lila," she said, and even though he'd tempered his reaction to her she could still feel that energy, that connection, when she took it and shook.

"Nice to meet you."

He dropped her hand even while she said, "Likewise."

Sterling emerged from the house again and came walking up behind Travis, that same goofy grin still in place. He clapped his brother on the shoulder and pointed at Lila. "Lila."

Travis's response came out in a near growl. "We met."

Sterling looked at June, who, Lila noticed, looked straight-up amused (and also like she was trying to hide her amusement).

"Well, are you going to show her the bunkhouse?" June pronounced each of her syllables with extra clarity, like she was speaking to a toddler.

Travis shook his head, blinked. "Yeah. Of course." He turned to Lila and nodded once. "Would you like a tour?" He sounded oddly uncertain, so much different from how he'd sounded during the interview.

She hooked a thumb at her car. "I've got all my stuff in the car. Should I get it now?"

Travis's mouth dropped open and June rushed to answer. "Not yet. Let Travis show you around, and then you can move your car over to the bunkhouse. It's a long way to carry everything."

Travis nodded as if he'd been waiting for June's instructions. He licked his lips. "Okay. Well. Are you ready?"

Nervous, Lila nodded. "Ready."

"Want to come?" Even Lila could hear the desperation in his voice as he looked at June, who responded with a smug, "I'm good, thanks."

Like a little boy—why was she suddenly picturing him as a cute, freckle-faced kid?—Travis started walking and motioned for Lila to follow.

"This is the big house." He motioned at the house as he walked along its side, his strides so long, Lila had to quicken hers to keep up. "Sterling's remodeling it."

Once they'd passed the big house, he pointed to a smaller one in the distance. "That's my place. I have all the paperwork in there right now. Figured I wouldn't move anything until you had a chance to look through it and see if it's even something you want to tackle. There's no use moving it twice."

"That sounds reasonable."

He lifted his arm again to point at a low building several yards past his house. "That's the bunkhouse, where you'll be staying."

"Great!" Still almost running to keep up with the man-god next to her, Lila marveled at how perfect this setup was. The bunkhouse was situated so far back, tucked safely into the arms of the property where no one would just happen to pass by and see her.

She should listen, focus on what Travis said, but she couldn't because all of a sudden, the breeze carried his scent right up to her and it was all pine and wood and she wanted to be closer to him and inhale every last morsel.

"Sound good?"

Oh, God, what had she missed? She couldn't let him know she wasn't paying attention ... and she especially couldn't let him know she wasn't paying attention because he smelled so. Damn. Good.

"Sounds great." She had no idea what sounded great, other than his voice, which sounded like sex and satin sheets and warm, smooth skin against hers and *what was she thinking?*

They'd reached his front door and he was opening it and

gesturing for her to walk past him and go in, just like a real gentleman, and she was inside his house and it felt way too intimate.

"The office is through there." He pointed at an open door and she stopped short just after walking through it.

He'd mentioned a mess. That was an understatement. A table along one wall was absolutely overloaded with file boxes, which were absolutely stuffed full of papers. From where she was standing, Lila could tell that if someone had implemented a system, it was a long time ago—and no one had used it in ages.

She had no idea what to say and was relieved when he spoke up. "I told you it was a mess."

A heavy sigh escaped her mouth before she even realized it was coming.

At that, Travis laughed out loud. "Worse than you were expecting, isn't it?"

"No! No, it's not that. It's just—"

He held up a hand. "One thing you're going to learn right away is that the Wilder family doesn't sugar coat anything. Which means you don't have to, either. Trust me. I know it's a mess. That's why I needed help."

"I mean, what *happened?*" It was obvious from the look of the arena, barn, and big house—and now this giant, disorganized pile of paperwork—that the most of the place had been sorely neglected. Lila realized right away that her question may come across as prying, and she held up her hand this time. "Never mind. That was rude."

Travis shook his head. "No, it wasn't. It's a perfectly reasonable question. One I will answer over a drink. What do you say I show you the bunkhouse so you can get settled in, and then we'll have dinner together? I'll tell you everything." After a beat he added, "Well not *everything* everything. But everything you need to know."

She nodded, simultaneously wanting desperately to be alone with him over dinner and wanting to get as far away as she could from him and the feelings he stirred up. And why wasn't he asking about the picture? Maybe she'd never have to talk about it at all.

He gestured for her to head back to the front door and as she walked through the entryway she tried to get a feel for what his house was like. From the quick glimpses she caught, the place was tidy; she didn't see any stray clothes or dishes laying around. She also didn't see any photos on the walls or tables, or anything personal, like knickknacks. From that, she deduced he didn't have a woman in his life, and she kicked her inner sex goddess for doing a fist pump and whispering a victorious, "Yessss."

From the outside, the long, low bunkhouse looked a little sad as it squatted in the shade of the giant trees. But inside, it was bright and clean. She let her gaze roam over the space and when she turned to face Travis she realized he was watching her carefully. He was worried about her reaction and she found that so adorable, she wanted to throw her arms around him and squeeze. Because that would be wildly inappropriate, she went with using her words. "This is really nice. I love it. You even thought of laundry detergent and dish soap."

He chuckled, the sound deep and satisfying like the engine of an old truck. "*June* thought of laundry detergent and dish soap. I cleaned the place and she did the finishing touches."

Another interesting visual image flared as she imagined doing domestic work with Travis.

"That is really nice. Thank you. I'll thank her, too, as soon as I see her again."

Meanwhile, she compiled a list of items she'd need to cleanse this place and keep it safe from negative energy: sage, salt, crystals.

"You want to get your car and unpack?"

"Sure. I didn't bring much, so I can go ahead and do that if you've got something else to do."

"I'll just help you carry stuff in. It's no big deal."

Chapter Eight

Travis was in trouble. Having just finished helping Lila carry her belongings into the bunkhouse, he returned to his house, and shut the door. Then he started pacing, something he realized he'd been doing a lot.

Lila Sullivan was the absolute worst-case scenario in terms of an accountant. She was drop-dead gorgeous. He could hardly tear his gaze away from her bright green eyes. And when he was looking at her—which was pretty much every time they were in the same space —he couldn't help but imagine running his fingertips over her skin. He just knew it was silky smooth, soft. He wished, desperately, she'd never mentioned her love for fitness. Because even though she wore jeans and a sweater, he couldn't help but notice her curves, which looked toned and strong. Touchable.

He'd already imagined all the ways he could make love to her and the was still a *stranger*.

To make matters even worse, those startling green eyes had a haunted look, one that both intrigued him and made him feel fiercely protective. If he were a knight, he'd wield chain mail and a sword and chase down anyone who tried to hurt her.

He'd had his suspicions the moment she said she could come to Arizona the day after their interview. Seeing her in person (and realizing she looked completely different than the woman in the picture she'd uploaded) confirmed it: she was running from something.

Every single rational fiber in his body screamed at him to tell her their situation wasn't going to work after all, to send her away. But all the emotional fibers clamored for his attention, telling him he'd be crazy to put her out into the world. He could protect her here.

When he remarked that she hadn't brought very much, just a medium-sized suitcase and a duffle bag, all she'd said was that she traveled light. He told her he'd give her some time to get settled and she said she'd come over to get acquainted with the paperwork in an hour.

So now, here he was, pacing his house, waiting. And, of course, thinking about Lila.

Through the narrow window next to his front door, he saw her approaching. In the slight hunch of her shoulders, the quick darting of her eyes, the small, close-together steps, it was apparent she felt unsafe. When he opened his front door, that seemed to change. Her body relaxed and her expression eased into a smile.

He stood back and gestured for her to come in. "Did you get settled in okay?"

"I did." She ducked past him and her scent, a summer bouquet, followed her. "Thanks to you and June."

"Good." He shut the door. "I should probably admit that I'm almost afraid for you to start going through these boxes. Once you dig in, you might lose interest, real fast."

Waving him off, she went through to the office. "My suitcase is unpacked. I'd say I'm committed."

The words shouldn't have made Travis's heart beat faster, but they did.

Now that she had a task on which to focus, Lila's movements became calm and certain.

"I'd like to start with one box. Let's move all the others over there and then I'll have space to lay everything out."

Travis nodded and grabbed the closest box. As they worked together to stack the others along one wall, Lila said, "I don't expect you to hang around. You mentioned you had other things to do. If I have questions or anything, I can just find you. Or holler at you, like Sterling said is customary around here."

The strange thing was, Travis wanted to stay. Before, the idea of going through all those papers terrified him. Now, there was almost nothing he wanted to do more.

That's not true. A little voice piped up from the back of his mind. *You'd like to get Lila Sullivan naked.*

As tempting as it was to hit himself over the head, he didn't. He smiled at Lila. "Thank you. That sounds great. I've got to finish riding the fence line before I bring in a new group of cattle."

She'd been lifting stacks of paper out of the box and setting them on the table and she paused to look at him, her eyebrows raised in the most adorable way. "You're going to get cattle?"

He wasn't sure whether the idea intrigued or repulsed her. "Yeah. Back in the day, Sweet Springs was a renowned cattle ranch. I'd like to build it back into that."

Lips pursed, she said, "It seems so weird to just go buy cattle."

"I never thought about it that way, but you're right. It's fun, though. I usually go to auction."

"They auction cattle?"

"Well, yeah."

"I guess I have a lot to learn about the business."

Heartened, he smiled. "You'll get it. You have reams of paper to go through. Anyway, it's going to take some time to make the ranch lucrative again, especially because of this *legacy* my dad left us." He gestured at the boxes against the wall. She nodded and continued removing papers from the box.

He'd been dreading telling Lila, but this seemed like the perfect opportunity. "Remember when I said I'd tell you everything?"

Still working, she nodded.

"I know I said I'd tell you over a drink, but now seems like the perfect time. I mean, we can still get a drink later. If you want. But —" He stopped himself, ran a hand over his face. "Let me just get back on track. I should mention that my dad had a gambling problem. I'm not sure how long it was going on—at least five years, I know that much—and he nearly ran the place into the ground, financially. I didn't really want to air the family laundry, but I figured you should know in case you come across anything that doesn't fit in with the traditional business accounting."

Lila had paused, and now she resumed taking papers out of the box. "That's good to know. I mean, not that he had a gambling problem and almost ran the place into the ground, but just that I might find paperwork relating to that. I'll set aside anything I find."

Only then did Travis realize his vision had gone blurry with nerves, waiting for her reaction. And whatever she thought, she had the decency not to seem alarmed or scandalized. "Thank you. I guess I'll leave you to it."

As soon as he left Lila, he wanted to be near her again. "Which is all the more reason to take a nice, long ride."

This time, he saddled up Leia. It occurred to him that he could invite Lila to go for a ride, saddle up both horses, let them both get a good workout. The way she'd wrinkled her nose when he talked about the cattle, though, made him wonder if she'd ever ridden. Not that he'd mind teaching her. His imagination went wild, broadcasting images of Lila in boot-cut jeans, their bodies close as he showed her how to mount.

He wasted no time getting the horses into a full-on canter and within minutes, they'd reached the next section of fence. As they slowed to a walk, a whistle cut through the air and Travis looked up to see Cash, on horseback, coming toward him.

"Who's this?"

Cash leaned forward and rubbed the horse's neck. "His name is Bernard."

"Where'd you get him?"

Cash chuckled. "Hendrickson. Old geezer is selling off most of his horses. I guess he finally realizes he can't ride anymore."

"You buying them?"

Cash shrugged, looked off into the distance. "Thinking about it. I wanted to get back in the saddle, first. See how it felt."

"And?"

When Cash made eye contact and smiled, Travis knew: he was hooked. "It's all right."

If he'd been within punching distance Travis would have taken a swing. "I can tell you're excited."

"I am, bro. Not gonna lie. I need to make a plan, though, for where to keep them and stuff."

Would it be too much to fall off his horse and onto his knees and beg his brother to move back to the ranch, horses and all? "You can keep them here. Well, I mean, how many are we talking?"

Cash laughed. "I don't know yet. Thanks for the offer, though. I'll keep you posted. Anyway, I see you're riding fences, but you sure had an interesting look on your face when I rode up."

Did he? "Did I?"

"Yeah, man. You looked like you were trying to solve the world's problems."

Travis sighed and the horse shifted beneath him. "I'm sure you heard I hired an accountant."

"Oh, I heard, all right." There was that twinkle in his brother's eyes.

Of their own accord, Travis's eyebrows drew downward. "And what exactly did you hear?"

Cash's dimple flashed. "Only that you'd hired an accountant based on her voice alone, and that she showed up looking like your worst nightmare. A super-hot but fragile young woman."

Travis swore. "Word travels fast."

"Don't I know it. I've already heard from Mrs. Wondrowski about you pouring me into a ride share the other night at A Cold One, believe it or not. I remember that evening distinctly and there was no pouring of anyone into a vehicle."

"You're right about that. And I guess even though I might not use the same words to describe the situation, you're right about the accountant. Well, mostly. I set up interviews only with candidates whose experience matched to the needs of the job. But yes, her voice did have quite an impact."

"Do you think, fifty years from now, we're all going to be sitting around the table, telling your grandkids, 'And this is where their love story started'?"

Travis eased Leia into a walk. Chewy fell into step beside them, and Cash and Bernard followed.

"Ha." That gave him a start. "Anyway. She's here now. She's in my spare bedroom sorting papers."

"You left her alone in your house?"

Travis looked across Chewy's back at Cash and shrugged. "Why not? It's not like I've got anything to hide, or anything worth stealing." His eyes on the fence line, Travis relaxed his grip on the reins. He wasn't in too much of a hurry to get back to the house.

"I guess that's true."

"I sort of wonder if *she* has something to hide, though." The words were out of Travis's mouth before he could stop them and he almost wished he could call them back. Lila's jumpy behavior reminded him of a rabbit that knew a snake was watching it, waiting to strike. She was scared, and he didn't want to blow her cover ... but also, this was his family. They'd agreed they wouldn't keep any more secrets.

"What do you mean?" Cash pulled Bernard to a stop, and Leia and Chewy stopped, too. As if she sensed Cash was the one calling for eye contact, Leia turned so Travis was facing his brother.

"The thing is, I selected the option to have applicants upload a photo when they applied." He held up a hand before Cash could make fun of him, accuse him of looking for a hot bookkeeper (partly because he'd gotten one). His face colored and he forged ahead. "Only because I wanted to make sure I wasn't going to hire someone local, someone we knew."

Amused now, Cash nodded. "Okay."

"Anyway, the photo she uploaded—it could have been anyone. It was a bit blurry, but in it, the woman looked like she had light brown hair, brown or maybe hazel eyes, and a medium complexion. But—"

"A raven-haired beauty with bright green eyes, creamy-white skin, and a jumpy disposition shows up on your doorstep."

Word really did travel fast. "Right."

"And you haven't asked her about the picture yet."

"Right."

"Well, why the hell not? I mean, it's a reasonable question."

Travis nodded, nudged Leia to get her moving again. "Honestly? I don't want to scare her off ... that is, if the paperwork doesn't do that on its own. It took me forever to admit this, but I can't handle the accounting on my own. Someone said yes to coming here, and I don't want to risk losing that."

Cash nodded. "Are you also afraid of her answer?"

Of course his brother would pick up on that. "I mean, yeah. What if she's in the witness protection program? Or worse, what if she's a hard criminal, running from a warrant in Alabama?"

"Do you really think either of those things is possible?" Cash looked at him sideways.

Travis chuckled. "No, I guess not. I mean, if she was in the witness protection program, she'd have some kind of handler guy, right? And he'd come to us and ask us if she could stay here. And if she was a criminal ... well, she's not. So."

"Let's hope not, bro. Because from where I'm sitting, this thing has potential."

Chapter Nine

Lila was glad Travis left her alone with the paperwork. The boxes and boxes and piles and piles of it. That way, he couldn't hear her when she leaned on the table and moaned. "What have I gotten myself into?"

He'd described the situation as a mess and that was a serious understatement. Lila was fairly certain no one had looked at any of the paperwork for years beyond opening envelopes (in most cases) and shoving correspondence into file boxes.

After sitting, frozen in complete overwhelm for a few minutes, Lila decided the best first step was to spend some time going through the boxes, just to see what she was working with. Then she could categorize and sort.

Some music would be nice, but nobody had radios anymore, and she didn't want to drain her phone battery. "Add a Bluetooth speaker to your cart," she told herself, then took out her phone and did so. "Add placing your order to your list." She nodded at that too, and added that item to her to-do list.

"Focus, Lila."

Already, she'd spotted a few repeat documents. Yellow carbon-copy receipts came from the feed and grain store and she wondered how long it'd been since anyone at Sweet Springs actually made an order. The first receipt she found was dated several years ago. Without looking too carefully at the yellow receipts, she began pulling them out of the piles and stacking them.

Another regular: half-page receipts from the fuel company. From what she could gather, Sweet Springs must have a big gas tank somewhere onsite, and at one time, they must have used that to fill up their tractors. Those receipts got their own pile.

Bank statements, too, seemed plentiful, and she started a stack of those as well, quickly noticing that many of them were unopened.

She became so immersed in her work, she jumped when someone tried to open the front door. She swore when she remembered she'd locked it as soon as Travis left, and rushed to open it. Through the window she could see his frustration.

"I'm sorry. I locked it when you left."

As soon as he made eye contact, his expression softened. "It's okay. I just didn't realize. I don't think I've ever locked this door."

That explained why he felt comfortable leaving a stranger in his house. Lila couldn't imagine what it would be like to navigate the world with such a sense of security. She refrained from telling him maybe he *should* lock it.

"You look shellshocked. Please tell me you're not ready to leave."

Her laugh came out as a strangled sound. "I was debating."

"Oh, God. I was afraid of this." His body sagged and this time, her laugh came out genuine and she put a hand on his arm.

"Not really. I'll admit, I had a moment when I was thinking, 'What have I gotten myself into?'" She inhaled and held her breath for a second, debating. "But it's fine. I'll get a system going and I'll have it organized in no time."

"At least, that's what you've been telling yourself for the past couple of hours." His eyes danced and she was relieved he could see the humor in the situation.

"Right."

"I promised you dinner."

She panicked. The idea was nice, but she couldn't bear the thought of going into town, of having someone recognize her. The absolute last thing she needed was for someone to post a photo of her eating in one of Prescott's restaurants ... how easy would it be for that madman to track her down then?

Once again, it seemed as though Travis discerned what she was thinking. "Want to stay in? If we're being honest, I'm a decent cook, but I'm just not feeling it tonight. We could order a pizza." Before she even answered, he held up his hands. "Wait. You're a fitness guru, right? You probably don't want pizza. There's a salad place. And a really good Thai place, too. They probably have healthier options. And now I'm rambling. You name it, I'll buy."

Charmed, Lila found herself smiling the first real smile she had in days. "You know what? I can't remember the last time I had pizza. Being an in—I mean, representing myself as a health and fitness expert, I always felt like I had to watch what I ate."

She'd almost slipped ... which she couldn't do, under any circumstances. What was it about Travis that made her so comfortable? Whatever it was, she had to tamp it down. Douse it. Bury it.

In fact, maybe she *shouldn't* stay. Getting comfortable with anyone—letting her guard down—seemed like a mistake at this point. But where else would she go?

"Pizza it is. What do you like?"

Her mouth watered while she thought about that. "Classic pepperoni."

"You know, how a person likes her pizza says a lot about her."

Why were his eyes so intense? What was he thinking? "What does classic pepperoni say?"

The smile he gave her lessened the intensity of his gaze, but she could still feel energy coming off him in waves. "It says you're a sensible woman who appreciates the simpler things in life."

"Scary how accurate that is."

"Yeah? Well, I like the spicy meat lovers'. What do you think that says about me?"

She laughed out loud. "I'm too demure to say."

Standing right there in the office, he ordered the pizza and offered her a beer. She accepted and told herself she'd have just the one. She couldn't get too relaxed. Relieved when he led her to the dining room table—sitting there felt more professional and less intimate—she sank into a chair across from him.

Almost as soon as she took a sip he said, "I need to ask you something."

She froze, the bottle just centimeters from her lips. Of their own accord, her eyes found his. Then she realized how silly (or guilty) she must look and she lowered her bottle onto the table. Her mind raced. What was he going to ask her? Did he know she was hiding? Did he know who she was? Would he let her stay? "Of course."

"On the employment application, you uploaded a photo..."

Crap. She'd hoped he'd forgotten about that.

"It wasn't you, was it?"

"It wasn't." Her voice came out in an almost-whisper.

For a long moment, she debated. She could tell him it was her, that it was an old photo and she'd since dyed her hair (which she had). Or she could tell him she'd wanted privacy (which was true). Or she could tell him she'd completed the application in a hurry and accidentally uploaded the wrong photo. None of these seemed believable.

Just tell him.

Somewhere, she'd read that if you don't want to tell someone the whole truth, you should tell as much of the truth as you could, while omitting as much detail as possible.

She cleared her throat. "As I mentioned, I've had some recent challenges with my company. Some of those challenges relate to my, ah, public image. This job looked so perfect on the application, and I really wanted it. By the time I'd come to the part where I had to upload a picture, I was already in, elbows deep. So I searched the Internet for my own name and found a different Lila Sullivan. I figured if my picture was the make-or-break element of that application, then I wouldn't want to work for you anyway. Not that I knew it was you at the time." Her attempt at a smile felt like a grimace.

For another long moment, Travis didn't answer. If she had to guess, she'd guess he was warring with himself over how much information to push for and whether this lie (however white it was) was worth terminating their agreement immediately.

She waited, without moving a single muscle.

"I reckon that makes sense. When I first saw you, I felt—well, I felt surprised, first of all. The woman in the picture you uploaded didn't draw my notice much at all. But you—let's just say I couldn't take my eyes off you."

He couldn't?

"I mean, that's not to say—I'm sorry. That was inappropriate."

Maybe it was, but it thrilled her to know he felt attracted to her, too. If she wasn't mistaken, a slow, coy smile was spreading across her face. To cover it up, she took a long drink of her beer.

"I'm sorry," he said again.

She waved him off. "It's fine. I understand." The less he told her, the less she'd feel obligated to tell him.

"I feel like I should explain why I chose to have people upload a picture."

Again, she waved him off. "You don't have to explain. Your application, your business, your choice."

"No, I want to." He, too, took a long drink of beer. "This whole thing—" he made a circle with one hand to encompass the ranch— "it's been humiliating. The fundraiser we had this summer went great and proved that like June said, the community supported us. And yet, I didn't want to hire anyone we knew ... I couldn't chance someone in this town airing our dirty laundry. Well, any more than it had already been aired. Because to tell you the truth, I have no idea what you're going to find in there." He gestured at the room where Lila had started laying some of the paperwork out on the table.

"I may have assumed you wanted pictures so you could choose the best-looking applicant." She knew he could hear the teasing tone in her voice because he grinned. "But now that I've seen the literal mountain of paperwork in there, and heard about your dad, I understand. And I promise, if anyone appreciates your need for discretion, it's me."

He gave her one business-like nod and then the pizza delivery person knocked on the door. Lila, of course, flinched and her head whipped toward the door. While she chastised herself, Travis raised an eyebrow at her and stood up.

He set the pizza boxes on the table. "Expecting someone?"

"No." She took the plate he handed her, opened the first box to find it was meat lovers', and then opened the second one and put a couple of slices on her plate.

"What was that, then?"

"I was just surprised, that's all."

"Huh." He pulled a piece of meat lovers' off the pie and the cheese stretched, making Lila's mouth water again.

She took a bite of her slice and groaned in pleasure, closing her eyes. The spice of the pepperoni and the tang of the tomato sauce and the creaminess of the cheese came together in what she'd definitely consider a divine experience.

When she finished chewing and swallowing and opened her eyes, she found Travis watching her with the most interesting expression on his face.

Was it arousal?

It'd been so long since she spent any time with a man, but she was almost positive Travis found her eating pizza arousing. And that aroused her. His eyes glinted. He licked his lips. He swallowed. He watched as she used a finger to wipe a little grease off the side of her mouth. His eyes followed her every movement.

Because she enjoyed that so very much, she put her finger in her mouth and sucked it clean, slowly and sensually. An actual groan escaped from his throat and she felt a flicker of triumph. She waited for his gaze to meet hers, and then she gave him her best I-know-you-want-me smile.

They couldn't be together—she was staying only for as long as it took her to organize his mess—but she could enjoy that sizzle in his eyes until then, couldn't she?

When he smiled, slow and sinful, she knew without a doubt: she could.

Chapter Ten

Travis didn't need all three of his brothers to help him repair the fence line, but he figured inviting them was akin to an impromptu family meeting. Which was perfect, because he wanted to get their perspective on *The Lila Situation*. That's what it had officially become after she watched him watching her eat pizza the night before.

Now here he was, lying in bed, thinking of the way she licked her bottom lip, an erection the size of Alaska pressing against his underwear.

Before even getting out of bed, he fired off a text to his brothers. He got up and poured coffee, then made his way to the shower, where he could hear his brothers' responses coming in. His phone continued to go off the whole time he showered, dried off, and pulled on his underwear. He toweled his hair dry and shook his head while yet another round of texts came in.

When he opened his texting app he had to scroll quite a ways to get to his original message: *Anyone up for repairing fence today?*

The initial responses were generic:

Hayes: *Sure, what time?*

Sterling: *You bet. I could use some time away from the big house.*

Cash: *I'm free all day.*

Then, naturally, the ribbing started. Hayes asked Cash why he was free all day, and Sterling jumped on that, wondering when he was going to get his act together and do something with his life. Cash, sounding wounded (at least, as much as a guy could sound wounded via text), responded that he might have some news about that by this afternoon. Then Cash asked what everyone else was up to that day, and Hayes and Sterling gave their typical BS answers.

Hayes: *I have a meeting with the president this morning. He wants my opinion on how to get the ladies.*

Sterling: *You know, the usual. Fighting zombies til noon and then taking a nap.*

Chuckling, Travis texted, *Sorry I missed all this. I was in the shower. Why don't we meet at, say, 1 p.m.?*

The three of them responded with thumbs-up emojis. Travis should have known that wouldn't be the end of the conversation. When Hayes asked how things were going with Lila, he wished he'd waited to start this thread until they were well into the workday. Then they wouldn't have time to converse.

He typed, *Well, the trial period isn't over yet, but she seems fairly committed.* He left out all the thoughts that had kept his mind racing overnight—he wanted to talk to them in person about those.

Cash: *But have you asked her out yet?*

Travis shook his head. *No. Not happening. This is a strictly professional arrangement.*

Besides, based on her jumpiness and her over-the-top need for privacy, Travis thought she might not be in the right frame of mind to start a relationship. He could hear Callie already: *Shouldn't let you let her decide that for herself?* Excessive honesty from his sister-in-law was the product of having grown up together.

He put his phone on silent and set it face down on his desk. Lila would be there any minute and God only knew what other comments his brothers would make that would leave him feeling awkward when she arrived. Sure enough, a knock sounded a couple minutes later. Travis opened the door and the sight of Lila stole his breath. She'd pulled her long hair into a bun on top of her head, which made her Kelly green eyes stand out in the most incredible way. She wasn't wearing any makeup and for the first time he noticed a light dusting of freckles across her nose. In that moment, he was fairly certain she could very well be some kind of mystical creature—a fairy or a sprite or a woodland nymph.

"Good morning." He wondered how long he'd stood there, staring.

"Good morning." She smiled. He could get used to seeing her first thing every day. He kicked himself for thinking that. Neither of them even knew if she was planning to stay. And even if she stayed long enough to get everything in order, he'd already told her she could work remotely if she wanted to. In Alabama.

So many reasons to keep things strictly professional, and yet ...

"Come on in. Coffee's on."

"It smells good. I should have gotten up a little earlier and made a pot with the coffee I ordered yesterday. I don't want to drink all of yours."

"I don't mind sharing."

The truth was, setting a mug on the counter for her when he got down his own felt domestic in the best possible way. Not that he'd admit that to her or anyone.

"All I've got is milk and sugar, nothing fancy."

"That's fine. That's what I use at home."

Why did even that—the simplicity of how she took her coffee—seem so significant?

He got out the milk and the bag of sugar. "I don't have a sugar bowl."

She laughed at his apologetic tone. "Why should you, if you don't take sugar? It's fine. I can just scoop it right out of the bag if you give me a spoon."

I could so fall for her.

And then they were standing in the kitchen, both of them leaning against the counter, sipping coffee, and he realized it was the most natural thing in the world.

Which is why he had to get back to his computer and bury himself in important tasks (real or made up). The hours ticked by, and Travis did his absolute best not to listen to the sounds of Lila working.

Finally, it was almost one o'clock.

Not every legacy Levi Wilder left behind carried sadness and grief. From the time they were small, Levi instilled in his boys the importance of being on time. So Travis wasn't surprised when he walked out of his house at five minutes 'til, and all three of his brothers were waiting for him. Cash, wearing that devilish grin as usual, lifted his chin at the front door and said, "We didn't want to knock. You know, just in case. Don't bother knockin' if this boat's a'rockin'." He rocked his hips forward and back.

Travis rolled his eyes while Hayes and Sterling whooped. "I'll have you know, we shared a very professional morning in two separate rooms for the most part."

"That's a shame, isn't it?" Hayes's question was directed at Sterling, whose shoulder he grabbed and gave a friendly shake.

Sterling took some pity on Travis. He smiled as if he agreed with Hayes, but he didn't say anything.

Travis groaned. "We can take my truck. I've got it loaded."

"I call shotgun." Cash hooted as he pulled open the passenger door and got in.

"Think he'll ever outgrow that?" Travis wanted to know.

Hayes and Sterling shook their heads and the rest of them climbed into the truck.

"So what did you really want to talk about?" Hayes had never been one to beat around the bush and his directness had only intensified since he and Callie got together.

Travis didn't bother trying to deny the ulterior motive behind asking for help with repairing the fence line. "You know, the whole thing about Lila uploading a photo of someone else on her job application."

Cash rolled down his window. "Can't really blame her, can you?"

"What do you mean?"

"I mean, let's face it." He shrugged. "She's a looker. She was probably afraid that if she uploaded a real picture of herself, you'd hire her just because she's hot."

Hayes reached over the top of the passenger seat and punched Cash in the arm. Cash threw up his hands, all innocence. "What? It's true."

Amused, Travis said, "She *is* a looker. I think we can all agree on that. But here's the thing. I asked her about it and she said something happened with her other job. Something about being in the public eye. She said she uploaded a different picture because she needed privacy."

"That's pretty ironic, right?" Sterling leaned forward. "You asked for a picture for the same reason."

Travis considered as the truck bumped along the dirt road that split the pasture in two. "Yes. But there're two things about her dishonesty." He held up a finger. "One is that it shows me she's afraid of something. I mean, she has a salt barrier inside the front door."

"A salt barrier?" Hayes's forehead wrinkled.

"I know. I had to look it up. It's to protect against bad juju."

"Yikes," Cash said.

Travis nodded. "I know. And I don't know why—I don't even know her, really—but that makes me want to protect her."

"She does seem a bit ... fragile." Sterling chuckled. "When she first pulled up here, she jumped every time someone dropped a board or hit a nail inside the big house."

Travis nodded, sighed. "Yeah. I've seen that. When the pizza guy came last night."

"Wait. Hold the train." Cash held up a hand.

"You ordered pizza and ate it together?" His eyebrows moved up and down, fast. Travis shook his head and plowed on. "But the second thing about her dishonesty is that I feel like she's hiding something. What trouble is she in? And do we want to risk her bringing it here? I think we can all agree we've had enough trouble around here."

"We have," Hayes said. "But if she was willing to run away from whatever trouble she encountered, maybe that means she doesn't have anyone else. It would be a shame to turn her away."

A sudden rise of emotion surprised Travis. "That's kind of what I was thinking. But I wanted to run it by you guys before making a decision."

"We appreciate it, man," Hayes said.

"Plus, if you let her stay here, you might end up, you know." Cash wiggled his eyebrows again, earning three more punches.

"Dude should not be allowed to ride shotgun," Sterling said.

They'd reached the northwest corner of the property. Travis stopped the truck and took his notebook out of his pocket, then pulled forward to the first problem spot he'd identified. They all got out and Travis opened the toolbox in the bed of the truck. "There are a couple of shrubs in the next hundred yards or so that need to be trimmed."

He handed the saw to Cash, who groaned, just like in the old days. "Why do I always get the crap jobs?"

Just like in the old days, Hayes snatched the saw. "Who cares which job you get? It's all got to be done."

While Cash mumbled something about being one of the middle children, Travis got out the drill and a box of screws. "Here. Here's a big-boy job. Let me get you a couple of boards and you can start replacing rails. I don't think you'll need the saw."

As they got to work, Travis felt the familiar ache of longing. He experienced it less frequently these days, but whenever it hit him, he wondered if there would ever come a time when he would stop wishing he could talk to his mom.

Physical labor had always provided a good distraction. Somehow, working until his muscles burned and sweat covered his skin released some of the tension that crept in whenever he thought about her.

As a child, the pain of her leaving, abandoning them, was so intense, he could feel it in every part of his body. His chest would ache and that pain would radiate, gnawing at his consciousness.

Before she left, Sophia Stewart—she'd never taken Levi's surname—gathered her four sons in the living room. Travis still remembered that childlike feeling of anticipation. He thought she was going to surprise them (it turned out she was, but not in the way he expected).

She called to them in her singsongy voice. "Boys! Come in here, all of you."

She had them sit down on the couch and Travis remembered squirming to make room for himself between Sterling and Hayes. He started to whine, but then he saw the look on his mom's face. Her mouth was drawn into a line and for the first time he noticed little pockets of skin on either side, like she was trying not to frown. He stopped squirming and waited, a sick feeling coiling in his stomach.

Once they were all sitting still, she knelt in front of them and spoke: "Dad and I have decided to part ways."

Silence.

The *parting of ways* didn't come as too much of a shock. Their parents had been fighting for as long as Travis could remember. Most of the arguments happened behind closed doors, but all of the Wilder boys heard the quiet, angry words their parents slung back and forth. When they were all in the same room, Levi and Sophia brought the tension with them. It hung in the air like a thick, cold fog.

Sterling was the first to find his voice. "What does that mean, exactly?"

Their mom cleared her throat. Her eyes darted from one of them to the next, and that's when Travis knew. She was leaving. His entire body vibrated with fear about what she was going to say.

While they waited for her response, all the whispers he'd heard around town floated into his consciousness. *Sophia is a literal movie star. She's meant for the big city, the silver screen. She'll never stick around. Can you believe Sophia Stewart has stuck with Levi Wilder all these years? It's only a matter of time until she realizes what she's done. There's no way Sophia is going to stick around this podunk town, but they already have four boys. What a tragedy.*

"I'm leaving." The words ended on a sob, and Sophia covered

her face with her hands. Sterling, the oldest, was the first to go to her, to get up off the couch and place a hand on her shoulder.

She was gone the next day.

At first, Travis noticed her absence daily. In the mornings, Levi started work early, so the boys had to fend for themselves for breakfast. There were no more stacks of pancakes, sizzling bacon, or fresh fruit. There also wasn't anyone to tell them to put on their shoes and catch the bus, and they missed it several times. After school, they were once again left to their own devices, and while making peanut butter and chocolate chip sandwiches was fun at first, the excitement wore off when they realized the monotony of making your own snacks, day after day. Their mom's place at the dinner table remained empty until someone finally moved her chair to the corner and started stacking laundry on it.

Soon, her absence was the new normal. But Travis still noticed it on special occasions, like birthdays or school performances or art shows. Her absence at those events stopped bothering him at some point—maybe by the time he was in eighth grade and all his friends seemed embarrassed of their parents—but he still wished for her every now and then. When he got deathly ill and had to get his own medicine or hot tea. When he had his first crush sophomore year and wanted advice from a girl. Not just one of his immature school friends, but a real, actual girl. High school graduation. The purchase of his first pair of horses when he was fifteen.

And now, as a grown man, he wanted his mom again. This ... *thing* with Lila, whatever it was, wasn't as simple as a school-aged crush. His mom would know what to do. She was worldly, experienced, wise.

"Earth to Travis." Cash stood in front of him, grinning, waving both hands like an air traffic controller. Travis jumped, snapped out of it.

"Where'd you go?" Cash smiled, but his brow was furrowed with concern.

Travis shook his head. "I was just spacing out. Thinking about..."

"Lila?"

Travis shrugged. "In a way, I guess. Anyway, what's up?"

"I think we're done with this first section. Want to move on?"

They did, and while Travis drilled and measured and cut, his thoughts returned to his mom.

Why hadn't she even called or come home? Didn't she care about them?

He knew she did. It was impossible not to remember the way she brushed back his hair when she tucked him in at night. The way she stopped to kiss him on the head when she walked by. The way she smiled at him when he said something funny. But how could she leave and not come back?

And what about their dad? Travis had seen it with his own eyes: his parents were in love at one point. When the boys were really little, it wasn't uncommon for their dad to sweep their mom into a dance when they finished a movie and the credits came on. Late at night, the two of them would often sit on the front porch and talk quietly. Travis could hear their murmurs and their hushed laughter through his open window as he drifted off to sleep.

And then she just up and left. Was the whole thing an illusion?

Whenever he tried to talk to his brothers about it, they shut him down. He learned that they didn't want to talk about her or think about her or even say her name. And Travis learned early on that you never mentioned her in front of Dad.

But the questions still plagued him. How could true love just slip away like that? It was supposed to be the foundation of their family ... the foundation of their very existence.

As they all got older and his brothers moved out and made their own way, Travis clung to his home.

He built a house on the ranch and poured himself into making it a home. He planted a garden and bought comfortable couches and hung art on the walls. It was empty of other people ... but wasn't that safer? If you didn't make people part of your sense of home, they couldn't destroy that when they left.

Chapter Eleven

L ila woke with a start. Her pillowcase and sheets were damp with sweat.

It was just a nightmare.

Safe and sound in the bunkhouse at the Sweet Springs Ranch, she went through the anxiety-fighting exercise she'd learned as a child: focus on one thing she could touch (the satiny-soft sheets June had chosen for her), one she could hear (the thrum of the ceiling fan), one she could see (the shadows of the leaves on the tree outside her window), and one thing she could smell (the scent of her shampoo on the pillowcase).

Although the bad dream shifted and changed every time it visited her, the theme was always the same: Lila was powerless.

The bullying started in fifth grade.

One night after a family birthday party, Lila's parents sat with her aunts and uncles around the kitchen table, playing cards and chatting after the kids went to bed. Lila fell asleep quickly, but woke up an hour later to use the bathroom. When she stepped into the hallway she heard one of her aunts say, "Lila's really getting that fifth grade chub, isn't she?"

Someone else tittered and Lila felt the heat of embarrassment flush her face.

Her mom was quick to jump in. "Oh, Tracy. You're always so worried about those things. She'll grow out of it in no time."

Lila was grateful her mom quashed that topic, but her words also confirmed what Aunt Tracy said. Her throat thick with wanting to cry, Lila tiptoed into the bathroom. For the first time, when she looked in the mirror she noticed her stomach did stick out more than it had before and her face was a little rounder.

Then, as if that evening somehow shined a spotlight on her changing body, the kids at school took notice, and they weren't shy about sharing their opinions.

"There's more of you to love this year, Lila."

"Now we know what happens when you swallow a watermelon seed."

"Maybe Mr. Hardy should assign you *two* seats."

Then the taunting started. During class, if someone got up to sharpen a pencil or get a tissue or go to reading group, he—it was usually a boy—would snort or whisper, "Oink," and then snicker.

She tried to cover up her midsection by wearing baggy t-shirts or oversized hoodies, but still, the kids were relentless. One morning when she came into the classroom, a Twinkie sat on her desk. After looking around and realizing hers was the only desk with a Twinkie on it, she panicked. Immediately, tears welled in her eyes, but she knew crying was the absolute worst thing she could do. She set her backpack on her chair and took out her binder, then slid her binder onto her desk and knocked the Twinkie onto the floor.

The teacher, Ms. Knock, an athletic woman with a booming voice, hollered at her. "Lila! Your Twinkie fell off your desk."

Great. As if the Twinkie itself wasn't embarrassing enough.

Lila nodded. Someone snickered, the sound echoing around the classroom (at least, in Lila's mind). Part of her felt like she should say it wasn't hers, but the other part of her knew that if she did that, whoever placed it on her desk would disagree with her, publicly, making her feel even more ashamed. So she said nothing and picked it up. Then when it was time to go outside for lunch recess, she dropped it in the trashcan next to the door.

The Twinkie became a cruel joke. She never knew when she'd

find the next one. Whoever left them put them in her backpack, at her spot in music class, inside her lunch box.

She didn't tell her parents. What could they do? Lila didn't know who was placing the Twinkies and even if she found out, that person could argue he was doing her a favor, leaving the baked goods as gifts.

Then one day the unthinkable happened, and she was forced to tell her parents everything. She was running late to school and it wasn't even her fault. Her little sister misplaced a shoe and took an extra five minutes to find it. The delay meant they were stuck in the middle of the morning rush and by the time Lila made it to her classroom, the bell was ringing. Everyone else was already seated, and twenty-four heads swiveled toward her as she came blustering through the door (which was precisely why she preferred getting to school ten minutes early).

By then she was flustered. When she took off her backpack, one of the straps got stuck on the belt loop of her jacket. Forty-eight eyes watched as she wrestled with her backpack and jacket. When she finally got her backpack unhooked, everyone went still. The room had been quiet—Mrs. Knock insisted on quiet while the kids did their morning journals—but now it went dead silent. And then she sat. She felt something squish underneath her bottom. She knew immediately what it was, but willed herself to believe she was wrong.

She didn't dare get up. She wouldn't give anyone the satisfaction of seeing what had happened. They all knew ... they'd all been waiting for it. But they didn't need evidence. For an hour, it was all she could do not to cry. Then it was time for group work. Lila and her group, the Diamondback Rattlesnakes, were supposed to get up and go to the math table. Lila pulled out the book she was reading and pretended to be so engrossed, she hadn't noticed everyone was moving to groups. That strategy worked for less than a minute before Mrs. Knock hollered, "Ms. Sullivan, wouldn't you like to join your group for math?"

Again, twenty-four heads swung in her direction. Lila cleared her throat. "I'm not feeling too well. I need to sit down."

"I can give you a pass to go to the nurse."

Lila held up one hand, just like she'd seen her dad do countless times when he didn't want to argue. "That won't be necessary. I think I just need to sit down for a few minutes."

Mrs. Knock quirked an eyebrow at her. "Okay, I'll bring your math to you."

She did, and in that way Lila managed to stay in her seat until lunch recess. When the rest of the class lined up to head out, she remained seated. Mrs. Knock gave her a look, but didn't say anything before she walked Lila's classmates to the cafeteria. When she came back, she sat at the desk in front of Lila's and turned around to face her. "Do you want to tell me what's going on?"

Lila shook her head and looked down at the cover of her book.

"I might be able to help."

Lila didn't want to tell Mrs. Knock what had happened—it was so humiliating—but she also knew she had to make her escape right then, while all the other students were at lunch. "I think I sat on a Twinkie."

"What? You're going to have to speak up."

A bead of sweat dripped down Lila's back, making her shiver. "I think I sat on a Twinkie."

"You think you sat—" Mrs. Knock's laughter cut through the empty classroom. Lila swore it bounced around the room, surrounded her like she was in a horror movie. Mrs. Knock slapped her knee. Threw her head back. Laughed some more. After what felt like an eternity, she stopped laughing just long enough to notice Lila's expression. Which was not at all amused.

"I'm so sorry, honey. It's just so silly. It reminds me of something I would've done when I was your age."

Lila wanted to tell Mrs. Knock the whole truth, explain that her sitting on the Twinkie wasn't an oversight but a cruel joke. She also knew that if she did, Mrs. Knock would be obligated to find out who was taunting Lila. And then Lila would be known not just as the chubby kid, but also as a snitch. She didn't know which was worse. So she did her best to return Ms. Knock's smile. "Do you think the nurse has some pants I can change into?"

"I'm sure she does, honey. Come on, I'll walk you over there."

With uncharacteristic stealth, Ms. Knock led Lila around the back of the building where no one would see her, and then walked behind her when they rounded the corner and made their way to the nurse's office.

To make matters more humiliating, the biggest pants the nurse had were the right length for Lila but too tight around the waist. Which meant Lila had to call her mom.

"Mom. Do you think you could bring me a pair of pants?"

"Why, honey?"

Lila couldn't bear to tell her mom the truth right there in front of the nurse, so she said, "My pants got dirty."

"Can't you just dab the stain with a little water? I've got a to-do list a mile long."

Lila swallowed in an attempt to keep the waver out of her voice. "It's in kind of an awkward spot, Mom."

"Oof." Thank goodness—her mom was picking up what she was putting down. "Sure, honey. I'll be there in about twenty minutes."

At the dinner table that night, Lila's mom looked her in the eye. "How in the world did you happen to sit on an unwrapped Twinkie?"

Face burning with shame, Lila told her—everything. Both parents looked at her with pity while she spoke, but her mom's expression reflected red-hot anger by the time she was done. "I'll go down to that school first thing tomorrow and talk to the principal about this."

Lila dropped her head into her hands. "No, Mom. You can't."

"Why the hell not? Nobody deserves to be treated that way."

"Because. If the principal starts investigating it, the kids are going to know I tattled. And the only thing worse than being the ... *fat kid*—"

Her parents gasped and her sister's mouth dropped open.

"—is being a snitch."

Fortunately, her mom acquiesced and Lila never made the mistake of sitting down without looking at her seat again. No one was ever cruel enough to play that same trick on her, either. But on the last day of fifth grade someone built an intricate Twinkie tower on her desk. She thought of it like a sendoff—figured she'd never see another Twinkie at school again—and was therefore extremely disappointed when, on the first day of sixth grade, she found a package of Hostess cupcakes on her desk.

For Lila, rock bottom happened freshman year. Something about the mix of hormones and the anonymity of being one fish in a school of 2,000 empowered the bullies to be even more brazen.

Once again, her fellow students oinked at her in the hallway. It seemed like the number of oinks increased exponentially. One kid oinked, two more caught on, and then two more for each of those two. Suddenly, her ginger hair was also an issue. If people weren't oinking at her, they were calling her out over her hair. And if they weren't doing either of those things, they were teasing her about her freckles.

She didn't tell her parents. She couldn't bear the idea of them saying anything to the principal or anyone else.

One day at lunch, a parade of boys marched by, each one dropping a baked good on the table in front of her. Mrs. Knock, who'd worked her way up to being the high school P.E. teacher, saw the boys, and undoubtedly their smirks, and came over to sit down across from Lila. By that point, Lila had mastered the art of looking like she didn't care even though her insides were absolutely churning.

"Does this have something to do with that Twinkie you sat on in fifth grade?"

"You remember that?" Lila could hear the emotion in her own voice and swallowed, hoping to clear it.

"Of course I do." A beat of silence passed. "So, does it?"

Looking down at her hands, which were folded and resting against the pile of Twinkies, Snowballs, and Hostess cupcakes, Lila nodded. "I'm pretty sure it does. And it also has to do with the oinking I hear in the hallways. And the name-calling. And the whispers."

She wouldn't cry.

Although she didn't look directly at her, Lila could tell Ms.

Knock was nodding. And she'd known her long enough that she could envision her expression: *I thought so.*

"Lila, you've always been great in school. But do you have any, I don't know, hobbies? Sports or crafts or dance or musical instruments?"

Again, Lila shook her head, pressed her lips together. She was too afraid to speak. If she did, she might start blubbering.

She'd tried a few things—Little League, soccer, ballet—but she never enjoyed any of them long enough to complete more than a couple of seasons. Her parents, satisfied that at least they tried, and she was succeeding in school and staying out of trouble, didn't push her. But Mrs. Knock didn't need to know all that.

"Listen. I'm coaching the cross country team. I'd like you to come out for it."

At that, Lila's head snapped up and her gaze met Mrs. Knock's. Mrs. Knock laughed. "Don't look at me like that! It's just for fun, and there aren't any tryouts."

"But don't the cross country runners run, like, a long way?"

Mrs. Knock chuckled. "Sometimes. But you won't be the only beginner on the team. We'll start out with shorter runs. And you can walk if you need to."

Lila considered. Before she could come up with an answer, Mrs. Knock raised her arm and hollered across the cafeteria. "Rebecca!"

A second later, a petite blonde with a giant smile and a high ponytail slid in next to Mrs. Knock, beaming at Lila.

Mrs. Knock said to her, "I'm recruiting for the cross country team."

Rebecca beamed some more.

"Rebecca meet Lila. Lila, meet Rebecca."

Rebecca held out her hand and when Lila took it, her smile got even bigger. "Nice to meet you."

In that moment, Lila knew she was joining the cross country team, for better or for worse. Because Rebecca was the first person her age who had looked at her and really seen her.

The first practice was *hard*. Lila hadn't run more than a 100-yard dash probably ever and Mrs. Knock expected the kids to run a full lap just to warm up. There were calisthenics and stretching, and then *more* running.

Every time she slowed down, there was Rebecca, that grin in place, encouraging Lila to "just keep going."

Her lungs burned and her legs ached, but she made it through, and her heart leapt in her chest when Mrs. Knock announced practice was over and had them circle around.

The second practice was *hard*. By the third practice, that new-activity shine had worn off, and Lila thought she might finish out the week and call it quits. But when the final bell rang the next Monday after school, Rebecca was standing outside Lila's classroom, waiting to walk with her to practice.

The second week was easier, and by the third week, all the exercise felt exhilarating.

Mrs. Knock came to jog with her during a warm-up. "Looks like you're getting into the swing of things."

The ease with which the smile came to her face surprised Lila. "Yeah. I am."

"I'm proud of how you've stuck with it. I know it's hard when you're first starting out."

In her chest, something bloomed. Pride, yes, but more than that, it was confidence. Something she hadn't felt in as long as she could remember.

She'd tried something new, something difficult, something totally outside of her comfort zone, and she'd done it. She'd probably never be the fastest runner on the team, but she was a runner. On a team. And she was having fun.

"It's hard, but I like it. I think it's showing me I can do hard things."

Mrs. Knock gave her a knowing smile. "I knew you could. But the important thing is that now you know it, too."

One afternoon on a longer training run, Rebecca said, "I overheard someone talking about how kids oink at you in the hallways."

Lila gritted her teeth. She'd thought cross country practice was the one time she was safe from the bullying and harassment. Safe from thinking about it, even. "They do."

"That's so mean." Rebecca's voice held no vitriol, only sadness.

"I know."

"Do you ever say anything?"

Lila laughed and glanced over her. "No. Of course not. What would I say?"

"I don't know. *Something*. Do you know who's doing it?"

"There are a few kids. Repeat offenders."

They jogged for a few seconds in relative silence, their feet hitting the trail in sync. "Certainly you can come up with a comeback."

Lila snorted. "Like what?"

"I don't know. Tell me who one of the kids is."

"Dane Jackson. He's the worst." Just the thought of him, the image of his face in her mind, made Lila wince.

"Oh, that's easy. The next time he oinks at you, you should say back to him, 'You know what, Dane? You have your whole life to be an idiot. Why don't you take today off?'"

Lila snorted.

"Good one, right? Or maybe, 'You should worry less about me and more about how bad your face looks.'"

"That's a good one, too."

"Or, 'You must have been born on a highway. That's where most accidents happen.'"

"Where did you come up with these?" They'd returned to the trailhead and slowed to a walk.

"Oh, you know." Rebecca shrugged. "The Internet."

It took Lila a full week to actually say something to Dane. But during that week, she and Rebecca spent any spare time they had researching and creating insults.

On a balmy Tuesday morning, Dane oinked at Lila for what must have been the hundredth time. He looked at his friends to enjoy their reactions, which made Lila angrier than ever. She took a deep breath and, voice wavering on the first couple of words, managed, "Hey, Dane!"

His eyebrows shot up and he made eye contact with her.

"Grab a straw, because you suck!"

It wasn't the best comeback, but his friends laughed, covering their mouths, and then started saying things like, "Ooh, what a burn," and "Yo, Dane, you gonna let her talk to you like that?"

Lila was beyond pleased when Dane, eyes still wide with shock, snapped his mouth shut and walked away.

So that's what it felt like to stand up for yourself. It was exhilarating, and she couldn't wait for her next opportunity. She vowed to herself that she'd never let anyone treat her badly, ever again. She'd devote her life to feeling empowered, and to helping others feel empowered, too.

That's what she reminded herself as she lay awake in her temporary new home at Sweet Springs Ranch. Adult Lila was not the powerless, meek fifth grader she'd once been. She'd poured sweat and tears into developing her confidence, and she wouldn't let anyone take it away.

Yes, but you're hiding.

She groaned when she heard that tiny voice in her head and drifted off to sleep telling it that she wouldn't be hiding forever. Just until she knew she was safe.

Chapter Twelve

Travis found it strange that Lila didn't seem interested in leaving the property. At all. True to her word, she'd made a grocery order and had it delivered. Aside from that—sustenance—she showed no interest in what lay beyond the Sweet Springs Ranch. He told himself maybe she was just a homebody, but that seemed unlikely seeing as how she'd jumped at the chance to travel across the country and live on the property of a stranger.

The evening they moved all the ranch files into the bunkhouse, Travis told her he'd see her the next day, and then went home to get ready for dinner with his family. While he got dressed, he had a lightbulb moment: as an experiment, he could invite her to join them. He didn't want to give her too much time to think about it, so a few minutes before he planned to leave, he went over to the bunkhouse.

He was certain she wasn't expecting anyone. When she opened the door, her eyes were wide and he could see her pulse at the spot where her chin met her throat. It was racing, and he felt somewhat guilty for not texting or calling ahead.

She stood back to let him in and the soles of his boots crunched on the floor. The salt. He'd forgotten. He wondered if stepping on it messed it up, and was about to ask her.

But then he noticed her outfit and he forgot all about his reason for coming over and the salt barrier. She was wearing workout clothes—mint-colored leggings and a matching tank top that hugged every delicious-looking curve. Instantly, the throbbing started below his belt. What he wouldn't give to run his hands over those curves, to feel the fabric stretched tight over her skin. Just a hint of cleavage showed above the neckline of her tank top and he had to clench his fists to keep from running a fingertip inside that edge. He must've stood there a while because Lila laughed and said, "Did you stop by for a reason? Or just to check out my outfit?"

When he dragged his gaze up to meet hers, he saw humor there. He should be embarrassed; she'd caught him staring. But he only felt more aroused. He scratched the back of his head. "Actually, I was coming to invite you to dinner."

Her eyebrows shot up. "With the *family*?"

He shrugged. "Yeah. I noticed you haven't left the property. I thought this would be a good way to show you around town a little."

He didn't miss the way her eyes darted to the side when he mentioned she hadn't left the property.

"I really appreciate the offer, but I wasn't exactly planning on going out." She gestured at her outfit. "Plus, I wanted to get in a workout."

"For the record, I think you look great." Her neck and cheeks turned pink and Travis kicked himself. "I'm sorry. I didn't mean—"

She shook her head. "It's fine. This is my favorite outfit. My power suit, if you will. So I'll take your compliment. Thank you."

How did she do that? How did she manage to take him from embarrassed and chagrined to charmed and bewitched? "You're welcome."

"Well, enjoy dinner."

"Thank you." For the second time in the span of two minutes, Travis stood there, staring at her for a little too long. She probably wanted to close the door and shut him out and although he felt like he should acknowledge his awkwardness, he decided not to call too much attention to it.

"Maybe next time," he told her. Then he gave her a nod, turned on his heel, and walked to his truck.

As soon as Travis walked up to the table a while later Callie stood up. "Travis Wilder, you sure as heck better have invited Lila to join us for dinner. Where are your manners?"

Feeling exactly like a little boy getting yelled at by his mama, Travis raised his hands in surrender. "Easy now, Cal. Of course I invited her. You know, for all his faults, Levi Wilder raised his boys to have manners."

Cash, mouth full of a hot buttered roll, nodded. "Damn straight."

Hoots of laughter erupted from the boys, and June and Callie exchanged exasperated glances.

"Well, all right then." Callie settled herself back into her chair and smoothed her napkin over her lap. "Did she say why?"

Travis thought about the salt barrier, the scared-rabbit look in Lila's eyes, her hammering pulse. That outfit. "Not that it's any of our business, but no. Just that she wasn't expecting to leave the house, wasn't dressed for dinner, and had a workout planned." He cursed his body for sending a blush straight to his cheeks.

Cash tore another bite off his roll. "You see that, y'all? What was she wearing, bro?" His grin was the actual definition of devilish and Travis closed his eyes and prayed for patience.

When he opened them, everyone looked at him, waiting, expectant. "You're a damn fool, Cash. Should we order?" He raised his arm to catch the attention of their regular server, Matt. Then he picked up his menu and held it in front of his face. More snickering ensued and he ignored it.

Everyone ordered and thanks to Hayes, the topic of the conversation changed. "Cash. You said you had something to tell us the other day when we went to work the fence line, but we never got around to talking about it because you were acting like a toddler."

"'I don't want to use that tool.'" Sterling's mockery had the rest of them laughing.

Cash held up his middle finger. "I'm thinking about a career change."

"You mean a career? At all?" Hayes elbowed Travis, who saw enough apprehension in Cash's eyes to tread lightly. "What career?"

Cash cleared his throat, wiped his mouth, and set down his roll. This was serious. "I'm thinking about becoming a cop."

Just a minute before, Travis would have believed silence impossible, but there it was, descending on their table like a heavy blanket.

"This is not the reaction I was anticipating." As he looked from one brother to the next, Cash's smile shrank.

"I'm just surprised, is all." Sterling set down his fork. "I mean, isn't there a limit to how many run-ins you've had with the police if you want to become one?"

"Funny. You know, I've never been arrested."

"That should count for something." Hayes elbowed Travis again.

Travis, conscious of his role as the peacekeeper, smiled. "I think it's a great idea, Cash. You thinking of staying local?"

Finally setting down his roll, Cash nodded. "Yeah. I saw an ad at the movie theater that said Prescott PD is hiring. I looked into it. There are background checks and an academy, but I could be on patrol within the next six months."

Callie's eyes went soft and misty. "Our little Cash, all grown up."

He balled up his drink napkin and threw it at her.

"I'm teasing. But in all seriousness, aside from seeing the ad, what inspired you to consider law enforcement?" She leaned forward, elbows on the table.

"I hear the ladies like men in uniform."

Sterling, Hayes, and Travis reacted, shooting straw wrappers and throwing napkins, themselves.

Laughing, Cash raised his arms to defend himself. "I'm only kidding, you morons. To be totally honest, you all inspired me." He made a circular gesture with one hand to encompass the whole group. "Callie, you're kicking ass as a lawyer. Hayes, you're heading up all those kids' camps at Cool Pines. Sterling, you're making national news with your business, and June, you're starting your own event planning business. And you, Trav, you've built this beautiful home and you're going to restart our cattle business. And what am I doing? Tending bar, sometimes. Horsin' around. I was already thinking about it. Like, what do I do, you know? How do I make something of myself? And then I saw that ad, and it just clicked."

Again, silence descended.

Hayes broke it. "Wow. That's great, man. I'm excited for you. I'm speaking for all of us—we can't wait to be at your graduation from the police academy."

"Thanks, man."

"To Cash, finding his purpose." Callie lifted her glass, but before anyone could repeat her words, Hayes added, "To Cash, finally getting his shit together."

"To Cash." Everyone drank.

A couple of servers brought their food on trays, and Travis was grateful for Cash's announcement. The ensuing conversation gave him a reprieve from being the center of attention (at least, where Lila was concerned). On the other hand, it also gave him time to think about Lila, which was not a reprieve.

He couldn't put his finger on why Lila affected him differently than any woman he'd ever met... he couldn't stop thinking about her and he wanted to know everything there was to know about her and he wished they could be in the same space, all the time. Which gave him an idea.

Chapter Thirteen

As soon as Travis left, Lila regretted not going to dinner with him. Although she was accustomed to being alone, she was unaccustomed to feeling so *lonely*.

For the first time since arriving in Prescott, she experienced a deep craving for the online community she'd spent the last past several years building and nurturing. In the bunkhouse with nothing but silence and her fear to keep her company, she couldn't quite tamp down the urge to get on social media.

She knew she couldn't reactivate her accounts. If someone was paying attention, she couldn't risk him noticing she was back, even if her return was temporary. So instead of using her phone, she opened an incognito browser window and typed in the URL for her favorite social media website.

She sighed when a pop-up prompted her to login or create an account. She'd just create a dummy account so she could see everything she wanted to. Still, she couldn't comment on or even like anyone's posts, however tempting that might be. A few keystrokes, a handful of clicks, and an email confirmation later, she was in business.

Chuckling, she told herself she would simply lurk, see what

everyone was up to. In that way, she could feel somewhat connected to her online friends and her regular life.

She started by entering the hashtags she usually followed—that should bring up many of the accounts in her community.

"Bingo." JewelsFitness was one of the first to come up, and Lila clicked on her profile. Scrolling through her posts—her signature tangerine color giving Lila a boost of dopamine—Lila felt some of her tension melting away. In the most recent post, Jewels shared that she'd hit her goal of ten reps of bicep curls with twenty-five-pound dumbbells. Lila felt a rush of pride. Jewels had been working toward that goal for weeks. Would it hurt to like the post? *Yes.* Yes it would. She couldn't afford to draw any attention to her fake profile. With a heavy sigh, Lila backed out of Jewels's account to look at her search results again.

She smiled when she saw a post from DeezGunz, a duo of bodybuilders who, like Lila, aspired to inspire others to use exercise for confidence. They beamed at the camera in a photo they'd taken at the gym. Again, her mouse hovered over the *Like* button for an instant before she reminded herself not to engage.

After scrolling through a few more of her online friends' accounts, Lila decided she was putting herself through a weird kind of torture and logged out. Someday she might be able to interact with her friends again. For the moment, though, she'd do better to focus on the task at hand, which was organizing this giant mess of paperwork. She remembered her mom saying something about busy hands and decided her best option was to make herself useful.

She turned on her Bluetooth speaker and found some upbeat music.

"And a candle, for ambience." She'd purchased several in her last order and selected lavender for calming.

Then she sat down at the big table where she'd set up. She'd already spent some time sorting paperwork and knew she was going to need some sort of filing system. So far, the paperwork fell into several categories: invoices, receipts, business correspondence, bills, and personal mail. Ideally, she'd like to match up invoices with receipts, and she figured the best way to do that was to organize each stack by date. But first, she had to go through the dozen or so boxes to sort those invoices and receipts from the rest.

Before she got too much farther, she figured she'd better order some folders so she could color code everything.

Oh, what she wouldn't give to go to an office supply store, in person. All those organizational treasures, all in one place. The colors, the textures, the smells. Her heart sank at the thought that she couldn't hop in the car and go to one now.

"Another online order will have to do."

Although perusing the online selection of folders, dividers, paperclips, and pens wasn't quite as satisfying as holding those items in her hands, she experienced a thrill when she saw the message, *Your order is confirmed.* The store's website even included animated confetti.

She closed her laptop and got to work sorting. Again. And again, she marveled at the sheer volume of what Levi Wilder left behind. She had to wonder at his mindset in his final years. If he was totally coherent, he probably suffered from some kind of depression. How else could anyone explain the complete negligence of the family business?

Her music went silent, and in the span of time before a text message alert chimed over the Bluetooth speaker, Lila panicked, wondering if someone had somehow cut off her streaming. Even as she picked up her phone to check the text message, she had to will her heart rate back to normal. She didn't recognize the number. But the message said, *This is Travis. I know you didn't want to come out, but would you like me to bring you dinner?*

Lila smiled. And when she did, her stomach growled, answering Travis's question. She glanced at the time and was surprised to see that an hour and a half had passed since she first got on her computer to order her filing system.

Another text came through: *We're at Stover's. They have just about anything you could want. Think diner-style food. Probably not the best menu for a fitness guru, but we can pick someplace healthier next time.*

She thought for a minute and then texted back asking if they had some sort of soup and salad combo.

The chicken and wild rice soup is, as Callie says, to die for. I'll get you that and a house salad. Is vinaigrette okay?

Her mouth watering, Lila sent back a thumbs up and a *Thank you.*

You got it. I'll let you know when I'm on my way.

Only when her phone chimed ten minutes later did Lila realized she hadn't stopped smiling. *Leaving now. See you in 10.*

As tempting as it was to get up and pace around the bunkhouse, Lila remained planted in her chair, sorting. She didn't even jump when Travis knocked on the door. "One gold star for you."

The warmth in his eyes took her aback. His smile proved he was so happy to see her and a warmth spread in her chest. She stood back to let him in, and felt wistful at all the scents his clothes carried: savory meat and fresh-baked bread (and she swore she could hear all the restaurant sounds: silverware against dishes, people talking).

The fear at the forefront of her consciousness insisted staying in was the safest bet, but she felt such a longing to be out on the town, amongst conversation, laughter, *life.* Waiters rushing from the kitchen to their tables, food sizzling, people tucking into their food.

With a sigh, she closed the door behind Travis, who remembered to step over the salt barrier before walking over to the kitchen and unloading the takeout containers. "Do you want to eat out of real dishes?"

She shook her head. "The takeout containers are fine. Thank you for bringing me food. I lost track of time and didn't realize how hungry I was."

"You're welcome. And because it's my favorite, I also brought you some peach cobbler." He held it up. Then, as if he felt guilty, he rushed to add, "I know! Again, not the healthiest option. But it's *so* good. And if you're only going to be in town for a short time, I thought you should experience it."

God, could the man be any more thoughtful?

She took the takeout container from him, opened it, and inhaled the scents of peach and cinnamon and just-baked dough. Eyes closed, she moaned in ecstasy. "Oh my God, I haven't smelled something this delectable and as long as I can remember. You are sent straight from Heaven, you know that?"

He chuckled, and although she wanted to keep her eyes closed and continue sinking into the sensory experience of smelling the cobbler, she opened them to look at him. Just like he had the other night while they were eating pizza, he watched her, and the look in his eyes made all the heat and pleasure swirling around in her body coalesce right between her legs.

A little devil appeared on her shoulder, legs crossed, hands on hips. *Really, what could it hurt to spend a little time with this man?* An angel, prim and proper, lips pursed, appeared on her other shoulder. *You couldn't possibly. You can't afford the distraction. And plus, you're not sticking around. It wouldn't be fair to you or Travis to turn this into a quick roll in the hay.*

The little devil crossed her arms and looked down her nose at the angel. *Who said anything about quick?*

Travis broke Lila out of her trance when he took the box from her and set it on the counter. "You okay?"

Lila laughed, the sound flirtatious. "I'm fine. Sorry." She let her gaze rest on his and then took his hands. "I guess it's been too long since I had a decent dessert."

She could feel the surprise come off his body in a quick, electric jolt. Then his eyes went molten and she was drunk on the feeling of power, the idea that her words could turn him on.

He took a half-step toward her, closing the distance between them. His mouth hovered over hers. "We probably shouldn't."

"Probably not." Her voice came out in a sultry whisper. "But that doesn't stop me from wanting to." If she leaned forward a smidgen, rose onto her tiptoes, their lips would touch. There was that little devil on her shoulder again, pumping her fist and screaming, *Go for it.*

Lila listened. She barely had to move to touch her lips to his. He made a sound—something between frustration and relief—and brought his hands to her upper arms. She wrapped her arms around his waist and leaned in, deepening the kiss, parting his lips with hers. He sighed, gave up resistance. Released her arms and slid his around her shoulders.

Her nerve endings lit up and she became hyperaware of every place their bodies touched. His mouth was gentle but firm. Insistent. His arms were strong and pulled her against him like he was desperate for contact. She could feel his arousal against her belly, and had to stop herself from touching him there. Kissing was nice, but she didn't want to do anything she'd regret. Instead, she ran her palms up his abs and over his chest, feeling a little delight as she skimmed over those planes. As his tongue teased hers, another pleasure-filled moan filled the air and the realization it came from her own mouth only turned Lila on even more.

"I could kiss you forever," Travis said, his lips still against hers.

Those words made her skin buzz with anticipation and her knees weak. "Same."

He ran his hands through her hair, pulling gently on the ends of it. Then she remembered her hair was part of her disguise, which was exactly why she couldn't fall for Travis Wilder, no matter how his eyes twinkled at her, no matter how many fireworks she saw when their lips touched, no matter how much she wished they could stay in this moment forever.

Breathless with the strangest mixture of arousal and grief, Lila ended the kiss and rested her for head on Travis's. "Well."

"I was thinking the same."

"We probably shouldn't do that again."

Travis's sigh carried genuine disappointment. "I'd like to say I was thinking the same on that point too, but I wasn't. Even though you're probably right."

This time, Lila took a half-step back. "If I'm being completely honest, I'm not saying I wouldn't *like* to do this again." Her lips twitched. "But it's probably not prudent."

Travis threw his head back and laughed, and Lila couldn't help but join in. His voice was weepy when he said, "Since when was kissing ever prudent?"

Lila shrugged, then threw up her hands. "Probably never. But still."

He wrapped his arms around her shoulders and kissed her on top of the head. "I think we should have a real conversation about this. But not right now. Some other time, when you haven't just kissed me senseless."

"Did I just kiss you senseless?"

"I'm pretty sure you did."

Lila didn't realize she was still smiling until Travis spoke. "And you're proud of it, too, aren't you?"

He'd nailed it. "How can you tell?"

"Oh, I don't know. Just something about the way you look."

"Huh. Well, I guess I'd better walk you to the door."

She took his hand and led him to the front door, where he made a show of taking her face in his hands and kissing her long and slow before he ducked out. Knees weak with need, she locked the door behind him, barely registering her usual fear, as powerful as she felt in the moment.

The shrill sound of her phone ringing jolted her out of her reverie even as she watched Travis walk back to his house. She half expected it to be him, calling to say how much he enjoyed kissing her. But it wasn't. It was an Alabama number and seeing it put ice in her veins. Then she realized there were words below the number: *Huntsville Police Department.*

At least she knew it wasn't the stalker calling. But knowing it was the police department? Her palms turned slick with sweat against her phone. She recognized Officer Gomez's voice right away. "I stopped by your apartment today."

Her heart, which had started racing as soon as her phone rang, thumped hard against her rib cage. "I'm out of town."

"I gathered that."

How had he gathered that?

As if he could read her thoughts, he chuckled. "My squad and I, we've been hanging around your apartment. A little double duty—hoping to scare off potential predators and doing a little surveillance.

It was pretty obvious you'd skipped town. You left your blinds closed and your lights haven't come on for several evenings now."

Great. If if was that obvious, her stalker would know she wasn't home. What if he tried to break in? She kicked herself for not setting her lights on timers.

"Would you mind telling me where you are?"

She considered. On one hand, Officer Gomez had seemed like a pretty decent guy. On the other, wasn't everyone a suspect at this point? On yet another hand, wouldn't withholding the information seem suspicious? "I'm in Arizona."

"Ms. Sullivan, I can understand why you wanted to skip town, but the investigation will go a lot more smoothly if you're available."

Black swirls and bright sparkles danced in Lila's vision. She sucked in a deep breath, exhaled, took another gulp of air. "I'm sorry. I—I was scared. I didn't know what else to do."

"Don't you have friends or family in Huntsville that you could stay with for a while?"

"Knowing someone's been following me, I wouldn't want to put any of my friends or family at risk."

"You have a point." She thought she detected humor in his voice, but she couldn't be certain.

"Forgive me for sounding rude, but is that the only reason you called? To find out where I'd gone?"

"No!" The sound of his deep breath came through the earpiece. "No, I called because we've got a lead."

A lead? "You mean you think you might know who was following me?"

Another sigh. "We don't want to jump to conclusions. I'd like to meet with you in person, but it sounds like you're two-thirds of the way across the country."

"I've never been good with fractions, but it's a twenty-hour drive."

Officer Gomez sucked air through his teeth, and Lila imagined his face turning red with frustration.

"Do you think you can make some time in the next couple of days to meet with someone from the local police department?"

"Why?" Her heart was at it again, knocking around like it was trying to give her a warning.

"I'd like to have someone show you several photos. See if any of the people in the photos look familiar to you."

Photos? Another spike of adrenaline hit. What if one of the photos was of someone she knew? With the identity of the creepy guy being a mystery, at least she didn't have to acknowledge it might be someone she felt safe with. She wanted to say, "Do I have to?" but she already knew the answer. "Of course."

Chapter Fourteen

Travis was not going to be able to sleep anytime soon. And much to his disappointment, instead of releasing some of the tension in his body—most of it of a sexual nature—kissing Lila had only increased its intensity. He could think of nothing other than putting his hands on her body. And undressing her. And laying her down on his bed.

What was wrong with him? Safely back inside his own house where he couldn't act on any of those impulses, he grabbed a beer and flopped down on the couch. After prying off his boots, he put his feet on the coffee table. He sipped his beer and reminded himself he couldn't afford to get tangled up with her. Not only because he was focused on building up the cattle ranch and she would be leaving shortly, but also because of whatever secrets she continued to keep.

Inspiration struck.

He didn't know why he hadn't thought of it before, but he grabbed his tablet and returned to the couch. His mouth dropped open when the search engine populated results based on his search term: *Lila Sullivan, Alabama.*

Apparently, when Lila mentioned her public image, she'd majorly downplayed just how public that image was. And, Travis thought as he scrolled through the results, she downplayed how that public image looked completely different from the image she'd presented at Sweet Springs Ranch.

Her name and picture appeared in many of the major publications; not that Travis read women's magazines, but he certainly recognized their titles. Article after article contained picture after picture, and in every single one, Lila Sullivan, personal trainer and fitness influencer, had the most beautiful mane of copper colored hair. Travis knew it was the same person because of her eyes. Those emerald green eyes were unmistakable.

"What in the world?"

What would cause someone who obviously had a successful career to pick up and move across the country ... and completely change the most remarkable element of her appearance? She hadn't mentioned any of this on her job application, and Travis wanted to know why. "What are you running from?"

But it was none of his business, was it? Already feeling like he was crossing some sort of line when it came to her privacy, Travis couldn't stop himself standing up and bringing his beer over to the window, where he could look at the bunkhouse. Just like she had for the past several nights, Lila had pulled the drapes shut. Still, because her lights were on, he could see her silhouette as she moved about the main room. She traveled the same pattern, and based on what he'd seen of her superstitions so far, he wondered if she had some sort of nighttime ritual. There was something about the way she moved and he could hardly resist the temptation to keep watching her. Thinking about how she looked with red hair.

He didn't know if he wanted her to see him watching her, or if he didn't want her to. But his body made the decision for him and he closed the blinds and turned away from the window.

He had to get his mind off of her. *And keep your hands off her.* Lila's problems were none of his business until she made them her business. As of now, she hadn't, and if she wanted privacy, she deserved it.

Cattle. Grabbing another beer, Travis returned to his desk. Researching cattle would take his mind off Lila. Instead of searching for good-looking bulls and cows, he would search for ugly ones. Mean ones. Ones that put the fear of God into whoever they made eye contact with.

He would make it his mission to restart the Sweet Springs cattle legacy with the meanest, ugliest looking bull he could find. He'd spent so much time looking for auctions lately, he already knew there were none in Arizona during the upcoming weekend. But who said he had to shop in Arizona? He liked keeping things local, but he also couldn't ignore his need to put some space between himself and the seductress living not more than ten yards from his front door. He glanced toward the window again and thanked himself for closing the blinds. Her skin was so soft and smooth and his palms yearned to touch her again. He balled his hand into a fist and rested his forehead on it. He couldn't think like that.

"Auctions."

He typed into the search bar *Cattle auctions in Utah,* and whooped with excitement when he saw one scheduled for that Saturday and Sunday. He followed the link to the auction website and whooped again when he realized he could view photos of the cattle that would be on the auction block.

He clicked the first link, which pulled up a page for the Leaning D Ranch. He whistled when he saw the first picture. "That's a beaut right there." *Bluebonnet.* Somehow, the photographer had caught the animal looking straight at the camera, a go-ahead-and-try expression on his face. He had long, thick lashes that would make any lady jealous, and the prettiest caramel-colored eyes. His horns were a creamy white and curved up and out like Travis imagined they would if they were sound waves from the most beautiful symphony.

"Hard pass."

The next bull was slightly uglier, with a gigantic lower lip and fur so light, it looked translucent. His eyes were a bit too close together (for Travis's liking anyway). He jotted down *Liberty* as a possibility.

"Bingo," Travis said when he looked at the third photo. This bull looked like he'd run headlong into the pasture fence. According to the website, he had a clean bill of health, but boy, did he look mean.

Either his eyes were two different sizes, or he'd had one slightly closed when someone snapped the picture. Most of his fur was a mottled brindle, but he had a bright white slash across his face like a scar. Suddenly, Travis felt giddy.

"Oh, yeah. Mayhem, you're first on my list."

Out of nowhere, he imagined taking Lila with him to the auction, showing her the ropes, explaining the process, describing how he chose which cattle to bid on (he wouldn't tell her he was going for ugly to distract himself from her). He pictured her, wide-eyed and full of questions, staying by his side all day. They could go out to dinner after the auction. They'd have so much to talk about—those events were always packed with colorful characters.

Dammit. He pulled himself out of that fantasy. The whole point of this exercise was to stop himself from thinking about Lila, and there he was, considering where he'd take her to dinner and what it would be like if he took her back to his hotel. Okay, he hadn't gotten quite that far, but didn't he wish that's where it was going?

"Get a grip, Wilder."

Feeling brazen and determined, he registered as a bidder at the auction. Then he opened a new tab to search for and book a hotel. He didn't bother stopping himself from trying to figure out which hotels Lila would like best, even though he knew she wouldn't be with him. When the hotel reservation confirmation came up, he finished off his beer, wiped his mouth with the back of his hand, and grinned.

It was official: he was going on his first cattle-buying trip that weekend. Which meant he had his work cut out for him for the next two days. Which meant his mind would be occupied. He sent a text to the group chat with his brothers: *Guess who just registered as a bidder at the Cedar City Cattle Auction. This guy.*

Hayes: *I told you guys, didn't I?* He added a smiling devil emoji.

Cash: *You called it, bro.*

Sterling: *You were right. I guess we owe you money.*

Travis felt his face twist into a frown. *What are you fools talking about?*

Hayes responded with another smiling devil emoji and then, *Oh, nothing. We just knew, after you brought Lila dinner tonight, that you are going to have to get out of town.*

Cash: *Things are getting hot.*

Travis rolled his eyes at Cash's use of the fire emoji. Three times.

Sterling: You've already booked the room, haven't you?

Travis: Shut up, all of you. Unless anyone wants to come with me.

Cash responded with a raised hand emoji. *I'll go.*

Travis was relieved. Buying cattle was exciting, but it was also a big job. The company, and a second set of eyes, would be nice. *Cool. I won't turn down a second opinion.*

Rapid fire, the other two brothers also responded with raised hand emojis.

Grinning, Travis said, "Looks like we're all going."

* * *

Travis was in the truck first, buckled in and ready to go.

"Cash is not getting shotgun this time." Hayes threw his duffle bag into the bed of the truck and got in the front seat, buckling his seatbelt as if to prevent anyone from taking that spot.

Before getting in, Sterling came to the driver's door, where Travis had the window rolled down. "Can I drive?"

"Screw off, man." Travis locked the door and rolled up the window. When Sterling got in, he said, "Nobody drives my truck."

Sterling huffed out a sigh, the sound of his exhale loud enough for Travis to hear. "Great, I have to sit back here with him. He always insists on getting the stinkiest snacks."

Cash got in next. "What? You don't like the mouthwatering aroma of gas station burritos?"

"Bro." Travis eyed Cash in the rearview mirror. "I think we're all more worried about being in an enclosed space with you during the aftermath of the gas station burritos."

Cash guffawed at that, and Travis pulled out of the driveway.

"I guess I get to be DJ." Hayes leaned forward and started connecting his phone to the truck's stereo system.

"Fine." Cash's voice sounded pouty. "But none of that sappy stuff."

"It's not sappy. It's classic country."

In his rearview mirror, Travis watched as Sterling leaned back against the side of the truck, crossed his arms, and put his hat over his face. "This is going to be a long drive."

As soon as they got onto the highway after their initial gas station stop, Hayes turned toward Travis. "So, Trav. Tell us what happened that's made this trip urgent all of a sudden."

Mouthful of burrito, Cash said, "I bet you're wishing I sat shotgun now, aren't you?"

"Don't talk with your mouth full." Hat still over his face, Sterling reached out to whack Cash on the shoulder.

Then they waited. Travis turned up the music and Hayes turned it back down.

Cash's voice came from the backseat, clear as a bell this time. "Must have been good, whatever it was."

Travis used the rearview mirror to shoot daggers at Cash, who feigned fear and held up his hands to defend himself.

"Might as well tell us." Sterling's drawl suggested they had nothing but time.

Travis weighed his options. He didn't have to tell them. He could keep the kiss to himself, and then he wouldn't have to withstand the teasing that would surely follow for an indeterminate period of time. Or he could tell them. He could tell them about the kiss but not about how it made him feel—like his insides were a tangled ball of yarn. "All right, fine. We kissed."

Behind him, Sterling whistled. Next to Sterling, Cash said, "I knew it."

Hayes punched Travis in the arm. "Hot damn. I guess you do still have it after all."

"What's that supposed to mean?"

"It means we wondered if you even like girls anymore." Cash's tone was playful, but Travis felt a twinge of hurt that they'd apparently discussed his lack of a dating life amongst themselves.

"Of course I like girls. I just haven't been around any that, you know, tickle my fancy."

Sterling reached over the back of Travis's seat and squeezed his shoulder, then shook it playfully. "But this Lila, she tickles your fancy, doesn't she?"

Travis shook his head. "It was just one kiss. And it won't go any further than that."

"Why not?" Hayes wanted to know.

Travis shrugged. He wished he could climb out of his own skin and leave the conversation. "I don't know. She's going back to Alabama, and I wasn't figuring on hitching up with an old lady anytime soon." *And she's running from something I don't know if I want to be involved in.*

"You know," Hayes said, and Travis knew what was coming next. "That's what I thought about Callie when I saw her at the Cool Pines Ranch. I thought, She's gotta go back to Phoenix and I've got to stay here. But then, what can I say? Sparks flew."

"Same," Sterling said. "When I met June, I thought, 'Wow, she's the prettiest girl I've ever seen.' I also thought I was the luckiest man alive, to get to spend that one evening with her in Great Falls. And then she showed up in Prescott."

Cash whistled. "And boy, were you pissed."

Sterling's bark of laughter filled the cab. "That is an understatement. Anyway. The rest is history."

"Ergo ... " In the rearview mirror, Travis could see Cash twirling his hand, indicating that this conversation should come to a natural conclusion.

"Ergo, this is totally different. Lila will be here just long enough to help with the paperwork. And then she's leaving, and that's that."

"It was a nice kiss, though." Hayes punched him in the arm again. "I could tell from the way your ears turned pink."

"My ears did not turn pink." *Did they?*

Cash snickered. "They're turning pink again right now, bro."

"Shut up. All of you."

"Okay, okay." Sterling leaned back again. "This is the last thing I'll say. I swear."

"Go ahead." Travis hoped his brothers could hear the dread in his voice.

"All I'm saying is, if you guys kissed and you felt like you had to hightail it out of town, I think it's fair to say it was a pretty great kiss."

His brothers were right on, but Travis didn't want to let them know that. They'd never let up. So he changed the subject, explaining how he was looking for the ugliest possible herd of cattle to get the ranch going again. He tried to listen as his brothers chatted, but his mind kept drifting back to Lila. He wondered what she was doing, what she was wearing. He'd asked Callie and June to stop by and invite her to share a meal with them, and he hoped she'd accept. He even made sure they knew she wouldn't want to leave the ranch.

Again, he wondered what had driven her away from home, away from what appeared to be a successful career by any standard. He decided he'd ask her once he got home. Once he had some space and time to clear his mind. Because no matter how short a time Lila was staying, he couldn't afford to forget that every time he was around her, he lost all coherent thought.

* * *

Travis figured his brothers came along to the auction solely to provide moral support. But Saturday morning when they all woke before their alarms and Sterling threw on his clothes and went to get coffees, he realized they were just as excited as he was. They'd spent much of the evening before huddled around a high-top table at a local bar, nursing beers and talking strategy.

"Wait," Cash said. "You're saying ugliness is your number one factor. Good genes is number two?"

Travis nodded, that gleeful feeling bringing the tang of adrenaline to the back of his throat. "You got it. The uglier the better. I want Sweet Springs cattle to be renowned as the worst-looking group of animals anyone ever saw."

All three of his brothers sat back at that. Sterling scratched his head. "Whatever floats your boat, man. Good thing the ranch is known for producing good-looking men."

The others nodded in agreement at that, and Travis rolled his eyes again. Then they'd gotten back on the auction website and made a list of bulls they'd be happy to buy.

And now, it wasn't even six a.m. and Sterling was returning with four coffees in the carrier. "I saw a couple of ranchers down at the diner. Sounds like they've got a lot of bidders signed up. We're going to have our work cut out for us."

Anticipation thrummed through Travis's veins.

The Leaning D Ranch absolutely teemed with people. As soon as Travis parked the truck and looked around, he realized most everyone here considered the auction an *event*. Dress boots and hats, bolo ties with turquoise inlays, and even some fine leather chaps adorned the cowboys, cowgirls, and ranchers who'd shown up.

Travis almost regretted his choice of outfit—a default more than an actual decision—his worn boots and jeans looked like working clothes, in stark contrast to the finery the other ranchers wore. Sterling shut his car door and clapped Travis on the back. "We may not look fancy or highfalutin, but at least we look like real ranchers. I'll bet you half the guys here couldn't even run a herd of cattle if they wanted to."

That perspective gave Travis the confidence boost he needed, and he nodded. "Thanks, man. I've never been to an auction quite like this."

"Me, neither. But you know what that means: an auction like this has never seen the Wilder boys in action."

They walked around the back of the truck to meet Hayes and Cash, and then the four of them went to check in.

"We've got an hour until the auction starts." Hayes pointed at the rows and rows of seats. "Reckon we should get a spot?"

They filed in behind him, and he led them to a spot on the aisle about halfway back.

Cash leaned over to whisper to Travis. "There's definitely some people watching around here."

Travis followed his gaze to a pair of young women who were dressed to the nines in short denim skirts, sparkly boots, and cropped shirts. "Those two look exactly like your type, Cash."

Cash waved him off. "I was just trying to see what you would say."

"Mm-hmm."

Cash didn't argue and his gaze stayed on the ladies until they went out of sight. Over the next hour, bidders filed into the seats until it was standing room only.

Sterling looked around at all the people gathered and whistled through his teeth. "There might be more humans here than cattle for sale. I guess we're going to have some stiff competition."

Chapter Fifteen

When Travis told Lila he and his brothers would be out of town for a couple of days, she almost had a panic attack. She forced the air into her lungs and a smile onto her face. "That's great."

She didn't have to wonder if he could read the fear on her expression. "You okay?"

"Of course! Couldn't be better. You know, if I have any questions—"

He reached out, uncertain of exactly what he planned to do with his hand until it came to rest on her shoulder. "You can call me. Any time. I may not answer right away, you know if I'm in the middle of a heated bidding war. But I'll get back to you."

Lila nodded, the movement so fast, she swore she could feel her teeth knocking together. She spent the next couple of days telling herself she'd come to rely on him too much. Maybe his absence would be good for her. Force her to rely on herself for her sense of safety.

Still, when he stopped by Friday afternoon before heading out of town and told her he'd asked June and Callie to check in with her, she experienced a sweeping sense of relief.

As tight-knit as their group was, she shouldn't have been

surprised when June texted her Friday evening and invited her to have lunch the next day. At that, too, she panicked. Then she kicked herself for panicking—why was it her first response to almost every situation these days? She grappled for ways to control the situation. How could she manage to avoid leaving the ranch? She could pretend she was sick, but the truth was, she craved the companionship. A solution struck her: she could invite them over to the bunkhouse. She'd never have to set foot outside.

She responded to June: *You all have done so much for me. I would love to make you lunch here at my place, where we can sit and talk for as long as we like.*

To her great relief, June accepted. Lila wasted no time placing a great grocery order, which arrived on her doorstep Saturday morning. Meanwhile, she made a mental list of conversation topics. The last thing she needed was for the two of them to start asking her questions.

At eleven, Lila swept up her salt barrier. Then she unlocked the extra locks she'd installed so that when the girls arrived at noon, they would hear only a single deadbolt being turned.

"We brought you flowers." June thrust a bouquet at Lila, who brought the flowers close to her face and inhaled.

"They smell heavenly. Thank you."

They bustled in, a storm of happy, feminine energy in which Lila let herself bask.

"I got us sparkling juice and Chardonnay," Lila said. "I mean, I don't even know if you drink wine, but I thought it would be fun."

"Are you kidding?" Callie was behind the counter and wielding the corkscrew in a flash. "Any excuse to drink wine, we'll take it."

Lila got down glasses and Callie poured while while June searched the cupboards for a vase. "I should have known there are no vases in here. I'll just use this giant cup."

Lila smiled. "I'm sure you have a name for that, right? Rustic floral or something?"

"Exactly." June grinned at her and within a few minutes, the three of them gathered at the table, the rustic floral centerpiece in the middle.

"This make-your-own-sandwich idea was genius." Callie took a big bite of hers, making the other two giggle.

Inexplicably nervous, Lila put the finishing touches on her own sandwich, rearranging the lettuce and tomato even though she'd considered it complete just a moment before.

"I feel bad that you went to so much trouble." June set down her sandwich and wiped her mouth.

Lila shook her head to protest but June plowed on. "The next time the three of us have lunch, we're definitely taking you out. Right, Cal?"

Callie nodded, the movement exaggerated for emphasis. "Absolutely."

Stay noncommittal. The food felt dry in Lila's throat. "It was no trouble at all, really. I mean—" she gestured at the platter of sandwich fixings before them—"I just laid everything out. Look, I tricked you into making your own sandwiches." She wondered if June and Callie thought her laugh sounded as forced as it actually was.

"Well, thank you," Callie said. "And—I should have said this before." She lifted her glass. "Cheers to new friends."

The sentiment made Lila's eyes prickle with tears. She told herself her over-emotional state resulted from gratitude, and definitely not from extreme loneliness. Maybe abandoning her real life hadn't been the best idea. But if this is where she ended up, maybe it wasn't the worst idea, either.

June wanted to know how things were going with the paperwork and in the middle of Lila's explanation of her new organizational system, a knock sounded at the door. A jolt of fear zapped Lila's consciousness, and she could feel it in every single one of her nerve endings. Her first instinct was to hide under the table but fortunately, common sense prevailed and she instead stared at the door, her heart in her throat. Enough time passed that whoever it was knocked again.

Forehead wrinkled in concern Callie said, "Do you want me to get that?"

Lila nodded, which made all the words in her head rattle around, echoing: *stalker, predator, danger, run.* She became hyperaware of everything: the exact position in which Callie placed her napkin, the sound of her chair scraping against the tile floor as she stood up, the way June wiped her hands and neatly folded her napkin before turning her head to see who was at the door, Callie's footsteps on the floor, the sound of the deadbolt turning, the way the sunlight poured in once the door opened. And the outline of a man in a police uniform.

Oh, right.

"Good afternoon. I'm Officer Rowland from the Prescott Police Department."

Suddenly, everything went soft again, and in the tips of her fingers, Lila felt her pulse slowing. She rushed to stand up. Hurried to the door. Stuck out her hand. "I'm Lila Sullivan. I'm so sorry. I completely forgot Officer Gomez said you were coming."

His eyes were so warm and friendly, she chastised herself for being afraid. "That's no problem. I'm just glad you're here."

"I see I'm interrupting, but this will only take a few minutes."

Lila didn't miss the look that passed between Callie and June. She gave each of them what she hoped was a reassuring smile and then gestured to the kitchen counter. "I guess you're here to show me some pictures."

Officer Rowland nodded. "Yep."

He set his folder on the counter and opened it up. There on top was a photo of Lila Sullivan, pre-makeover. As Lila reached down to turn it over, officer, Officer Rowland got one last look at it and then peered at her. He seemed to realize she was the same person from the photo because he gave a little nod, cleared his throat, and picked up the envelope that had been under the photo.

Lila noticed then that Callie and June stood next to the table, watching, frozen. She jumped. "You guys." She flapped a hand at them. "Go ahead and eat. Should just take a minute. Everything's fine. Don't look so worried."

Another look passed between them, but they did sit.

"Officer Gomez sent over several photos." Officer Rowland ran his thumb under the envelope's flap. "I'm going to show them to you, one at a time. I'd like me to tell me if you recognize any of the people in them."

Short of breath, Lila nodded.

Without so much as a twist of his wrist, Officer Rowland removed a photo from the envelope and set it on the counter. Lila's first thought was that she didn't recognize the guy in the mug shot, who looked very unhappy. *Sad*, even. His eyebrows were two horizontal caterpillars on a protruding brow bone, and his short haircut made his small, C-shaped ears stand out.

"I don't recognize him."

Officer Rowland adjusted the position of the photo on the counter, lining it up with the edge. "You sure?"

She licked her lips. "I'm sure."

He pulled out the second photo, which featured a younger guy with light skin and hair and icy blue eyes. "Him, either."

The third photo showed a man Lila wouldn't look at twice— except when it came to his eyes. They were the epitome of cold. Although his features looked ordinary, his gaze sent a shock to her system. "Nope." She turned the photo over. "But just looking at his picture is terrifying."

Officer Rowland grunted. "Agreed. Next one."

He turned over the fourth photo and Lila gasped. "Yes. That's the guy who was standing outside my apartment before I came here." The thought of that moment, when she saw him looking up at her window, made her skin crawl.

"You sure?"

"Yes." She glanced at Callie and June. They were staring at her.

He pulled a little spiral-bound notebook out of his shirt pocket and made a note. "I still have to show you the rest of the pictures. You know. Just in case."

She nodded. Licked her lips, which had gone suddenly dry. "Okay."

He flipped over two more photos and she was relieved she didn't recognize the man in either one.

Officer Rowland stacked the photos and slid them back into the manila envelope. "I'll be in touch with Officer Gomez. He'll reach out to you if he needs anything else, okay?"

In the minute or so it took him to make his exit, Lila mentally repeated a mantra: *I'm safe right now.*

Once he was gone, she turned to face June and Callie, who continued to stare at her.

"Lila." June stood up. "Do you want to tell us what's going on?"

She didn't—of course she didn't. She didn't want to speak of it or think about it at all. But she couldn't refuse, could she? Not when a police officer had interrupted their new-friends lunch and they'd seen him show her the photo line-up. Moving carefully again, doing her best not to let her feet make any sounds on the floor, Lila returned to the table and sat.

"It's a long story."

Callie and June remained still, hands in their laps, eyes on her. It was almost as if they were saying, "We have all the time in the world."

Before she could even begin, Callie gasped, covering her mouth with her hand. Her eyes were wide. She pointed at Lila. "You're Lila Sullivan. The actual person behind FearlessLila. Aren't you?"

At that, *Lila* gasped. "How did you know? Never mind. It's obvious, isn't it? Dyeing my hair wasn't enough, was it? I know. I thought about getting colored contacts, but I was afraid I couldn't wear them all the time. Wait. You know who I am?"

"She's the fitness influencer I was telling you about." Callie had turned her attention on June, whose mouth also dropped open.

"The one who had those fifteen-minute workouts?"

"The very same."

Both of her new friends' heads swiveled toward her. She grimaced. "The very same."

"Oh, my gosh." June's voice came out in a near-whisper. "She's, like famous, isn't she?"

"She is." Callie nodded, authoritative. "So famous. I love your videos! I do them on my lunch breaks all the time. Well, I did, until you took down your accounts."

Lila's heart swelled. That was exactly how she'd designed her workouts—so busy women could do them anywhere, almost any time, and reap the benefits ... primarily increased confidence. And Callie—who before Lila moved here had been a random stranger—knew who she was. Still, as Lila now knew, with fame came danger.

"But—why are you *here?*" Callie interrupted her thoughts. "And why did you dye your hair? It was so *pretty.*"

"Like I said. It's a long story. And I'm gonna need more wine." Lila brought the bottle to the table, refilled their glasses, and started talking.

It felt so good to share everything that had happened—how she'd been flying high in her career, hearing from people whose lives she was helping to change, only for everything to come to a complete stop when someone started stalking her. She told the girls about the pictures, the messages, the guy standing outside on the sidewalk. She finished with how she'd shut down her online accounts.

"And that's when you decided to move. Look for a job, and get the hell out of town." June nodded, confirming her own conclusion, and then drained the wine from her glass.

"Exactly."

"And Travis has no idea who you are," Callie said. "Seeing as how he avoids social media at all costs."

"Which is an added bonus. I had no way of knowing that when I applied for this job."

"But why Prescott? And are you really an accountant?" June wrinkled her nose. "I mean, you're so good at the fitness stuff. I just never pictured you as an *accountant.*"

That made Lila laugh out loud. "I was an accountant before I got into fitness. It's how I supported myself as I built my FearlessLila brand."

June and Callie both nodded, as if her explanation told them everything, revealed all the world's secrets.

"And I came to Prescott because it was more than halfway across the country. Honestly, in the job posting, Travis seemed desperate. And so was I. Match made in Heaven."

She shrugged. *It's that simple.*

"So do the police know who's stalking you?" Callie's demeanor had shifted. She was in full lawyer mode.

Lila gulped her wine, remembering the face of the man in the photo—the man who'd stared up at her from the sidewalk. "I think so. But they haven't caught him yet, I don't think. At least, that's what Officer Gomez—the guy from Huntsville—implied on the phone last night."

"No wonder you don't want to set foot off the property," June blurted out before quickly covering her mouth.

Lila looked from June to Callie. "You guys noticed?"

"Well, yeah." Callie's demeanor softened. "You've ordered everything for delivery. And Travis said you'd put up a salt barrier, which I researched—"

"You researched it?"

June closed her eyes and Callie looked somewhat chagrined. "Yeah. I mean, if you were crazy, I wanted to know."

Her honesty made Lila laugh out loud—again. "Fair enough. You're right. I am afraid to leave the property. It seems unlikely anyone would track me down—maybe to Arizona but not as far as Sweet Springs Ranch. I figure I can help with the paperwork here until the stuff at home blows over."

"It sounds like the police are on it," Callie said.

June narrowed her eyes. "And now..."

"What do you mean?" Lila knew what was coming, and she knew she was trapped.

"You think Travis is hot." Callie pointed at Lila, her grin wicked.

A furious blush rushed up Lila's chest and neck and onto her face. "Isn't that beside the point?" Her voice was squeaky.

"Ohhh, I don't think so. You're here now, aren't you?" June was giggling, and that made Lila want to giggle, too.

"I mean, I am. But not for long." She held up a hand. "Not that I don't like it. It's just—I miss my life. I've worked so hard, for years, to build FearlessLila. And I just had to shut it down." She snapped her fingers.

June and Callie looked sympathetic, which made Lila want to cry.

"Look. You guys. Don't worry, okay? Travis and I—we're just going to be friends. I'm here to do the accounting, and that's it. We talked about it."

This time, the look that passed between June and Callie was anything but subtle.

"They talked about it." Callie spoke in a barely contained squeal.

"I heard that."

"Why did you talk about it?" Callie's direct stare gave Lila an idea of what facing her in the courtroom would be like—and it was scary.

"Oh, you know."

"No, we don't." June, giddy, took another sip of wine.

"Did you guys—never mind."

"We kissed." Lila had no idea why she said it, but the words came tumbling out.

"I knew it." Callie spoke quietly, eyes locked on Lila's. "Didn't I tell you?"

June nodded. "You did. But I wasn't sure."

"Now we know."

"You guys talked about this?"

"Of course we did," Callie said and June added, "For months, we've been discussing Travis and when he's going to get himself a girlfriend. Wait. That sounded so sexist. But you know what we mean. He's just such a great guy and he has this nice house and he has so much going for him. Whoever landed him would be so lucky … we were just hoping he'd find someone."

Quite suddenly, Lila felt dreamy. Travis *did* have so much going for him. Whoever landed him *would* be so lucky. But it wouldn't be her. That thought made her feel melancholy. "His future girlfriend will be so lucky. But that's not me."

"Okay," Callie said, the word singsongy.

"We hear you." June pointed at Lila. "But we also see your face. You *like* him."

Her face had cooled, but when June spoke, it flamed again.

"Even if I did, it wouldn't matter. I'm leaving soon, and there's no room in my life for a relationship."

"Hmm," Callie and June said.

"Let's change the subject."

"Tell us everything." June dug into her sandwich again. Mouth full, she said, "Tell us how you became an influencer, what you do every day and what it's like to be *practically famous.*"

The two of them listened, rapt, as Lila shared the story of her journey from bullied kid to cross country runner to fitness enthusiast to bonafide influencer.

"Sometimes I have to pinch myself. When reporters or other influencers message me asking if I'll talk to them or share some quotes for an article or post, it's just ... amazing. It's even more so when I hear from people who read those articles or posts and resonated with whatever I said. The little-kid version of Lila can't believe we're out there, helping other people claim their power, you know?"

June, eyes filled with tears and she fanned her face. "You're going to make me cry, Lila. That's so amazing. I know I barely know you, but I'm so proud of you for everything you've done."

"Me, too," Callie said. "And even more determined to make sure this stalker asshole, whoever he is, doesn't screw up your chances for continued success."

Another wave of gratitude hit Lila then, threatening to overwhelm her. "Thanks, you guys. Your support means so much to me. But there's just one thing."

"Oh." Callie made a dismissive gesture. "We won't tell Travis. At least, not unless we have to, for some reason. As long as you're a legit accountant."

Lila laughed. "Oh, I'm a legit accountant, all right. I can show you everything I've done so far."

"That won't be necessary." June stood up and started clearing dishes from the table. "We trust you."

Joining June in clearing dishes, Callie stood, too. "We do. And we want you to know that you don't have to be afraid of this stalker asshole, whoever he is. As long as you're here, you're part of our crew. We won't let anything happen to you."

The fact that Lila believed them didn't stop her from putting down another salt barrier the moment they left.

Chapter Sixteen

Travis and his brothers were heading home with five of the ugliest bulls in the southwest, and had plans for a company to deliver twenty-four head of cow later that week. The Sweet Springs Ranch was on its way back.

With help from the auction staff, the four Wilder men had just finished loading their bulls into a rented trailer. Travis was practically giddy as he jogged to the driver's door and the guys piled into the truck to make the drive home.

"Shotgun." Sterling pushed Hayes out of the way to get to the front passenger door and Hayes cursed and got into the back.

"I promise not to get another gas-station burrito," Cash said. "The last one did some serious damage."

"To all of us." Hayes buckled his seatbelt and like Sterling had done on the ride north, leaned against his side of the cab and put his hat over his face.

The sun had set and they were about halfway home when Sterling turned down the music—contemporary country rather than Hayes's classic—and turned toward Travis. "So. What are you going to do about Lila, now that we're heading back home?"

Travis groaned.

"What, man? Did you forget about her?" How did Cash always manage to sound like he was wearing a shit-eating grin?

"Of course not." The cattle auction had provided a wonderful distraction, but Lila had been there the whole time, just outside the periphery.

"You've got to talk to her about the kiss." Cash punched Travis in the arm.

Travis made a move to elbow him, but he sank into the backseat too fast. "We should have made you ride in the trailer with our ugly bulls."

"Shut up, man. I'm serious."

One hand still on the wheel, Travis used the other to rub his forehead. "You're right. I have to talk to her. I just don't know what to say."

"What would you say if it was someone else?" Hayes asked.

"Nothing! If it was someone else, she wouldn't be living on our property, a stone's throw away from my front door. I could avoid running into her if I wanted to. I'd never have to talk to her again."

"Wait." Hayes piped up from the backseat. All innocence, he said, "Are you saying you want to avoid running into her?"

"No." The word came out harsher than Travis intended, and his brothers snickered.

"I guess you're gonna have to figure something out, man," Cash said. "Or do you want me to talk to her?"

"Again, no."

They pulled into Sweet Springs Ranch several hours later and Travis drove into the corral. Before the guys had even gotten out of the truck, Callie and June came out of the RV in front of the big house. Travis felt a pang of disappointment Lila wasn't with them, and then he saw her come down the stairs, shut the door, and jog to catch up with them.

Gratitude rushed in to replace the disappointment—he'd been gone for less than forty-eight hours and the others had brought Lila into the fold, made her one of them. By the time the guys assembled at the back of the trailer, the women had closed the corral gate and gathered there, chattering away about a show they'd been watching.

Both Sterling and Hayes pulled their women into their arms. A flash of jealousy rushed through Travis's body. Did he want that, with Lila or anyone else? Until a few days ago, the answer would have been a resounding "No." But now? If he gave into his desires, he'd be wrapping his arms around Lila's waist, kissing her hard, and, if he was anything like Hayes, grabbing her ass. Callie yelped and pushed Hayes away.

Travis and Cash worked together to open the trailer's back doors and put down the ramp, and they all stood back as the bulls turned toward the opening, ears and noses twitching, tails flicking.

"Oh, my God." Callie sounded incredulous and Travis's mouth quirked into a smile even as he watched Lila for her reaction. "Those have got to be the ugliest creatures I have ever seen."

The Wilder boys exchanged fist bumps all around while the women looked at them like they were crazy.

"Is that what you were going for?" June wanted to know, and suddenly, they were all laughing, even Lila, and Travis felt the pieces of his life clicking into place.

The bulls, sniffing the air and the ground, slowly made their way down the ramp and into the corral.

Still hooting, Travis explained how he'd selected only bulls with good structure and sound legs and feet, but also that he wanted to make a statement by restarting the Sweet Springs Ranch line of cattle with the absolute homeliest he could find.

"I'm fairly confident you've made a statement," Lila said.

They were the first words Lila had spoken to Travis that evening and his body responded to her voice by developing a sudden and unmistakable yearning to touch her. He stuffed his hands in his pockets and his body leaned toward her as if it were magnetized.

Callie broke the spell: "We put out a bunch of hay and turned on the watering system. These, ah, good-looking fellows should be good to go for the night. You guys hungry?"

They all replied with variations on "Famished," and June said, "Good, because we cooked enough to feed an army."

While the bulls wandered off to find the hay, the guys closed up the trailer and moved the truck out of the corral. Within a few minutes, Travis was swept up in the energy of the group as they trooped into Sterling and June's RV to eat the dinner the women had prepared.

"You should have seen Travis, man." Cash filled his paper plate with food and sat down on the couch. "He was an animal in there."

Callie snickered. "I mean, I can't imagine it was much of a fight to snag those particular bulls."

"That's why he was an animal." As usual, Cash's mouth was full and his brothers said, "Don't talk with your mouth full."

Everyone was laughing then, and by the time they were all settled, Travis found himself seated next to Lila in the dining booth. "So, how'd you get roped into being here this evening?"

She laughed. "After we had lunch earlier, Callie and June invited me for dinner, too. We had such a nice afternoon, I couldn't turn them down. Plus, I wanted to see the bulls you brought home."

"And?"

She smiled. "I've never seen bulls up close before. They're terrifying." She laughed. "And I know everyone else said they're ugly, but there's also something kind of majestic about their giant chests and their horns and the way they move."

I think I'm in love.

"Did you say *majestic*?" From her spot across the table, Callie gave Lila an exaggerated sneer.

"I did." Lila grinned at her. "I mean, they're such giant, powerful animals, aren't they? I'm pretty sure they symbolize strength, in part."

"When you put it that way ... but they're also stubborn. And, if you're dumb enough to make one angry, they're *mean*."

"I'll keep that in mind, try to stay on their good side."

"Is that why you cooked chicken instead of steak?" Callie held up a piece of chicken on her fork.

"You cooked this?" Travis quirked an eyebrow.

"Lila! Hit him for me." Indignant, Callie swung her arm at Travis. "He said that like he can't believe you cooked this delicious chicken!"

Travis flinched away from Callie's swinging arm and rushed to defend himself. "That's not what I meant! At all! It's just that I think of Lila as a guest."

That didn't help his cause; Callie started her assault fresh. "Now you're saying it's rude that June and I let her cook!"

"That's not what I'm saying! I just meant—"

Lila put a hand on his arm and looked at him. "It's fine. Don't worry. I know what you meant and I volunteered to cook the chicken because I wanted to contribute."

"Yeah, you ninny." Callie crossed her arms and Hayes, laughing, did the same. "Ninny."

They spent the rest of dinner in relative peace, and Travis enjoyed listening to Lila talk to his friends like they were her friends. A tiny part of him wished she'd come to feel so comfortable at Sweet Springs, she'd want to stay. But a bigger, more sensible part of him knew she needed to return to her hometown, where she had friends and a business and an apartment.

Before long, plates were empty and the dishes were done and it was time to head out. Travis stepped out of the RV first and offered Lila his hand as she descended. She held onto his arm as they made their way down the ranch's main road toward his house.

Crickets sang and the stars sparkled in the sky. The fall-evening scents of damp earth and hay rose from the ground. In a few short months, frost would crunch under their feet. *And Lila will be gone.* A cold, sick sense of dread swirled in his gut.

"Can we stop and say goodnight to the bulls?"

He would have laughed—his family had never considered bulls pets, like they had horses—but when he glanced down at her, he could see she was serious. "Sure."

To his surprise, when they approached the corral fence all five bulls meandered over to where they stood.

"Hey, guys." Her voice, soft and calm, conjured images of the two of them in a bedroom with dim lighting and soft sheets. *I should not be getting aroused right now.*

One of the bulls, Mayhem, came close enough to stick his nose between the fence rails, and Lila reached out a tentative hand. "Can I pet him?"

Travis shrugged. "Sure. I don't know if he's ever been petted before, but you can try. Just know that he might be surprised."

Lila nodded and put her palm close to the bull's nose. Mayhem sniffed, and when he didn't back away, Lila smoothed her hand over his cheek. He blinked and remained still. She turned her head, slowly, so she could make eye contact with Travis, and her smile made him wish for a million more moments exactly like this one.

Her focused returned to the animal. "Just coming to say good-night to you on your first night here. Welcome to Sweet Springs Ranch."

The rest of the bulls came in closer, as if they too were jealous of the intimate moment between Lila and Mayhem. Travis couldn't believe the bull actually stood still while Lila's hand remained on its nose. It blinked at her once, twice, and then a third time before turning and walking away, the moonlight casting its giant horns into silhouette. The others followed.

After Lila watched them go, she turned around to face Travis. "Okay. *Now* we can go home."

The longing that hit him—for them to go home together—almost knocked him off his feet. Again, he offered his arm and they walked toward the bunkhouse. He'd been fine for the past two days. Yes, he'd thought about her almost constantly, but right now, the idea of separating from her was putting his body into panic mode. Inviting himself in was out of the question. Maybe he could send her a mental signal—brainwaves—urging her to invite him in. Or, he could invite her to come over to his place. But it was late. Surely she'd say she was tired and had to go to bed. It sounded like she'd spent a bunch of time with June and Callie that day, and she may be done socializing. He'd better make up his mind. They were only a few steps from her door.

"I know it's late." She stopped, turned toward him, and grabbed both of his arms. "But do you want to come in?"

His reaction was completely childish. He could barely contain the laughter rising up inside his body, and jumping and dancing and pumping his arms seemed to be the only solution. Responses like,

"Absolutely!" and "You bet I do!" and "I can't believe you're inviting me in!" came to mind and he tamped them down.

"I'd love to." He kept it casual, but her eyes lit up like *she* was a child and he'd offered her the biggest swirl of cotton candy. "Oh, good. I really wanted to hear more about the auction. And this might be weird, but I missed you."

She missed me?

His grin in response to her words was completely involuntary and he didn't try to hide it. "You missed me?"

She shrugged, bit her lower lip, looked away. If the bunkhouse's porch lights were any brighter, he knew he'd be able to see her blushing. Which was adorable.

"I did." She grabbed his hand and started walking toward the bunkhouse again. "I guess I've gotten used to having you around. And, until June and Callie invited me to hang out with them—which was lovely, by the way—you were also my only social outlet."

She continued talking while she unlocked the deadbolts. Travis counted four, and although he wanted to ask her about it, he pushed his curiosity from his mind.

For now, he'd enjoy spending time with Lila, this charming woman who talked to his bulls and said she'd missed him.

Inside, the lights were already on and Lila stepped over the salt barrier and headed for the kitchen. "Want a beer?"

"Sure."

She handed him one and then went to work uncorking a bottle of wine.

"Not a beer drinker?" he asked.

"Not really. But I've noticed everyone else around here is, so I figured I'd better stock up." She got down a tumbler and poured the wine, then picked up a deck of cards. "Want to play a game of speed?"

Travis laughed. "You're going to have to give me a refresher on how to play. It's been forever."

Within a few minutes, they were going head to head, slapping their cards down as fast as they could, laughing when they knocked their hands together in a rush to use up their cards and win. He was slower than her at first, but after several rounds he caught up and the competition was fierce. They'd each gone through two drinks when she won the fifth tie breaker and giggling, told him, "We'd better quit now, before this ends up in a fistfight."

The timing was right: he could (and should) ask her about the articles he'd seen online, the makeover she'd obviously given herself, and what she was so afraid of. But he couldn't. They'd had such a nice evening together and this was the most carefree he'd seen her. So he stacked all the cards and shuffled them before setting them in a neat pile on the table.

"You're just afraid I'm going to win the next tie breaker."

"You might be right." She winked at him, interlaced her fingers, and put her elbows on the table. "But you might be wrong. As you've now experienced for yourself, I'm quite skilled at speed."

"Quite skilled, indeed. But I'll bet I could take you in an arm-wrestling contest."

Her expression went instantly serious. "Oh, you think so, huh?"

Too late, he realized his miscalculation. "Never mind."

She brought her hands up, rested her chin on them, and gave him a smile that held all the feminine magic in the universe.

"We got so caught up in speed, I didn't have a chance to ask you about the auction. Is it too late?" She tapped her phone screen to check the time.

Because he was apparently addicted to being with her, he said, "Of course not."

"Let's go sit in the living room."

She snagged another beer and poured another glass of wine and he followed her to the couch. He sat first and was immensely pleased when she sat close enough that their thighs touched. She smelled like citrus and vanilla and he wanted to wrap his arms around her.

"Tell me everything."

"Where to start? As you've seen, the end result of the auction is that I brought home five awesome, if ugly, bulls. I've also got a small herd of cows coming via delivery this week. I've been to lots of auctions—especially before my dad started gambling away his life savings—but never one like this. Sterling called it a highfalutin auction and that's accurate."

"How could you tell?"

"I mean, just knowing the price points of the boots walking around that place, you could tell. Guys were wearing thousand-dollar boots to bid on cattle."

"Thousand-dollar boots?! Those exist?!"

"You'll probably see receipts for them in all my dad's paperwork."

She shook her head. "That's amazing. I mean, I remember being just this side of buyer's remorse the first time I spent more than a hundred on workout shoes."

"I guess I'm not surprised. And how many pair do you own now?"

"Let me picture the closet at my apartment." She looked wistful as she counted on her fingers. "I have twenty-two."

Gasping, he sat up straight. "Twenty-two?! Holy cow, woman! What are you gonna do with that many shoes?"

"Very funny." She slapped him on the arm. "I've gotten some of them from sponsors or whatever, so I didn't pay for them all. And, I'll have you know, they complement my outfits."

"I'd love to see your closet."

Suddenly serious, she said, "I'd love to show you my closet."

In that moment, Travis knew: he had to clear the air.

"Lila?"

"Yeah?" She turned toward him, her eyes luminous.

"The other night, I looked you up on the internet."

"Oh." Her gaze morphed from soft and dreamy to intense and ... afraid?

Desperate to reassure her, he smiled. "I love your red hair."

Her smile came and went so quickly, he thought he imagined it. "Thank you. But that's not all, is it?"

He shook his head. "No. I mean, I *do* love your red hair. And you look beautiful with black hair, too." He wrapped the end of a strand around two fingers, then released it. "And I'm so glad you left your eyes that shade of green. Anyway. Based on everything I've seen, I'd wager a guess that your hair-color change is more than just a fashion statement. And I know you mentioned you had a public image issue, but before I looked you up, I didn't realize quite how public your image was. *Is.* Lila Sullivan of FearlessLila is a household name. Which means your issue must be commensurate. I want to respect your privacy, but I also want to be able to help protect you if you need it. So, why did you really leave Alabama?"

Chapter Seventeen

Lila knew the conversation would come up eventually and she'd mentally rehearsed what she would say. But now that it was here, she found she couldn't recall the words she planned. Her mouth worked, opening and closing without emitting any sound.

Travis waited, his eyes on hers, his posture relaxed.

He probably thinks I look like a deer in headlights.

"Well, it's a long story."

"I suspected as much." He flashed a grin but said nothing more.

She swore she could hear a clock ticking, notifying her of the passing of time, the silence stretching between them while she considered her response. "Where do I start?"

"At the beginning, I suspect."

She nodded. "At the beginning. Okay."

Could she tell him *everything*? What if she did, and he started picturing her as the chubby-cheeked ten-year-old she'd once been? What if his feelings for her shifted and he saw her through a lens of pity? Could she risk it?

Not just yet.

She glossed over that part, streamlined it, told him she'd encountered some bullying as a kid and gained confidence through the high school cross country team.

"I fell in love with fitness during college, and that's when social media was taking off. and I started sharing posts. I shared workouts, health tips, and motivational stuff—I wanted to help people grow their confidence like I had. Almost inexplicably, my account blew up. I had brands contacting me, asking me to be an ambassador, reporters calling me for interviews, and best of all, regular people writing in to thank me for sharing my story and helping boost their confidence."

"That sounds wonderful."

"It was. I was in seventh heaven. I mean, I kept having to pinch myself. I could hardly believe I'd gone from being this shy, insecure little girl to a confident, strong woman."

"And then."

Lila nodded, gulped. "Right. Recently, I started getting messages from these anonymous accounts. They were nice, things like, 'Hey, I loved your video on how to use a foam roller,' and, 'Great workout.' I make a habit of responding to every message, and before I knew it, I was receiving comments daily from the same anonymous account. It seemed so nice, you know? I did think about the account not having a profile picture; but I just figured the person who owned it was shy or insecure like I was at one point."

Travis nodded. "I could see that."

Her stomach swirled, giving her an unpleasant, nauseated feeling as she remembered when the messages had started crossing the line. "He started talking about how pretty I looked in the videos."

"Of course he did."

She gave Travis a look. "Actually, at first I thought it was a woman. Most of my followers are. But then those comments started getting more ... detailed."

He winced at the disgusted look on her face.

"'Your ass looks great in those leggings. Let me take you to dinner.'"

"That's over the top, right? I mean, even if it's true?" He smirked and she rolled her eyes.

"Right. But there's more."

He shifted so their torsos touched, and he put an arm along the back of the couch. Taking that as an invitation, she leaned against him.

"The guy started sending me pictures of myself. Pictures I assume he took while I was out and about. He always added compliments. 'Looking good today,' or whatever."

"That ratcheted up the creep factor, didn't it?"

"It did."

"I assume you called the police?"

"I did. They basically agreed with me that the guy's behavior was creepy, and said I should definitely be aware of my surroundings. But they *also* said he hadn't broken any laws. So they couldn't do much."

"Doesn't leave a person feeling very safe, does it?"

Finally, Lila felt like she could breathe. Travis seemed to understand exactly where she was coming from. "It doesn't. And then, after the policeman came by, I saw a guy standing outside my apartment, looking up at my window. I *know* he knew I'd called. And I was afraid of what he might do."

"So you decided to get out of town."

She nodded. "Right. I shut down my social accounts, applied for this job, and moved two-thirds of the way across the country."

"Are the police doing anything about this guy?"

Lila shrugged. "I mean, they're doing extra surveillance. They think they might have seen him. Officer Gomez—that's the guy who came to my apartment—he called me the other day and said they saw someone standing outside. He couldn't give me too many details, but said he'd send some pictures to the local police department to show me. A Prescott cop, Officer Rowland, showed up today during lunch to do a photo lineup. *That* was humiliating. I never thought I'd be involved in a police investigation. And it's unfolding right here, in front of people who I'd like to call friends."

"If there's anything I've learned since my dad nearly gambled our home away, it's that giving too much weight to what other people think is sentencing yourself to a life of misery. I was so humiliated by my dad's behavior, but when I got over that and we put on that kick-ass fundraiser, I realized my thoughts about other people's feelings were just projections."

Lila nodded. "That makes sense."

Travis inhaled, held his breath, exhaled. "Lila?"

"Yeah?" She turned to face him and his eyes held an intensity that made her breath catch.

"I never talk about this to anyone." He paused, as if reconsidering whether he wanted to share it now. "My mom left when we were kids. It's something I never understood, never quite got over. For many reasons, obviously. I remember when it first happened, the rumors flew. Kids talked about it at school, teased us about it. Said she left to be with a boyfriend, to live childless in Hollywood. She was a movie star." He added the last part as an aside, his mouth quirking into a wry smile even while his eyes held a deep sadness.

Her heart ached for him, and she slid her hand down his thigh to his knee, where she let it rest. "First of all, I'm really sorry. That must have been hard."

He nodded, and she squeezed his knee.

"Second, that explains why all four of you Wilder boys look like you stepped off the silver screen."

"You think so?"

"Yeah. I do."

"Thanks." He kissed the top of her head. The casual, intimate gesture made her all warm and fuzzy inside. "I think."

"Trust me. It's a compliment. When you told me you were hiring for a position at a ranch in Arizona, I looked it up and saw a picture of the four of you. I thought, 'What have I gotten myself into?'"

Laughing, he wrapped his arm around her and pulled her closer. "You know something else I learned from everything I went through with my family?"

"What?"

"I learned that you never know when it'll be the last time you talk to someone. So you should always say what's on your mind."

Suddenly nervous, her body feeling shaky, she sat up straighter and turned to face him. "And what's on your mind, Travis?"

His grin dissolved some of her tension. "I was hoping you'd ask. I really like you, Lila. I enjoy spending time with you. In fact, I want to spend as much time with you as I can. This is different for me. It's special. And because of my past, I can't ignore it."

She almost couldn't believe her ears. Was he saying he wanted to be with her? But, why? She was a walking disaster.

He took her hands and went on. "I know neither of us is sure how long you'll be here, and it might not make sense or be reasonable to try to be together. But I'd like to. I'd like to be with you, Lila. I'd like to take you on trail rides and out on the town. I'd like to cook dinner with you and spend evenings with you and be your person for as long as you'll have me."

While he spoke, a warmth spread through Lila's chest, making her feel pliable and content. She leaned forward and rested her forehead against his. "I really like the sound of that." She licked her lips. "But in case you haven't noticed, my life is a bit of a mess right now."

"I've noticed." He cupped her head with one hand. "But isn't life always a bit of a mess? Look at mine. My dad nearly gambled away our family property and we had to ask the community for help to save it. That was just the first step. Now we have to figure out how to make it profitable again so we can keep it. And who knows what you're going to uncover as you go through years' and years' worth of paperwork? Now, *that's* messy."

"Well, when you put it that way ..."

And then she was tilting her face up so their lips met and his hands were in her hair and that little devil on her shoulder was pumping her fist, reminding her how much she wanted this.

The kiss was everything she remembered from the first time, everything she imagined the next time would be, and so much more. Travis's lips were insistent and gentle and his hands felt strong as they moved to her shoulders. Everywhere their skin met, Lila felt a pleasant shiver, physical proof of the effect their connection had on her.

Her own hands began to explore, too, moving from her lap to his shoulders and then upwards to wrap around the back of his neck.

As quickly as he'd started kissing her, he stopped, his hands still clutching hers, a wry smile on his lips. "Is this a 'yes'?"

How she could experience delight and arousal at once, Lila didn't know, but there she was, wanting to giggle and get naked all at the same time.

"It's a yes."

She didn't know what the hell she was doing—they had no way of telling where this thing would end up. But at the moment, she didn't care. All she knew was that being around Travis made her feel safe and secure and confident and she liked that. So she decided to go with it. She could deal with the future when it happened.

Hoping to convey just how much she wanted this, wanted him, she sat up and pushed him onto his back on the couch. She raised herself up over him, then lowered her body onto his while brushing her lips against his again.

"Since the first time I laid eyes on you, I've wanted to kiss you. And I've thought about kissing you ever since."

His response was a guttural groan. He ran his hands from her hips to her ribcage and then took her face and kissed her deeply again. His arousal pressed against her, and she slid her center along it while their tongues danced.

"May I?" He tugged at the hem of her top, and she sat up, strad-dling him, and lifted her arms.

He groaned again when he removed her shirt, and her initial wave of self-consciousness gave way to lust as he cupped her breasts, enraptured.

"May *I*?" She tugged on his shirt until he sat up just enough for her to remove it.

The angel and devil on her shoulders both cheered when they saw his six-pack. Even that little angel could appreciate a nice, glorious set of muscles on a hard-working man.

"Nice," she told him, running her hands along the ridges of his abs.

"I was going to say the same." His eyes were on her breasts still and watching him watch her gave her a thrill like she'd never experienced.

Using a forefinger, he tugged down the edge of her bra to reveal her nipple and then he pulled her toward him and took the peak into his mouth. She gasped and continued to ride him, the friction bringing her closer to the edge. He released the first nipple and moved on to the second and she nearly came undone.

Her body humming with need, she reached down to unbuckle his belt and unbutton and unzip his jeans. He sprang free and he moaned with pleasure when she took him in her hand and started to stroke.

Drunk on power, she moved her hand faster until he released her breasts and brought her face down to his again, murmuring, "You're killing me," before crushing his mouth to hers. Then they were scrambling, desperate, removing each other's clothes and tossing them aside as they moved toward Lila's bed.

Travis laid down first and Lila climbed on top of him, causing him to groan again as he ran his hands from her knees to her waist. Smiling, she lifted her hips and sank down onto him. They both gasped and then started to move. She could actually feel her vibration shifting, rising, as their bodies melded.

Once again, Travis took her face in his hands and their eyes locked while they continued to move.

I'm falling in love with him.

She'd known she felt differently with him than she had with anyone else. Until this moment, she had chalked it up to this place being a safe haven as she escaped from her own reality.

But no ... it was more than just that.

Looking into his eyes, the spark, the bond, the sense of knowing she experienced was her undoing, and almost without warning, she shattered, the orgasm ripping through her. Travis cried out as he drove into her. She collapsed on top of him, the shudders subsiding as he stroked her back, creating pleasant little shivers all over her body.

"Wow." His mouth was somewhere near her ear, his voice muffled by her hair.

"'Wow' is right." She turned her head so she could kiss him on the neck, and he wrapped his arms around her waist and held her.

She sank into the connection, breathing in his scent—the fresh air, the sandalwood soap, the sweat—and relishing it, relishing *him*.

This feeling, the sense of comfort and safety and belonging, would stay with her forever, even if she didn't stay with Travis forever. The thought of leaving him made her chest constrict.

After a few minutes during which their breathing settled into a rhythm, Travis's whisper broke through Lila's reverie. "I'll get us a towel."

Before she could roll off him, he smacked her naked ass, making her yelp. Grinning, he went into the bathroom and returned a minute later with a hand towel. He surprised her by climbing back into bed, opening his arms, inviting her to join him.

She slid her body along his. "You going to stay a while?"

"Can I stay all night? I'm not quite done with you."

The words sent another thrill through her body and she snuggled closer. "You can stay all night. But what will the bulls think when they see you come out my front door in the morning?"

His bark of laughter punctuated the air. "Oh, I think they'll understand what happens between a male and a female. If they don't, then they're not up to the job of re-launching the Sweet Springs Ranch cattle line."

"You have a point."

Travis curled himself around Lila. She could tell when he fell asleep—almost instantly—because his breathing slowed and his body relaxed. His tranquility was intoxicating ... she couldn't think of a time in the past weeks when she'd been able to sink into the mattress like he was doing at the moment. But within a few minutes, the comforting weight of his arm and the even sound of his breathing and the scent of his skin made her eyelids heavy.

The next morning when she woke up, she realized she'd actually slept all night—which she hadn't done in forever. Just as she was finishing that thought, Travis woke too, and moaned dramatically. "I slept so good, and that is not how I imagined last night going."

Lips twitching, Lila said, "No? How did you imagine it going?"

"I had so many plans for us." He squeezed her waist a little tighter. "It was going to be a night you'd never forget."

"Believe it or not, I haven't slept that well in ages. For that reason, it's a night *I'll* never forget."

"I guess that's something. Want to make this a morning you'll never forget?"

Lila giggled. "That sounds lovely."

And then they were at it again, limbs tangled, skin sliding over skin, bodies connected and moving as one. Afterwards, they lay on their backs, fingers intertwined.

"Now I'm hungry. Want me to make us breakfast?"

"Ooh." She rolled toward him and stroked the bare skin just below his belly button. "A man who cooks immediately after a mind-blowing lovemaking session? Yes, please."

He kissed her on the nose, put on his underwear, and went into the kitchen. She wrapped herself in the sheet and watched him work from her spot on the bed. The muscles in his back flexed as he opened the fridge and got out the eggs, and Lila decided him making breakfast was just as arousing as him kissing her until her toes curled. He knew his way around the kitchen; without asking her where anything was, he got a bowl and began cracking eggs into it, then found a whisk and whisked them, adding salt and pepper.

I could watch this man make eggs every single day for the rest of my life.

"You want toast with your eggs?" Hearing his husky morning voice made a bolt of heat rush down and settle between her legs.

"Sure. I can toast it."

"Nah. Stay in bed. I'm coming back for you."

And so it was that they ended up eating breakfast in bed—eggs and toast and bacon on a tray—before he kissed her senseless and then told her he had to go home and get ready for the day.

"Do you have to?" She ran a fingertip along his cheek and over his lip. He took it in his teeth, gently, and grinned. "I don't *have* to. I could shower here. But I do have to run errands today. You're more than welcome to come with me."

Lila nearly panicked at the idea of leaving the cocoon she'd built around herself at the bunkhouse and on the Sweet Springs property. But part of her yearned to get out, to see the town where Travis and his brothers and Callie had grown up.

She loved and hated that he could see her warring with herself, but then he grinned at her and said, "Tell you what. You can think about it while we shower."

Chapter Eighteen

Travis felt the tiniest bit guilty using shower sex to convince Lila to come to town with him. But, he wanted to spend more time with her and he thought maybe getting out would be good for her, show her she was safe here. Those two reasonable justifications assuaged his guilt and he decided to go all out.

He wished they'd already gotten dressed so he could peel her clothes off her again, but he took his time and savored pulling the sheet away from her body and running his tongue down her torso, dipping it into her center a few times until she was gasping, her fingers wrapped around his head.

He pulled her to standing and led her to the bathroom, where he turned on the shower and lifted her onto the counter while they waited for the water to warm up. He kept them busy by lavishing her breasts with his hands and mouth.

Steam curled into the air, making their skin dewy. Again, Travis took her hand and pulled her off the counter, leading her to the shower. Because he was so turned on and didn't want their fun to end too soon, he grabbed the bar of soap she had on the little shelf, rubbed it into a good lather, and began massaging her shoulders and neck, kneading the knots that had undoubtedly formed as a result of the stress she'd been under.

Her head fell back and she moaned in pleasure—a different kind of pleasure than he'd brought her before ... and delivering relief in this way made him rock hard against her lower back.

Hands still slippery with soap, he cupped her breasts and toyed with her nipples until she was arching against him, begging him to take her again.

He gripped her waist and plunged into her and she braced herself on the shower wall so she could push back against him. The water pouring down over them, they rocked together and when he could tell she was near release he slowed the pace. "I love this view." He ran one palm from her lower back to her shoulder and tugged her against him.

Her response was half-laugh, half-grunt, and when she turned around to look at him over her shoulder, he found himself slipping over the edge. "Come with me."

She grinned then, and they both came fast and hard, shuddering with release.

When it was over, he slipped out of her and turned her around to hold her. She tipped her head back and kissed his mouth, then brought her mouth to his jaw and then his throat. The tenderness surprised him and unwound him and he knew he'd never be the same.

Wanting to pamper her, spoil her, he poured shampoo into his hand and began rubbing it into her hair, his fingers making circles on her scalp, sudsing her long locks. He thought about her natural color but decided not to bring it up and instead began rinsing out the shampoo. Eyes closed, she tilted her head back, and he took extra care because he knew she was being vulnerable with him. After he conditioned her hair and rinsed her body she picked up the shampoo. "My turn."

He would have believed it impossible, but the glint in her eyes made him jump to attention again. She noticed, giving him a little chuckle as he leaned against her as she brought his head down and began rubbing in the shampoo. Her fingers on his scalp were pure heaven and he turned his head to allow her access to every square centimeter. She rinsed his hair and applied conditioner, then massaged his shoulders while she let it sit.

Travis couldn't remember a time when a woman had taken care of him in this way. Not only that, but he couldn't remember a time when he'd wanted to take care of a woman in this way. Once he was clean and rinsed, Lila turned off the water and grabbed a towel off the rack next to the shower. She dried him off from head to toe in what had to be one of the most erotic experiences of his life. Throbbing with need for her, he returned the favor, even wrapping her hair when he was done.

They stood facing each other in the steamy bathroom, each of them wrapped in a towel. It took every ounce of self control not to cart her back to bed. Meanwhile, he wanted to wrap her in his arms, protect her and care for her, not just on this day, but every day. The thought startled him and he gulped. "So. About going to town with me."

One of her hands wrapped around one of his. "I have to say, you're pretty convincing."

He did a fist pump with his free hand, making her laugh. "I brought out the big guns."

"I would say so."

Afraid of changing her mind by saying anything, and absolutely desperate for her to go with him, he waited. After what felt like forever, she took a deep breath, stared into his eyes, and said, "I'll go."

He exhaled and managed to resist the temptation to make a handful of promises about how he'd keep her safe, how they'd have fun together, how she'd love Prescott. "Good. You'd better get dressed, though, because if you keep standing there in that towel, we're going to wind up back in bed."

"Not that I'd mind that."

God, did she have any idea what she did to him? "I wouldn't, either. But I do need to get to the feed store to make that order so the new cows have something to eat. How do you think they'd feel if we told them we couldn't feed them because we were too busy in bed?"

That made her laugh and brought the color to her cheeks. "I guess you'd better get dressed, then."

Thirty minutes later, he'd put on fresh clothes and was back at the bunkhouse. She opened the front door and he didn't stop himself from reaching for her.

"This is a nice greeting," she said between kisses.

"Isn't it?" *I'm falling for her.* Alarm bells blared in his mind. He had to be careful—this situation risked breaking both their hearts. Keeping hold of her hands, he stepped back. "Ready?"

"Ready. Let me just grab my stuff." After retrieving her purse and a sweater, she locked all four deadbolts, double-checked the door, and clipped her keys to her purse.

They got into his truck and he could see the rate of her breathing increase. Her grip on her purse was so tight, her knuckles went white. "You okay?"

When she looked at him, her eyes were wide, even as she nodded. "Fine. I'm fine." Her attempt at a smile was more like a grimace. He reached across the console and took her hand.

"You sure? You don't have to go with me." He'd already started the truck but kept a hold of her hand to show her he wasn't in any hurry. "You can stay here and relax and we can hang out again when I get back."

She nodded, the movement rapid. "I know." She licked her lips. "But I want to. I'm terrified even though I know I'm safe here. At least, I think I am. I want to go. I know leaving this house, getting off the ranch will seem less scary once I've done it." She rubbed her hands together. "Let's go. Put this thing in drive."

He nodded and did as she asked, then took her hand again, interlacing their fingers. He'd already devised a plan to keep her distracted: he'd talk and talk, giving her the most thorough tour of Prescott that anyone had ever received. So, as they pulled out of the ranch and onto the main road, he pointed to the north. "That's where most of the ranch properties are. We're heading south, into town, but we should definitely take a drive out there one day. It's all rolling pastures and grazing horses."

"Sounds beautiful."

"It is." They smiled at each other as they turned left. "I'll drive you through downtown, first. You've got to see the courthouse plaza and all the Victorian houses. And you've definitely got to hear some of the stories. Not *all* of them." He winked.

This time her smile looked a little more genuine, a little less grimace-like.

He pointed off to the west. "That property there is the Bar C Ranch. Their family—the Carreras—had four girls. We all went to school together and I can't tell you how many shenanigans we all got into. They were almost like cousins to us. In middle school, the second-to-youngest daughter, Lena, was getting picked on by some girl. She made Lena's life miserable. I can't even remember now exactly what they did, but I'm pretty sure it had something to do with her nose and eyebrows. They're Italian, you know. Big eyebrows are in, now, but back then, all the girls had the skinny eyebrows." He glanced at her and was happy she was looking out the window, taking in the Bar C Ranch's tree-dotted landscape.

But then she looked at him, her nose wrinkled. "I'm not sure 'big eyebrows' is the term women would use nowadays to describe what's popular in eyebrows."

He shrugged. "You know what I mean. Anyway, one night when our families were having dinner together, the oldest sister, Carla, was telling us about these bullies. And Sterling said, 'Are we gonna let them get away with that, boys?'"

Lila smiled, eyebrows raised as she waited for the response.

"And we all said, 'Of course we aren't.' We put our heads together to make a plan. It was our goal to make those two bullies as miserable as possible."

"So what did you do?"

Good. She looked calm now. The crease between her eyebrows had smoothed out and her hands were relaxed in her lap.

"Well, like I said, we all made the plan, but I was the lucky one who got to put it into play because I was in the same grade as Lena." He remembered that day with such satisfaction, he was positive Lila could see the evil glint in his eyes. "I was systematic. You see, this girl—Janie Robertson—all she cared about was her grades. For the next month, I'd wait for her to turn in her assignments and then I'd turn in mine. I'd steal hers right out of the basket and stow them in my backpack. It was a waiting game, right? She didn't know for *weeks*. And by the time the teachers noticed and confronted her about it, it was too late. I'd stolen dozens of assignments, several from each class. She was so far behind, she'd never be able to catch up. I remember seeing her crying to one of our teachers, swearing she'd turned in absolutely everything. I should have felt bad, but I didn't. Because I'd seen Lena crying at home. I'd seen her face go beet red at the dinner table when Carla told all of us what was going on. So all I felt when I saw Janie's misery was glee. I couldn't wait to go home and report it to my brothers and all the Carrera girls." By that time, they'd reached town, and Travis was pulling into the feed store parking lot.

Rapt, Lila remained still when he parked and took off his seatbelt. "So then what happened?"

"Let's go in. I'll tell you the rest after we make this order."

Inside, Lila's eyes went round as she took in all the inventory. Heavy duty jackets, jeans, and work boots took up one section, and shelves on an opposite wall held stacks and stacks of bagged feed. The center aisle opened up to side aisles containing buckets, rolled rope, fencing supplies, dog beds, seeds for planting, and gardening supplies. Travis had grown up coming to the feed store, but looking at it from a newcomer's perspective, it seemed magical.

"Lots of stuff, right?"

"Yeah." Lila gestured at the wall of feed. "I never would have guessed that many different types of animal food exist."

Before he could answer, she gasped and jogged ahead of him to the center of the store. He grinned when he realized what she'd seen: the *Chicks Are Here!* sign hung on one side of a chainlink enclosure. Inside that, a half-dozen containers sat on the floor, each one bearing a sign for a different type of chick. Lila stood outside the chainlink, peering down into a container labeled *Leghorns*. Countless tiny, fluffy, yellow chicks zoomed around on the floor of the container, making *cheep* noises.

"Aww." She crouched to get a better look and Travis crouched, too. "These guys are just about the cutest things I've ever seen."

"They *are* pretty cute. But they grow up into adult chickens, you know."

She elbowed him, smiling. "I figured. Did you guys ever have chickens?"

"When my mom was still here we did. They were her babies. She had a bunch of these—leghorns—and a few fun ones, too. Ameraucanas. Those are the ones that lay blue eggs. Frizzles, silkies, you name it."

"Frizzles?"

He pulled out his phone, did a quick Internet search, and showed her.

"Oh, my gosh. I *want* one! It's so *fluffy!*"

"Yeah, they're pretty cute." He was thinking *she* was pretty cute. "Sometimes they get frizzles in here. They get new shipments every week. We could come back."

"Let's!"

He didn't comment on how excited she seemed to make a return trip; he acted like it was the most natural thing in the world. "Should we go order food for these cows?"

They straightened up and she slipped her hand into his as they walked to the back of the store. Although their interlaced fingers made him almost giddy, he pretended that, too, was the most natural thing in the world.

Hank, the feed guy, looked at Lila with unbridled curiosity when the two of them walked up to the desk.

"Hey, Trav. What can I do for you?"

"Hey, Hank. I've got twenty-four head of cattle coming in this week and I've got to feed them."

"Are you going to introduce me to your lady friend?"

Lila's demeanor had shifted, closed off. Travis made a quick introduction and Lila offered an even quicker half-smile.

Hank couldn't seem to tear his gaze away from her, which made Travis uncomfortable. Die he recognize her, or was he just curious?

Travis never brought women into the feed store and had gone on only a handful of dates.

As if Hank had asked, Travis said, "Yeah, twenty-four head. Can you believe it? I may have bitten off more than I can chew. Anyway. How many bales do you suppose I need?"

Travis ordered the feed and got them out of there. Back in the truck, Lila buckled her seatbelt at warp speed and sat up stock straight, staring through the windshield.

"You okay?"

"Fine. I'm fine. I just panicked all of a sudden. I'm sorry." She wasn't convincing.

"No apology necessary. I got the feed ordered and we don't have to go in anywhere else. Can I take you on a quick driving tour, and then we'll head back home?"

"Sure." She grabbed his hand, looked into his eyes. "That sounds really nice. And you can finish telling me the story of you stealing Janie Robertson's assignments to get revenge for Lena Carrera."

"Deal." As he drove away from the feed store, Travis wondered if he'd tried for too much, too soon. Lila had told him she was up for a quick trip into town, but was she, really?

He almost regretted the shower sex. Almost. "The courthouse plaza is only a few minutes from here. It's the city center—there's a fair going on almost every weekend in the spring, summer, and fall. We used to come downtown to get ice cream, and we'd always end up messing around, getting into trouble."

Lila looked over at him, smiling, and relief flooded his veins: she seemed at ease again. "Sterling loves telling the story of the time we were playing Frisbee and knocked a bunch of jewelry off a lady's displays. We hightailed it out of there so fast. Another time, we had this stupid fart machine. It had a remote control, and you could set up the little speaker and then hide and play the fart noises. So we set up the speaker right next to a light pole and then hid in this drainage pipe under the street. We'd play the fart noises as people walked by."

"I can just picture you guys, peeking out of the grate. I'm sure you thought you were the funniest."

"Oh, we did."

"Sounds like you had a pretty good life here."

Why was he imagining building a life here with her? "That's true. It was the best."

They'd reached the courthouse, and he drove around its four sides, pointing out the ice cream shop he and his brothers frequented as kids, the rooftop where they hid after nailing the woman's jewelry display, and the lamp post where they'd hidden the fart machine speaker.

He was about to point out the fountain, with the water flowing down its tiers, when he remembered visiting it time after time, throwing in the shiniest pennies he could find, wishing for his mom to come back.

Obviously, it didn't work. He returned for one final visit to curse that damn fountain, to swear he'd never give it another coin, shiny penny or otherwise.

"That's pretty much it." He squeezed Lila's hand and turned the truck toward home. "And now I'll tell you what happened with Janie Robertson."

Eyes glinting, she rubbed her hands together. "Can't wait."

"Well, like I said, I spent some time stealing all her assignments out of the turn-in basket, and the teachers eventually caught on. They called in her parents and everything. And she swore, up and down, that she'd been turning everything in. Only, no one believed her. Apparently her parents had recently found some notes in her backpack—notes from boys—"

"Uh oh."

"Right. And they thought she'd gone boy crazy. So much so that she wasn't doing her work. Well, her parents grounded her. Not for life, but for a long time. Meanwhile, she took matters into her own hands. I'd see her in the halls, trying to intimidate kids into telling her who was stealing her papers. Only, no one knew except the Carrera and Wilder kids, and none of us were about to snitch. She started handing her assignments directly to the teachers. So I started changing her grades in the grade books."

"You did not."

"I did. See, we were from an upstanding family." As an aside, he said, "No one knew the family was falling apart. But anyway. The teachers never suspected me."

"But did Janie ever realize she was suffering because of what she'd done to Lena?"

"Oh, yeah. By the end of the school year, she was failing almost everything. And she'd been set to be valedictorian. Back then, they did a big eighth-grade graduation ceremony. Right before the valedictorian speech—the kid who earned it was Juan Cortez—I whispered to her that I'd been responsible for everything. I told her it was because of how she'd treated Lena, and that if she told anyone, I'd deny it. Based on the demise of her schoolwork by that time, I was the more believable character. You should have seen her face."

"I wish I had."

With that, they'd arrived back at Sweet Springs Ranch. Travis parked the truck and turned to face Lila. "It was so satisfying. I told myself then that whenever I encountered a bully, I'd do everything in my power to stop him or her."

"That's really sweet. And probably one of the reasons I feel so safe with you."

Chapter Nineteen

Over the course of the next few days, Lila had to warn herself not to get too accustomed to the rhythm and routine she and Travis fell into—or to Travis, himself. But she found she was defenseless.

They woke up together, made breakfast, and went their separate ways, then reconvened for lunch, worked separately until dinner, and then spent the evening and the night together.

Travis proved, again and again, that he was the most thoughtful man she'd ever met. He seemed to anticipate her needs, sometimes before she even realized what they were. And while the sex was out-of-this-world, she craved the conversation equally. Their post-dinner chats, usually on the couch in front of the fireplace, filled a void she'd recognized but never put a name to.

Although Travis didn't normally set an alarm—he woke on his own at five a.m. most days—the Thursday after the feed store trip, his phone jarred them out of sleep. Lila blinked awake, orienting herself—they were at his place this morning, and his bedroom was dark because the sun rose on the other side of the house. He sat up straight and she reached out to put a hand on his arm.

"It's delivery day." His voice held equal parts excitement and nerves.

As tempting as it was to pull him down beside her and make love to him before they began what promised to be a busy twelve hours, Lila sat up too and kissed him on the cheek. "You're going to need a good breakfast."

She was at the kitchen counter whipping up an omelette when he came up behind her and wrapped his arms around her waist. "If you'd told me, even two weeks ago, that this morning routine would become the highlight of my day, I would have said you were crazy."

His breath on her neck sent shivers all over her skin.

"Same here."

"I wish we had time to stay in and cuddle." His lips trailed, light as a feather, along her shoulder and up to her ear.

"Is cuddling really what you have in mind?" She'd finished whipping the eggs and he stepped back as she poured them into the hot pan.

From the coffeemaker, where he refreshed her cup and poured his own, he said, "Not really."

She glanced at him and he gave her a wicked grin as he brought over her coffee.

"Want to get the cheese out of the fridge for me?"

"What's it worth to you?"

At that, she rolled her eyes, but couldn't help the smile that remained. "What's breakfast worth to you?"

"Touché."

A few minutes later, they sat across from each other at the dining table, pulling cheesy bites off their omelettes.

"Want to go over the schedule for the day again?"

Travis sighed and wiped his mouth. "Actually, I do. Are you tired of hearing about it?"

She laughed. "A little. But I'm willing to hear it, in its latest rendition, if that helps remove some of the stress."

"Well, after breakfast, we're going to have a quickie."

"Travis Wilder. The schedule you made for today doesn't leave time for even the quickest quickie."

He looked down at this plate. "You're right. Fine. After breakfast, my brothers are coming over and we're going to ride the fence one more time to make sure it's in good shape. Then we're going to come back for lunch, and I'll sneak over to where you are, and we'll have a quickie."

She balled up her napkin and threw it at him.

"Kidding." He held up his hands in surrender. "Anyway, after lunch, the cows should be arriving, and we'll help unload them. At which point I will spend the rest of the afternoon watching them, agonizing over whether they're going to be happy here." He cut off another bite of omelette and stuck it in his mouth, smiling while he chewed.

"Did you say that last part for my benefit?" She pointed her fork at him. "Because I happen to know you have plans for this afternoon and I'm the one worried about their happiness."

"Okay, you've got me. After they're unloaded and blissed out on all the feed we ordered for them the other day, I'm going to start looking at equipment for the ranch."

"Because women think tractors are sexy, at least, according to that one country song."

He smiled. "According to that one country song *and* to all the women this side of the Mississippi."

"Okay, big boy."

"Did you just call me big boy?"

"Isn't that what the ladies call the men who drive the tractors?"

Polishing off his omelette, he shrugged. "All the ones I've heard."

"If I hadn't already thrown my napkin at you, I'd do it now."

"Ah, but you wouldn't. You adore me." Plate in hand, he stood up, pushed in his chair, and leaned over to kiss her cheek. As he put his dish in the sink she told him, "I'll do the dishes if you want to get on with your day."

She stood too, and set her own plate in the sink.

"What's your plan for the day?" he asked.

"Oh, you know. Some riveting paper sorting and accounting. Maybe going out to check on the cows once they get here, to welcome them and make sure they're going to be happy here."

Travis leaned against the counter and put his hands on her waist to pull her close. "You know, you're just about the sweetest woman that's ever set foot on this ranch."

Tasting his lips, she leaned into him. "You think so, huh?"

"I do. And while I reckon I could spend the rest of the day proving myself right, I'd better start tackling my to-do list."

She gave him one more kiss. "You do that. I'll clean up."

"Thanks, darlin'." He smacked her ass, making her yelp.

The sounds of him getting ready, putting on his jeans and belt, sliding into his flannel shirt, brushing his teeth, had become like a soundtrack for her mornings. She turned on the water and started rinsing the dishes and loading them into the dishwasher. Travis came out just as she started scrubbing the skillet.

"Thank you for breakfast and cleaning. I'll come get you when the cattle get here. I figured you'd want to see them right away."

"I think *you* might be the sweetest person to ever set foot on Sweet Springs Ranch." Again, he nuzzled her neck and kissed her, and again, her body responded with shivers. "Get out of here."

Almost immediately after he left, a knock sounded at his front door. Lila had almost quashed her knee-jerk fight-or-flight response to every unexpected encounter with another human, but her heart still leapt and her hands still shook as she went to answer.

"Good morning!" June and Callie stood on the front porch, their in-unison greetings singsongy and full of smiles.

"Good morning." Lila stepped back and pulled open the door before realizing her salt barrier was still in place. The girls hugged her as they came in, both of them spotting the salt and stepping neatly over it.

"Is there coffee?" Callie wanted to know. "If not, I'll brew some."

Before her experience in Arizona, Lila would have found this behavior intrusive, but she was becoming used to and (maybe even enjoying) the comfort with which Travis's crew moved amongst each other.

"There's still half a pot." She got down coffee mugs and set them on the counter, and June and Callie helped themselves.

Just as she was about to ask why they were there, Callie said, "We're here because we have an idea we wanted to run by you."

"Yeah?" Butterfly wings beat against the inside of Lila's chest.

"Yeah. Sit." June pointed at the table.

"If we're having a meeting, I feel like I should at least put on real clothes." The girls made matching dismissive gestures, and Lila laughed. "Okay, maybe not. Pajamas it is."

They sat.

Callie spoke first. "Lila, how much do you miss making your fitness posts?"

Lila sat up straighter. "Why?"

June laughed out loud. "Why do you look so suspicious?"

"We've been talking." Callie's eyes were big and serious.

"Have you?" Lila realized the two of them talking—about her—was another symptom of this closeness they all experienced. She wasn't sure how she felt about it.

"We have." June smiled.

"We think you should start making your posts again."

Lila inhaled, ready to object, and June held up a hand. "Wait. Hear us out."

"We've thought about your safety. We'll help you build a studio here, one where nobody would be able to tell where you are."

June nodded. "We've already figured out where we could do it—in the bunkhouse, over by the bunk beds. We could build backdrops on two sides. In front of that first set of bunk beds and in front of the window there. And you could set up your phone across from that. It would be easy. Right, Cal?"

"Right. It would be so fun to decorate it. And then you could get back to doing what you love."

Fear moved in, hot and fast. "But I—I have to do the paperwork. The accounting." *And what if that crazy person sees my videos and starts stalking me here?*

"Right." June drew out the word, like she was explaining this concept to a toddler. "But is that fulfilling to the same extent your fitness stuff is?"

"No, but—"

"We get it." Callie was no-nonsense, just like Lila imagined she would be in a courtroom. "You're afraid of some crazy stalker person seeing your posts. But you're safe here."

Am I? "I mean, he found me once. Don't you think he'll be able to find me again?"

"We're informed now. We'll take precautions."

Nauseated, Lila nodded. "I'll think about it."

"You will?" June was practically squealing, and Callie's eyes held the same barely contained excitement as June's voice.

"That's all we wanted." Callie stood up. "Our work here is done."

Nodding, June stood up too, and all of a sudden, Lila felt bereft. "What else are you guys doing today?"

They moved toward the sink to pour out the final drops of their coffee.

"I've got to read through some documents for a new case." Callie rinsed her cup and put it in the dishwasher.

June did the same. "And I'm going to check out a new event venue."

They said their goodbyes and stepped back over the salt barrier. The house was almost eerily quiet after the girls left, and Lila rushed through the rest of breakfast cleanup before returning to all her files at the bunkhouse. Still feeling just this side of lonely, she put on some music, lit a candle (ginger, to ease her fear), and sat down at the table where she'd set up her new filing system.

She'd made her way through most of the boxes and categorized their contents. Once she finished that, she would get into the bank accounts and make sure everything reconciled. Then she would create an accounting system Travis could use.

And he wouldn't need her anymore.

The weight of melancholy pressed down on her shoulders as she opened the next box. While she worked, she glanced over at the space Callie and June were suggesting she use as a studio. They were right: she could envision a two-walled backdrop there. If she set up her phone directly opposite the corner, no one would be able to tell where she was.

Even during her time here—as distracted as she'd been—she hadn't been able to kick the habit of keeping a running list of post ideas. Her entire being thrummed as she imagined creating the posts she'd come up with: an "I'm-back" post, a post sharing tips for a quick confidence boost, and one with do-anywhere leg exercises to incorporate into a busy day.

Once she had the setup, it wouldn't take long to create and post each video—she'd become a master at efficiency and would have plenty of time for posting *and* accounting.

Was it possible?

She knew it was. But it was also scary. At the same time, she reminded herself in a stern voice, she couldn't just *never post again* because of one stupid guy.

Pulling another stack of papers out of the box, she sighed. She'd told Callie and June she'd think about it, and she would.

Another knock at the door. Another mini heart attack. Another jolt of happiness when she saw Travis.

He spoke before she even finished opening the door. "They're almost here!"

The two of them made it to the corral just as the delivery truck, with its giant livestock trailer, pulled onto the property.

Lila felt the emotion rise in her chest. "I bet they're going to be so excited to get out of that trailer."

"I'm sure they are." Travis put his arm around her shoulders and kissed the side of her head.

"I know you're just humoring me."

Lips still against her temple, he said, "Never."

The truck driver parked and climbed down from the driver seat. He and Travis discussed where Travis wanted the cattle and by the time they were done, Sterling, Hayes, and Cash were there. Lila marveled at how well they worked together, Cash and Hayes pulling open the big gates, Sterling and Travis guiding the driver into the pasture. Just like they had when the bulls arrived, everyone assembled at the back of the trailer once the gates were closed. The driver opened the doors on the back of the trailer, and Travis helped him with the ramp.

Sure enough, as soon as the cows saw the open space, they moved quickly toward the end of the trailer. Once their feet touched the dirt, they took a few tentative steps. And then, just as Lila had predicted, they started frolicking around. Heart brimming with happiness and eyes brimming with tears, she made sure to throw Travis an "I-told-you-so" look. He raised an eyebrow and smiled. When all twenty-four of the cows had emerged, he and the truck driver loaded the ramp back into the trailer and closed the doors. The driver handed Travis an invoice, which he immediately handed to Lila. That, too, made her eyes prickle and she wondered what was wrong with her.

After the driver left and the gate was closed, they all stood watching the cows, which had settled in and were grazing, ears and tails twitching periodically.

Travis came up to stand next to Lila. "Okay, I guess you were right. They do seem happy."

She gave him a smug smile.

Sterling whistled. "These are some good-looking cattle. I'm glad you brought us along to that auction, Trav, so we could help you. We needed some good-looking stock."

Travis shot him a dark look but his lips were twitching. "Agreed. I think it's a great start."

Cash elbowed Travis. "You're looking a little green around the gills there, Travis."

Travis's laugh sounded almost forced. "I *feel* a little green around the gills. Things just got real. *Really* real. Five bulls was one thing. But two dozen cows? I guess we're doing this thing."

Hayes cackled. "Isn't this what you wanted?"

"Yes. It's exactly what I wanted. And also, I'm terrified."

"It's going to be great." Sterling gave Travis a reassuring smile. "I felt the same way when I started my business. Having it down on paper was one thing. But buying a truck and a trailer and all the equipment? That scared the crap out of me."

"It did?" Travis took off his hat and scratched the back of his head.

"Hell, yes, it did. But I'd recently read this quote."

"What was it?"

"I don't remember exactly, but something like, 'Think about everything you miss out on when you choose to stay safe. And imagine what could happen if you took that one action that had the potential to change everything.' And I decided then and there—I could change everything."

Lila listened to their exchange with interest. Their situations weren't exactly like hers. But the fear they felt? That was similar. Sterling had moved past his fear to build a successful business. So successful, in fact, that clients paid him to travel the country and he was on the cover of nationwide magazines. And Travis was right in the thick of it, doing the thing that scared him.

Maybe Callie and June were right: maybe Lila *could* go back to making her posts. Yes, she was scared, and she had no idea whether she could restart. But she did know that if she didn't try—if she stayed rooted in her safe zone—she'd never know if she could have changed things. And she'd regret that for the rest of her life.

"You must be deep in thought." Travis stood in front of her, his mouth smiling but his expression uncertain.

Startled out of her contemplation, she jumped before looking around and realizing everyone else had left the corral. Just she and Travis—and the twenty-four cows—remained. "Yes, I was. Sorry. I guess the unloading is done and it's time for everyone to get back to work."

"Everything okay?"

She nodded, suddenly confident about what she had to do. "Everything's fine. Cash's green-around-the-gills comment got me thinking."

"Are you afraid to spend the evening with me? Don't worry. I'm not sick or anything."

"No, it's not that. It's just—Callie and June came over this morning and were encouraging me to start posting again. I want to. But also, I'm scared."

He wrapped his hands around her upper arms and inhaled to respond. She held up a hand.

"I realized, me being scared doesn't mean I can't do it. Sterling was saying how he was scared when he bought all his equipment, and this delivery of cattle made you a little scared."

He faux-coughed, turning his face toward his shoulder.

"Okay, a *lot* scared." She smiled. "But Sterling kept moving forward with his business, and you're moving forward with yours. I can move forward with mine, too."

"I love this line of thinking. You can move forward with yours. And as long as you're here, or even after you go back to Alabama, you can count on me to help you."

Lila's heart melted for what must have been the millionth time, and she wrapped her arms around him. "Thank you."

"You're welcome. And now, as you know, I've got work to do. I expect to hear about your plans at dinner."

As she watched him walk away, she smacked his butt—it looked so damn perfect in those jeans—before heading back to the bunkhouse.

Out of habit, she checked her phone. Seeing a missed call from the Huntsville Police Department, she gasped.

She'd almost forgotten that Officer Gomez had said he'd be calling after Officer Rowland had her go through the photo lineup. And of course it had to happen practically the moment she'd decided to start posting again.

Was this a warning from the universe? Hands shaking, she called him back.

Chapter Twenty

At the end of the day, Travis felt more gratified than he had in ages. Hearing the cattle (*his* cattle) low, watching them graze, and seeing them gather under the shade trees ... it was exactly what he'd dreamed of. He couldn't wait to get to Lila's for dinner, and he practically jogged up to her door.

He found it unlocked. She was in the kitchen at the stove, and turned to smile at him when he came in. Something inside him uncurled in that moment, and he realized this—this particular woman, greeting him at the end of each day—was part of what he wanted.

That realization sent a shock through him.

"Smells good." He wrapped his arms around her from behind and kissed her cheek.

"I hope it tastes good. I tried a new recipe. Chicken and mushroom soup."

He kissed her neck. "Delicious."

She turned to kiss his mouth. "You haven't even tasted it yet."

"I know. But *you're* delicious."

She kissed him once more and returned her attention to the soup. "We have business to discuss."

"Looks serious." Releasing his hold on her, he retrieved a beer from the fridge and leaned against the counter.

"It's not that serious. It's just that I finally came up with some figures. Operating expenses, that sort of thing."

"Sounds serious."

Her eyes twinkled. "It is. But from what I can tell based on all the paperwork from the past, you should be able to pay those expenses once you get going. Hey, have you ever thought of making this a dude ranch?"

She glanced at him and he raised an eyebrow. "Like, where people come here for the experience?" Sarcasm coated his words and she laughed.

"Yeah. I did some research and aside from selling cattle and hay, it's one of the top moneymakers for ranches." She turned off the stove and gave the soup one more stir.

"I don't know..." He got down bowls. "Having strangers on the ranch seems a little intrusive."

This time, she raised an eyebrow at him.

"Right. You were a stranger when I invited you to come to the ranch. But your voice—it had this magical quality. I couldn't help myself."

She'd picked up the bowls and was carrying them over to the stove. She froze. "Are you telling me you invited me to the ranch because of my voice?"

Heat flushed his neck and face. "So what if I am? It seems to have worked out, doesn't it?"

Back in motion, she started ladling soup into one of the bowls. "Yes, but what if it didn't?"

"I guess we don't have to worry about that, do we?" He took the bowl she handed him and headed to the table. "In fact, I'd say it's working out quite well for both of us."

He was half-tempted to ask her to stay, permanently, but figured he'd gotten caught up in the excitement of having his own cattle on the ranch again. Just because he was finally building business back up didn't mean he could actually have a real relationship. Ranching was all-consuming. In fact, he remembered overhearing many arguments between his parents in which his mom said she felt lonely even though she was surrounded by people—her husband, her sons, all the ranch hands, and a hundred animals.

Travis remembered empathizing with his mom: his dad rose before the sun and spent most of the day out on the property, tending to cattle or machinery or fences. He came in for dinner, but went to bed almost immediately after the dishes were cleared.

Could Travis do things differently?

"It is." She sat down across from him.

Her words brought him back to the present moment, and he raced to remember what he'd said before she spoke. Oh, right. He'd said the situation was working out quite well for both of them. He smiled.

"Everything okay?" Her eyebrows knitted together in concern. "Oh, no. It's the soup, isn't it? You tasted it. What is it? Too much salt? Not enough salt? Too much pepper?"

Amused, he held up a hand. "I haven't even tasted it, yet. I was just thinking about ranching, that's all."

"Well, judging by the face you were making while thinking about ranching, I'm not sure if it's the right lifestyle for you, after all."

She'd meant it as a joke, but he was about *this* close to panicking —and she could tell.

"I was just kidding." She set down her spoon.

"I know you were. I just panicked for a minute because I was remembering how all-consuming ranch life was when I was a kid. Bills and hard work—it's my new reality."

"But that's not your entire reality. You're surrounded by people who love you. Your reality includes all these fun dinners and trips to A Cold One and probably more brother road trips."

And you. He wanted to say it, wanted to include her in the list of distractions from bills and hard work. But he didn't know how long she'd be here.

"You're right. I'm sure everything will be fine. Tell me what you came up with for numbers."

She did, and he felt his eyes nearly pop out of his face.

"See why I brought up the dude ranch idea?" She set down her spoon. "But I think we can make it work."

She said, 'we.' How could he be deliriously happy at her use of "we" even as he could barely choke down a bite of soup due to the stress?

"But how?"

"As you know, I've become intimately familiar with how your dad was running things before he started gambling. He was a savvy businessman. Do you know much about how he was bringing in revenue?"

Travis shook his head. "I feel like an idiot saying this, but this whole time, I've been focusing on selling cattle. I didn't even think about other income streams."

He wanted to throttle himself.

"I think you're going to need them."

Travis nodded. "I mean, whenever we'd complain about doing chores, Dad would remind us that the ranch was our livelihood and we had to keep it running if we wanted food on the table. And how he knew we wanted food on the table because all we did was eat. But no, I never knew exactly where our money came from, aside from cattle sales, obviously."

Lila nodded. "Okay. Obviously he sold cattle. He also bred cattle. People paid to use his bulls as sires. That's something you can do."

His appetite returning, he took a bite of soup. "This is good, Lila."

"I know. Not my idea, of course, but like I said, your dad was a savvy businessman."

"I meant the soup."

"Oh." Her eyes lit up. "Thank you."

"You're welcome." He took another couple of bites. "What else?"

"He also leased land to other ranchers. From what I can tell, he moved the cattle around—to let the grass grow in one area while they grazed another."

Travis nodded. "It's all coming back to me. I remember him

mentioning the grazing when I was a kid. What else? Wait. Before you tell me, I have to say, I'm so impressed with how quickly you're picking up on the business end of all this."

He could tell the compliment pleased her. "It's what I do. Your dad didn't do this, but I was thinking you could build stables and rent those out for people to board their horses. You've got the space. I know it's an investment, but I think it would pay off."

"That's brilliant."

"I'm fairly brilliant."

They sat there smiling at each other, and Travis started to think maybe Lila was right. Maybe with the right strategies and the right people, he could make the ranch work. And it wouldn't be as all-consuming as he feared.

"Tell me about your day."

"My day?" She had that deer-in-headlights look he hadn't seen in several days, and his sixth sense perked up.

"Yeah." He played it casual, wiping his mouth and taking another bite of soup. "Your day. How was it?"

"Oh, you know. It was fine."

"Obviously you were busy with the paperwork."

She blurted out her next words, like she had to hurry up and get them into the airspace, before they disappeared. "And I had a phone call from Officer Gomez, the guy who came to my apartment in Huntsville before you hired me."

"Yeah? What did he have to say?"

"Only that the guy I picked out of the photo lineup the other day is the guy they had their eyes on. He has a record—he's gotten misdemeanor harassment charges before, but the cops could never get enough evidence to actually book him into jail. He repeated what he said before, which is basically that being a total creep isn't a crime. And this guy is a creep, but because he hasn't broken any actual laws this time, they still can't arrest him."

Travis felt his blood heating, close to a boil. "So he can just go around, terrorizing people?"

Lila shrugged. "For now. Officer Gomez said he's passed the case on to detectives and they're going to try to catch him in the act, question him, see what they can get out of him. But it could take time." She shivered and goosebumps rose on her arms.

A muscle twitched in Travis's cheek. "Don't feel like you have to be in a hurry to go back. You can stay here as long as you want."

"Thank you. It means a lot."

"You're welcome. But just know that if you stay here, I'm going to expect us to continue taking turns cooking."

That earned him a laugh. "Actually, there's one other thing I wanted to talk to you about. It's not cooking."

"Shoot." Finished with his soup, he leaned back in his chair.

"Callie and June stopped by today. They think I should start making my fitness posts again."

He sat up straighter. "They do?" A whole different fear—the fear of something happening to Lila—made his heart pound.

"Yeah." She shrugged. "They were saying we could build a little filming studio right here in the bunkhouse." She pointed at the corner where two bunk beds came together. "We could make a backdrop right there, and I could set up my phone to film from next to the table."

"But aren't you worried about this stalker guy?"

"Honestly? Yes. But I'm also worried about what happens if I just stop posting because of some crazy stalker guy. I don't think I'd be happy laying low indefinitely. Not that I don't enjoy accounting, but ..."

"But your fitness and health brand is what really lights you up."

"Exactly."

"And you want to go back to having your red hair."

She blushed. "I don't know ... black hair is more anonymous. And it's kind of nice not feeling like someone's going to yell 'Ginger!' when I come around a corner."

"Has that happened?"

"Believe it or not, it's happened countless times. More when I was a kid, but even now, once in a while, someone will shout it at me when I'm in a public place. The mall, a park, the grocery store. Nowhere is safe." She gave a little giggle. "It doesn't bother me like it used to, but it's a little like opening up a scab every time. It never quite heals."

"I can relate." He didn't want to go into all the details of his mom's leaving—that, too, was a wound that would never quite heal.

Lila nodded, as if she understood not only that he could relate but also that he didn't want to spell out why. "My hair color is the least of my worries, though. What do you think about me posting videos from here? I mean, in my spare time, of course. It wouldn't take away from what I'm doing for you, for the ranch."

"I love the idea. I'm not worried about you becoming derelict when it comes to your ranch duties. If you do, I can think of ways to keep you in line." He wiggled his eyebrows at her, and she laughed again.

"I think we'd better start dinner cleanup before you distract us."

They did, and again Travis felt himself sinking into the simplicity, the togetherness, yearning for more of it. But hadn't their conversation just proven that he wouldn't have the resources to pour into a relationship? Not the kind of relationship he wanted with Lila, anyway.

Hands in warm, soapy water, he contemplated.

On one hand, the idea that Lila felt she couldn't return home infuriated Travis. She shouldn't have to live in fear. But on the other hand, knowing she was likely to extend her stay at the Sweet Springs Ranch made him—like his dad would say—happy as a pig in mud. And, horny as well.

As they worked together to clean up from dinner, he found every excuse to touch her. A hand on her hip as he slid past her to get to the sink, his shoulder against hers as they loaded the dishwasher. His fingertips brushing hers when she handed him a plate. As they finished up, he offered to pour her a glass of wine. He got himself another beer and they settled onto the couch. As had become customary when they sat together, Lila extended her legs and tucked her feet under his thighs. He took one of her feet in his hands and began to knead it, running along her arch and the inside of her ankle, making circles until she groaned with pleasure. He worked his way up her calves, using his fingertips to release the tension. He moved onto her thighs, letting his fingers brush the place where her legs met. As he worked, she became relaxed, pliable, heavy-lidded with pleasure.

He became hard, his dick straining to be released from the prison of his jeans. Still, he kept going, working on her fingers and hands and arms until she'd laid out on the couch in surrender. With very little pressure, he let his palms trail over her collarbone and chest, then down over her breasts.

By then, little sounds, half-moan and half-whimper, escaped her lips. It was all he could do not to groan with desire, and he let his hands continue their dance over her stomach and down to her waist.

Finally, her voice thick with desire and sharp with impatience she said, "Travis Wilder, you'd better go on and get naked right now."

He laughed despite the seriousness of her command. After standing up and stripping off his own clothes, he removed hers in a very un-gentlemanly way.

"Now take me to bed."

"Yes, Your Highness. Your wish is my command." He swept her up into his arms and they kissed all the way to her bed, where he dropped her on the mattress and climbed on top of her.

"Wait." She slid out from under him and pushed on his hip so he fell onto his side. She gave him one more gentle push so he was on his back. "My turn." She kissed his collarbone and then his chest, and then ran her tongue down the center of his stomach to where he throbbed, waiting for her. Then her mouth was on him and it took every bit of his willpower to remain still, to stop himself from plunging deep into her throat. She took him deeper, using her tongue to create so much suction, he thought he might come then and there.

"Get up here." He pulled her up so they were eye to eye, and if it were even possible, her smug expression turned him on even more. She straddled him and hovering just above him, she quirked an eyebrow. "Now?"

He lifted his hips so his dick brushed her warm center. "Yes. Now."

"Are you sure?"

He grabbed her hips and plunged into her. "So, so sure."

She lay down, elbows on either side of his head, mouth on his, and they began to move together. He used both hands to comb back her hair, then pulled her head back gently so he could look into her eyes. "I've never wanted anyone like this."

The smile she flashed went from triumphant to sweet, and eyes still on his, she gave him a light peck on the mouth. "I haven't, either."

She continued to ride him, slow and deliberate, the gentle, tender pace bringing him to his peak in no time at all. Almost as if he were having an out-of-body experience, he heard himself cry out. And then he zoomed back in, watched her eyes glaze over in pure pleasure before she, too, went over the edge, her body shuddering and her breath coming fast.

They rolled onto their sides, facing each other, and Travis ran a fingertip up her arm, relishing in the sheen of sweat their love-making had created. "I would say that was a pretty nice way to round out a day."

She ran her fingers through his hair. "I would say so, too."

They cleaned up and got back in bed, and when he spooned her, she tucked her feet between his calves.

He hissed. "Woman! Your feet are freezing! Let me get you some socks."

Laughing, she pulled them on. "You know, I think that's about the most romantic thing anyone ever did for me."

"It's self-preservation, not romance."

Still, as they both drifted off and he listened to her breathing beside him, he knew something had changed. To him, Lila was no longer temporary. She belonged with him, and he was going to do everything in his power to prove that.

Chapter Twenty-One

The next day during their lunch break, Lila presented Travis with a list of money-making ideas for the ranch.

Her heart was in her throat while he looked it over—she didn't want him to feel like she was overstepping—but then he grinned and said, "I could kiss you right now."

She grinned back and leaned in to give him a chaste peck, which turned into a full-on make-out session right there at the dining table. Her blood was heating and shivers traveled over her skin when he ended the kiss.

"I have something for you, too." He pulled a folded piece of paper out of his shirt pocket, smoothed out the creases, and handed it to her.

"Is this what I think it is?" She held in her hands the blueprints for a filming backdrop, complete with measurements and a supply list. Someone—Sterling, she assumed, since building was his business—had even sketched a little table against the backdrop and put a houseplant on it.

Travis shrugged. "It's rough, according to Sterling. But it's enough to get you started. You know, since you're going to be here a little longer and I know you're anxious to get back to making your posts. No pressure though."

"*I* could kiss *you* right now." She got up from her chair and straddled him in his, covering his mouth with hers while he wrapped his arms around her, claiming her.

"If our lunch continues this way, we're not going to eat," he said after another several kisses.

"Who cares? This is definitely satisfying my appetite."

He laughed, the sound throaty and alluring and making her want to do anything but eat her lunch. "Mine, too. But duty calls. I've got to talk to Cash about a new feeding system I have in mind, and he said he'd help me with the measurements."

"Oh, all right." She slid off his lap, giving him one more long, deep kiss before returning to her chair. "You think I could talk June and Callie into going to the hardware store with me to get all this stuff?"

Travis froze, his fork halfway to his mouth. "You're just going to go to the hardware store? Just like that?"

"Yeah. What do you mean? Oh, you're right. All that stuff probably won't fit in my car. Think I could borrow your truck?"

He stared at her, mouth open, eyebrows raised in shock.

"What? What are you thinking? It's the truck, isn't it? Never mind. I shouldn't have asked. I'll just rent a little trailer."

He set down his fork. "It's not that. You haven't wanted to leave the bunkhouse since you got here. I thought we made big progress in terms of you feeling safe when we went to the feed store. And now you're jumping at the chance to go to the hardware store."

Huh.

"That's true. I hadn't thought of that. I was just so excited about posting again—I forgot to be scared." She gasped. "Do you think I should be?"

He shook his head. "I don't think there's a should or shouldn't to the feelings you have. What's important is to move forward anyway, to do the things you love, to be with the people you care about, despite feeling fear. If you let your fear stop you from doing those things, then you're not really living, are you?"

The words stunned her. She hadn't considered her situation from that perspective. She'd been so caught up in the fear, so absolutely saturated in it, that she hadn't stopped to think about what it was preventing her from doing.

"No," she said, finally. "I'm not. But that's not happening anymore. I'm going to be a strong, confident woman. I'm going to get the girls, go to the hardware store, and buy the stuff to build the backdrop. And then I'm going to come back here and ask for your help building it."

As she intended, he laughed at the last part. "Sounds perfect."

"In fact, I'm going to text June and Callie right now." She did, and their responses came back right away—they were in. She arranged to grab June from the RV outside the big house and to then drive into town and pick up Callie from her office.

"I'll get the dishes if you want to get going." Travis stood up. "Take my truck." He tossed her the keys.

She managed to stop smiling just long enough to thank him and kiss him, and then she was out the door.

The first thing she noticed when she got into the truck was that it was huge. She wasn't sure if she could drive it through town without hitting anything. "You can do this, Lila." After adjusting the sideview and rearview mirrors, she put the key in the ignition and turned it. The truck thundered to life, vibrating underneath her. "You can do this." Fortunately, she didn't have to back up right away; she could make a wide loop around Travis's house and then pull up at the RV.

June bounded out, called goodbye to Sterling, and stood on her tiptoes to look into the cab. When she saw Lila alone in the truck, she squealed and then opened the passenger door. "He let you take his truck?! He must *love* you!"

Her tone was light, but the implications struck Lila like—well, like Travis's giant pickup truck running her right over. Did Travis *love* her? Surely he didn't. Did she love him? *You know you do*. Both the angel and the devil piped up from the back of her mind.

"He's just being practical. All the stuff Sterling says we need won't fit in my car, so..."

"Whatever. He *loves* you." June smiled across the cab, looking more mischievous than Lila had seen her. "Sterling showed me the blueprints. This is so exciting. Do you have a color scheme in mind? I can't wait to look at paint chips."

Pulling herself out of thoughts about whether Travis loved her, or she loved Travis, and how this all could have happened so quickly, she nodded. "I have a few ideas. But I wanted to get your input."

"You've got it!"

With June giving her directions, Lila drove downtown and parked along the curb in front of Callie's office building, an impressive turn-of-the-century structure. In her old life, Lila would have snapped a selfie with it, and used the hashtag *#coolarchitecture*. But not now.

"I'll text Cal, let her know we're here."

"What a beautiful building to work in."

"Yeah, it is," June said. "It's one of the oldest in town. Can't you just imagine what this place was like back in the early nineteen hundreds? I would have loved to be here then."

"It's so charming. And I love how all these buildings overlook the courthouse plaza."

June pointed to a redbrick building on the corner. "That's the hotel where Sterling and I were both staying this summer when we started spending time together."

"That's so romantic." Calling on her new sense of calm, Lila took her time to truly look around at the quaint downtown area. "This whole spot is so cute. Travis said the Wilder boys used to spend a ton of time down here."

June laughed. "Cause a bunch of destruction, more like."

"Do you think you guys will have kids?" For a second, Lila worried she might have been too nosy, but June smiled. "Yeah, we will. We've got to get a house first though, don't we? I'm not sure I want to have a newborn in that RV."

Lila felt a twinge of envy at how relaxed, how comfortable June seemed in her life. She'd found her place in the world. Lila yearned for that. Her throat tight, she swallowed. "Are you going to stay on the ranch?"

"Yeah. Sterling doesn't want to live in the big house, necessarily, so we might build another house, like Travis's. But we've got to finish the construction on the big house first so we can start having events there. The guys wanted that for an income stream. Travis mentioned your other ideas."

Lila's breath caught. What if June and Sterling hated her other ideas? But again, June was smiling. "A dude ranch? I love it. Think about how much fun it would be to have people here visiting."

"That's what I thought. I mean, I'm enamored with the place. I think people have this fantasy about ranches, so to get to spend time on one without too much responsibility? Seems like a win to me."

Before June could answer, Callie's arrival caught their attention. She came through the double doors on the first floor and then practically ran across the wide sidewalk in her suit and heels, her shirt coming untucked and her hair blowing up around her head like a crazy halo.

She blew in the back door. "Sorry, guys." Her movement ceased. "Wait." She circled her pointer finger. "Are we in Travis's truck?" She pointed at Lila. "And are *you* in the driver's seat?" Before Lila had a chance to respond she rushed to say, "Not that you can't drive a truck, but I can't believe he *let* you drive his truck. Nobody drives this thing."

While Lila let this bit of news sink in, June was twisting around in her seat to look at Callie. "Are you *okay*, Cal?"

"Fine! I'm fine. Just working on a tricky case. I really needed a break." She pulled her phone out of her purse and started typing, her fingers flying across the screen.

June grimaced at Lila. "Let's just give her a few minutes. You good if we head for the hardware store, Cal?"

"Go on." Callie waved one hand and Lila pulled away from the curb.

Between directions, June chattered away, giving Lila the history of buildings and parks they passed and telling little stories about places she'd gone since moving to Prescott. Callie interjected now and then and Lila marveled at how easily the conversation flowed. Aside from Rebecca, she didn't have many friends, and certainly not any close ones. So it was alien and surprisingly fun to let herself get caught up and carried along in the tide of these new, built-in friend-ships with Callie and June.

When they walked in through the sliding doors of the hardware store Lila paused, uncertain what kind of cart they needed. Callie pointed off to the right and June steered Lila over to the flatbed carts. "We're going to need one of these. For all the wood you're getting."

Her tone serious but her eyes playful, Callie said, "Are you getting lots of wood, Lila?"

While June tittered, Lila blushed.

"She's just kidding, Lila." June put an arm around Lila's shoulders and squeezed. "She knows you're getting lots of wood."

Callie snorted and pointed June and Lila toward the lumber section. "You can see it all over Travis's face."

Could they?

"It's kind of weird to think about Travis having sex." Callie's lip curled. "I mean, he's like a brother to me."

Leaning forward to look at Callie around Lila's body, June raised an eyebrow. "Sorry, but isn't *Hayes* kind of like a brother to you?"

Callie shook her head and made a gagging noise. "Don't say that."

They'd arrived at the lumber and Lila took out the blueprint and unfolded it. "According to Sterling, we need seven two-by-fours."

"Those are at the end." June commandeered the cart and a couple minutes later, the three of them had collected seven two-by-fours that met June's exacting criteria. They were straight enough, had minimal splinters, contained minimal knots, and didn't look too dry.

"MDF." Callie pointed across the aisle, and they maneuvered the cart over to the sheets that would make up the visible part of the backdrop. Again, they inspected each sheet before loading it onto the cart. Then they went and got screws (at which point Callie and June couldn't resist making more Lila-and-Travis jokes) before heading over to the paint section.

Giddy as they stood in front of the rainbow of paint chips along the wall, June bounced on the balls of her feet and clapped. "I'm so excited about this."

"Me too," Callie said, already pulling chips from their slots. "This creative stuff is such a far cry from what I deal with at work."

"You have anything in mind in terms of color?" June wanted to know.

Lila considered. "We definitely need something neutral so the backdrop doesn't clash with any of my outfits."

June tapped a finger on her lips. "You have a color scheme, right? Like a brand pallet?"

Lila found June's use of the lingo amusing and endearing. "Yes. My aesthetic has always been pastel colors. I almost always wear what fashion gurus call aqua or tangerine."

They debated the merits of several different colors for the backdrop and decided white would be too stark, black might make Lila fade into the background, and gray was too boring. They looked at pale shades of lavender, peach, and sea foam, before finally deciding on a pale sky blue.

"While they mix the paint, do you want to go look for a little houseplant, like Sterling put in his drawing?"

Lila shrugged. "Sure. That was a cute idea, and it'll make my videos feel homey."

They left their cart out of the way near the paint section and headed over to the houseplants. "That's the one." Lila pointed at a jade plant. "It's supposed to bring prosperity."

The girls didn't have to know she was getting it for Travis as much as herself. Callie picked up the plant and cradled it in her arms.

"Aww," June said. "Maybe we need to get Callie a plant of her own."

"Nah," Callie said. "I'll just be the auntie to this one. I don't have time to care for a plant." June rolled her eyes at Lila, and Lila laughed. And just like that, she felt like she'd been inducted into the girl gang. They went back to get the paint and retrieve their cart.

When they rolled it up to the back of Travis's truck, someone drawled at them from a couple spots over. "You ladies need a hand with that?"

Lila panicked, her skin crawling like she'd just walked through a wall of spiderwebs, but June was already answering.

"We're fine, thanks." Her tone held the kind of finality that would ensure the guy didn't insist.

The three of them loaded all the materials into the truck with no problems whatsoever. And then they were off, Lila in the driver's seat, bringing home the supplies she needed to get back to doing what she loved to do.

About halfway back to the ranch, June turned toward Lila and rubbed her hands together. Her eyes glimmered with excitement and mischief. "I have the best idea. We should take this back to the bunkhouse and build your backdrop. Wouldn't it be fun to surprise the guys?"

Build it themselves? Lila wasn't sure if that was the best idea. "That does sound fun ..."

"But?" Callie picked up on Lila's hesitation right away.

"But with all the things I know how to do, building stuff isn't one of them. I'm sure I could hammer in some nails. And I've used a drill before. But I think we're going to have to saw things, right? And whatever we make has to remain standing."

The corners of June's eyes crinkled. "We are going to have to saw. And your backdrop will have to remain standing. But I'm your girl. We've got this."

Lila found her confidence inspiring, but the doubt must have shown on her face.

Callie's tone matter of fact, she said, "June *is* your girl. You should've seen her when she first came to Sweet Springs a few months ago. We're building this beautiful stage and the dance floor, you know, for the fundraiser. June marches right onto the job site, the lone woman in a sea of men. And she volunteers to cut boards. You should have heard Sterling afterwards. 'I walk up, and there she is in those jeans. Leaning over that table. Cutting wood like she was born with a circular saw in her hand.'"

Lila couldn't help but laugh at Callie's deep-voiced imitation of Sterling.

"'And all the guys are suddenly so productive, rushing to put up the boards so they can bring her more.'"

June shook her head. "Never underestimate a woman who knows how to use power tools. That's your lesson for today, Lila. Within the next few hours, you're going to know how to use tools and build stuff. At least the basics."

A sense of excitement bubbled up inside of Lila, electric. "I have to admit, I'm feeling all-powerful all of a sudden. I get the sense that once I lay my hands on a drill or a circular saw, there's no coming back."

"There's no coming back from it." Callie sat back in her seat and crossed her arms. They made eye contact in the rearview mirror and Callie gave Lila a single nod. "After today, you're going to be a whole new woman."

Ultimately, the women decided to build the backdrop inside the bunkhouse so, as June put it, "The guys don't come along and try to rescue us."

Once they lugged everything inside, Lila told them, "I feel like I should offer you guys a drink. But I don't think I should be tipsy my first time using power tools."

"We can make some iced tea." Callie went into the kitchen and busied herself by filling the teapot then lighting the stove, and again Lila marveled at the comfort these friends shared amongst themselves. And with her.

June set to work organizing the materials. Lila followed her instructions, laying out the two-by-fours in one spot and the MDF in another.

"I'm going to run over and get the tools," June said.

"Want help?" Callie turned away from the counter where she was filling an infuser with the loose tea leaves she'd found in Lila's cabinet.

June shook her head. "I want to keep it on the down low. Sterling will definitely notice if we all show up together. Be right back."

While Callie put the lid back on the teapot, Lila said, "Tell me more about the case you were working on today."

Someone less attuned to human behavior might have missed the pause in Callie's movements, but Lila didn't. Something about this case didn't sit well with Callie.

"Technically, I can't talk about the case—attorney-client privilege. But let's just say someone very close to my heart is going through the worst betrayal imaginable. I might share some hypotheticals with you when June gets back. You know, just some scenarios."

Lila nodded. "Fair enough."

Chapter Twenty-Two

At the end of the day, the women were hunkered down in the bunkhouse on some sort of secret mission, so Travis invited his brothers to go for dinner at the burger joint. While they all sat reading the menus—arguably a pointless exercise since they'd all end up ordering their usuals anyway—he looked around the table.

What would their mom think of them if she could see them all now? Had they turned out like she'd imagined they would? And wasn't she curious? These thoughts and questions hadn't plagued him for a while.

So, why now?

The answer wasn't completely obvious, but it had been taking shape in Travis's mind over the course of the past couple of weeks. *Because of Lila.* Travis was vaguely aware of the others setting down their menus, discussing what they would order (their usuals, of course). But he couldn't quite disembark from his train of thought. If a mother could leave her home, her husband, her children, for God's sake, without looking back, how hard would it be for a woman—like Lila—to leave Travis behind?

"Earth to Travis." Cash leaned into his field of view and waved. "We lost you for a second."

Travis blinked once, and then again, hoping the physical movement would help him shift gears. "Sorry. Just deep in thought."

"You know what you're getting?"

"The usual."

They ordered and then Cash drummed his fingertips on the table. "Surely one of you guys knows what the women are working on." He looked at Sterling, Hayes, and Travis in turn.

Travis couldn't help but smile. "I have an inkling, but I think they want to surprise us."

Hayes shrugged. "You got me. I'm just happy to see Callie hanging out with the girls rather than buried in paperwork from this case she's been working on. I've barely seen her and I've talked to her even less."

"Sounds stressful." Cash sipped his beer. "I guess you probably can't tell us anything about the case, right?"

Hayes shook his head. "No. She hasn't told me anything, anyway. So I don't even know what it's about. But I do know I haven't seen her this emotionally invested in a case for a while."

"Well, hopefully tonight's giving her a chance to relax." Travis didn't tell them he was grateful Lila was getting a chance to relax, too.

"What's got you so deep in thought, Trav?" Cash's eyes were on him, and before he could fully consider the ramifications, he blurted out what he'd been thinking. "Do you guys, uh—" his voice stalled out. "Ever think about Mom?"

Everything stilled: his brothers' bodies, their voices, their breathing. In unison, their heads turned. Three pairs of eyes focused on him. If he were in a movie, the special effects would show Travis experiencing tunnel vision as he froze in fear.

He didn't know exactly what he was afraid of: them saying they didn't think about her, saying they did, or asking why he was even asking.

They'd rarely talked about her once they became teenagers.

"Why are you asking, man?" Sterling looked guarded.

Honesty's the best policy. "I don't know. This will probably sound weird, but she's been on my mind a lot since Lila came." He explained what he'd been thinking about how their mom could just pick up and leave and what that might mean for someone he had feelings for. "It sounds crazy when I say it out loud."

"This is deep, bro," Cash said. He cleared his throat, and Travis's fear of being ridiculed rushed in.

"Never mind."

"No," Cash said, holding up a hand. "I know you're expecting me to give you shit, but that's not it at all. First of all, let me just say that the fact that you're thinking about this means your feelings for Lila are, like deep."

The others nodded, as if Cash were some kind of sage.

"But also. To answer your question I *have* thought about her. During all the milestones, right? On every special occasion. For a long time, I asked myself why. Why would she leave us and never come back? Why wouldn't she contact us? Why didn't she love us?"

Sterling, who'd just taken a giant gulp of beer, nodded. "Same. But then after I found out about Dad's gambling, I figured maybe there was something going on that we didn't know about. You know? I thought about contacting her, back then, but I decided against it." He gave a half-laugh. "I'll admit, I was afraid she'd reject me. She'd been gone so long without reaching out to us, if she wanted to talk to us, she'd call, right? Or email. Or whatever. It's not like we're hard to find."

Something inside Travis started to heal as his brothers spoke. It had been so long since they talked about her, and knowing his brothers still struggled made him feel less alone.

"Right," Hayes said. "When I fell for Callie, I *so* wanted to tell Mom. It was weird. I'd pushed her out of my mind for years. And then, *bam!* There she was, occupying my thoughts. Because, you know, she'd always told me she thought Callie and I would end up together. It was coming to fruition and I could just imagine that look in her eyes."

"That 'I-told-you-so' look?" Sterling's smile was subdued.

"Yep," Cash said. "The one she gave me when I insisted on carrying my lunch in a paper bag instead of a real lunch box and my ham sandwich made me sick. Not one ounce of sympathy."

"Same one she gave me when I ate my entire bucket of Halloween candy in one sitting." Travis's stomach roiled at the memory.

"Do you remember her chicken noodle soup, though?" Sterling rubbed his stomach. "She'd make that for us when we were sick and it was so good."

"So good," they all said.

"Like Sterling said though, I can't help but believe something else was going on with Mom and Dad." Hayes paused, sipped his beer. "Maybe it's because I want to believe that—that she didn't leave us because of something fundamentally wrong with us, or her."

"I'm embarrassed to admit I never thought of that." Travis grimaced. "I just figured motherhood had ruined her dreams of being a famous actress, and regret and her drive finally beat out her love for us."

"Me, too." Cash looked down at the table, giving Travis a view of the long, thick eyelashes their mom had always envied.

That made Travis think of Cash as a little boy—all of them as little boys—and his heart ached for what they'd lost.

"I know she loved us." Hayes smiled, wistful. "She wouldn't have tucked us in every night if she didn't. Or checked on us in the middle of the night—do you guys remember waking up to her just watching you sleep?"

"Yep," Sterling said.

"I remember her coming to the school and yelling at me in the middle of lunch for forgetting my lunch." Cash squeezed his eyes shut. "Most embarrassing moment of my young life."

"And the moment you realized you weren't exempt from her consequences even if you were her baby." Travis winked at him.

"Well, that's the truth."

They sat in silence for a while.

"So." When Cash looked at Travis, his eyes were twinkling. "This Lila thing. You gonna tell us how serious it is?"

Travis made a show of sighing dramatically, letting his chest rise and fall. "I don't know. I mean, we've spent every spare moment together during the past week. I think about her all the time. Whenever something happens during the day—like when a cow dances through the grass—I add it to my list of things to tell her. I can't wait to see her, first thing in the morning or when I get done with my stuff for the day. It's like I'm addicted to her."

Hayes nodded, the movement slow and exaggerated. "Hear that, boys?"

"Hear what?" Travis could tell Sterling was just egging Hayes on.

"He said, 'when a cow dances through the grass.' He's got it bad."

Nodding in time with Hayes, Sterling grinned. "Oh, yeah. Our little Travis is in *lo-ove*."

"Shut up."

Fortunately, the server came with the food and Travis pretended no one could see him blushing. As soon as his plate rested in front of him, he scooped up his burger and took a hearty bite.

Cash did the same, and then, with his mouth full, he said, "So when are you going to tell her?"

"Tell her?"

"Stop talking with your mouths full," Sterling and Hayes said.

Cash, smiling around his gigantic bite, said, "Tell her how you feel."

Sterling had picked up his own burger and was poised to dig in. "Some people might argue that there's no time like the present."

Travis felt an actual jolt of energy race from his heart to his fingertips and toes. He hadn't even considered telling Lila how he felt.

For one thing, she had no plans to stay in Arizona. She loved the city and Travis didn't suppose she could be happy on a ranch in a small town.

Second, she liked him fine right now, but that was probably because she knew their situation was temporary. A girl could put up with a guy's quirks if she knew they had only a limited time together.

Third, the magnitude of his feelings for her terrified him. If they went unrequited, he didn't know if he could live with that. Or himself.

Hayes's long, low whistle brought Travis back to the present moment, where all three of his brothers stared at him from their spots around the table. "What?"

"What do you mean, 'What'?" Sterling picked up a French fry and pointed it at Travis. "You're afraid to tell her." He looked pointedly at Hayes and then at Cash. "Well, boys, isn't this something? Our Travis has fallen in love."

Cash held up his arms, pretending to defend himself against Sterling's words. "Ahh, the L-word! He said the L-word!"

Travis rolled his eyes while Hayes and Sterling laughed at Cash. "You guys are hilarious."

"But again, boys, isn't this something? He doesn't deny it." This time, he turned to Travis. "You don't deny it, do you?"

It was like a strange moment of truth. With all of his brothers laser-focused on him, he couldn't lie. "I don't deny it."

There. He'd admitted it: he loved Lila Sullivan. Now what?

"Cheers, boys." Sterling lifted his glass and Hayes and Cash tapped theirs against it. They all held their glasses up to Travis, who sat unable to move.

"Cheers, Trav," Cash said.

In slow motion, Travis lifted his glass so the others could tap it, and then he set it back down.

"It's fine, bud." Sterling patted his shoulder. "You're just in shock. Pretty sure it happened to me when I realized I was in love with June."

"Happened to me when I realized I was in love with Callie." Hayes took another drink.

"It's never happened to me." Cash winked at Travis. "Probably never will."

Sterling set his glass down with a thunk. "Some people might argue that the Wilder boys are falling like dominoes ... and you're next."

"Nonsense." Cash wiped his mouth with the back of his hand.

"When all the ladies love me, as they do, how can I ever choose just one?"

"That's the spirit," Hayes said. "Anyway. Let's get back on topic. You've got to tell her, bro."

"It's pointless." Travis's voice sounded whiny and childish to his own ears.

"Why?" Cash asked.

"Because." He counted on his fingers. "One. She's not staying forever. Two. She's a city girl. And three. What if she doesn't feel the same way?"

"Or, what if she does?" Sterling said.

Travis hadn't considered that. Yes, she did seem happy to see him at the end of each day. But he'd figured that was because he was one of her only social outlets. And yes, they did have a lot to talk about. He smiled when he thought of how often one of them said, "Just one more thing" before they went to sleep. And obviously, their chemistry was pretty much off the charts. He couldn't remember ever wanting a woman in the way he wanted Lila.

Was it possible she *did* feel the same way he did?

"There's only one way to find out." Hayes pulled out his credit card. "Go to her," he said in his best dramatic, stage-worthy voice. "Go to her and tell her."

Was it that simple?

All three of his brothers stood up, urging him to do the same—and leave the restaurant to head home to Lila. After he pushed in his chair, they surrounded him, patting his back and muttering inspiring words as if he were about to embark on an important and life-altering mission. Maybe he was.

Their words of encouragement echoing in his mind, Travis went out to his truck. When he closed the door, he noticed something in the handle. He pulled it out and nearly said, "Aww" out loud when he realized the object was one of Lila's hair ties. Liking the idea of keeping such a small part of her with him, he put it back in the handle and started the truck.

Although the drive home lasted only a few minutes, it felt interminable. The lights were on in the bunkhouse, but he couldn't tell if

June and Callie were still there. He raised his hand to knock, but Lila opened the door before his knuckles made contact. She threw her arms around him and he thought some people might take that as a sign.

"I'm so glad you're here!" She was breathless, her eyes bright and her smile wide. "Come in, come in. We have something to show you."

She grabbed his hand and pulled him farther into the bunkhouse, and he felt a stab of disappointment when he saw June and Callie. He was *not* going to declare his love for Lila in front of them.

Then he saw what they'd been working on: the backdrop for Lila's posts stood in the corner, exactly where he and Lila had talked about putting it. Time seemed to slow down. All three women beamed at him, expectant, waiting for him to congratulate them on a job well done. And it was.

Only, he'd wanted to help Lila with it ... he'd wanted to be the one to help her breathe life back into her dream and her passion.

But this wasn't about him. It was about Lila. So he beamed back at them, one at a time, his eye contact landing finally on Lila, who said, "Isn't it great?"

"So great." And it was. It looked perfect and would serve its purpose exactly as she intended.

Lila started talking then, explaining how they'd decided to go ahead and build the backdrop to surprise him, Sterling, and Hayes. And how much fun she'd had learning to use power tools. And how empowered she felt, and how excited she was to get back to doing her videos and posts.

And right then, Travis's momentary jealousy slipped away. Because even though he hadn't gotten to help her build the back-drop, she'd wanted to surprise him. And her excitement about showing him was palpable—it radiated off her body in little bubbles that burst against his skin.

"I can't wait to see you filming here. Do I get to watch? I've been wanting to see more of you in your sexy workout clothes." He gave her his most devilish smile and she slapped his arm.

"And that's our cue, Junie." Callie grabbed June's arm and steered her toward the table where they'd laid all the tools. "I'll help you pick up your things."

Laughing at that point, Lila went over to help them pack the tools into their bag. Travis watched them work, in awe of how quickly June and Callie had brought Lila into the fold—and how quickly she'd accepted their embrace.

Within a couple of minutes, the women had gone, leaving him alone with Lila in the bunkhouse.

"Well, what do you think? Be honest."

She's asking for honesty. "It looks great. Exactly to plan."

She put her arms around his waist and squeezed. "Doesn't it? I didn't know June had those hidden talents, but she really led the charge on this one."

"I'll admit, I was a little jealous I didn't get to help you, but it turned out really well. Just as well as if I had helped."

She tilted her head back so she could make eye contact with him. "You were jealous?"

He shrugged, wanting to play off his reaction like it was no big deal. "Yeah. But I moved past it."

"I love that." She tucked her head back underneath his chin. "I love that you were jealous. It means you care. I feel a tiny bit guilty, but I still love it."

Travis could just imagine what his brothers would be saying if they were in the room, flies on the wall: *She's giving you an opening. Just tell her. Say the words, bro. It's only three little words.*

"Don't feel guilty." He kissed the top of her head. "It looks great. I'm excited for you."

Chapter Twenty-Three

Lila's heart was actually melting. She felt herself going all warm and gooey at Travis's admission that he was jealous.

"When are you going to make your first video?"

Sinking into his embrace, she sighed. "I'd like to make one right now! Kind of an 'I'm back' post, you know? I've been thinking about what I'd say. But I should probably plan out a few before I get started, so I can have them ready to go."

The idea of putting herself out there again was slightly terrifying, but also she knew she didn't want to live in fear any longer.

"That makes sense. I guess I never really thought about the process of it all, but it makes sense to have posts in the queue if you're doing this as a business. Gosh, you really are an amazing businesswoman. I only wish I'd met you earlier."

She stepped out of his embrace and kissed his lips. "Thank you. I wish I'd met you earlier, too. But, alas. Here we are." She winked at him and went to the fridge to get him a beer, which he accepted with a smile.

While she poured herself a glass of wine, he said, "I was serious about watching you film."

Her nose wrinkled of its own accord. "I've never had an audience. Want to sit? I'm exhausted."

"What do you mean you've never had an audience? Callie and June said you get millions of views."

They sat on the couch and Lila extended her legs and put her feet on his lap. "That's a slight exaggeration. More like tens of thousands."

"Don't you consider that an audience?"

She shrugged. "Yes, but it's not a *live* audience."

He set his beer on the side table and started massaging her feet. His thumbs were so strong, and her whole body responded to his touch. "Never in my life have I met a man who could massage my feet and make me weak-kneed with desire."

His posture changed from relaxed to alert and when he looked at her, his eyes glinted. "Oh yeah?"

She laughed. "Don't get any ideas. It's true, but I'm also too tired to hop into bed with you, as lovely as it sounds."

"Perhaps I could persuade you."

Arousal flared in her core, molten. "You can try."

He grinned, quite wickedly, making her laugh again. And then he did try, working those magical hands from her feet to her ankles to her calves and thighs, just as he had a few evenings before.

And just like she had a few evenings before, Lila found him impossible to resist. As tired as she was, her body responded. Wherever his fingers touched, her nerve endings woke up and stretched and begged for more. And then it was her who was touching him, unable to keep her hands off the planes of his muscular body.

Instinct took over and the first coherent thought Lila formed was when he entered her, looking into her eyes, conveying so much sweetness: *I love him.*

Even as she thought the words, he said them, his voice husky. "I love you, Lila Sullivan."

"I love you, Travis Wilder."

She came undone, and so did he, and afterward, they lay breathless, limbs tangled up, bodies slick with sweat.

The rational part of her mind wanted to know what this all meant, and kept demanding, *Now what?* But the emotional part? It wanted to curl up inside Travis's arms and stay there forever. *Forever.*

Was that even possible? Did it matter? Could they just ride this wave for now, without thinking about the future?

Apparently finally able to move again, Travis stroked her hair, creating a fresh wave of goosebumps.

Lila propped herself up on her elbows and gave him a soft kiss. "That was nice."

"It was. And now that I've had my way with you, I guess I can let you go to bed."

"I'm awake all of a sudden. Maybe I should take advantage of that and plan some posts. Then you can help me film tomorrow."

He ran a hand down her back, from her shoulder to her hip, and then gave her ass a light smack. "Sounds good to me. Do you mind if I go to bed, though? It was kind of a long day."

"Of course not."

He did, and she sat down at the dining table with her notebook, her excitement building as she began brainstorming ideas. Although only a few weeks had passed since she'd stopped posting, she missed it. She couldn't wait to immerse herself back into the community she'd spent years building. She couldn't wait to talk to her followers, to read their comments, and to create more and more content. When she was FearlessLila, she was the best, most confident version of herself.

Once she'd narrowed her original brainstorm down to ten solid ideas, something switched in her brain and she couldn't stay awake another moment. In the bedroom, she stripped down to her underwear and slid between the sheets, curling her body around Travis's. His breathing was deep and even and just before she fell asleep she realized her own breathing fell into rhythm with his.

She woke the next morning to Travis clapping once and announcing, "Today's the day!"

He rolled toward her and wrapped his arms around her, nuzzling her neck, scraping her skin with his whiskers in the most delicious way.

"You're going to need a good breakfast." He rolled out of bed and pulled on his sweatpants. "I'm on it."

For just a moment, she lay in bed and wondered how she'd gotten so lucky. She'd found that job posting—and Travis—out of the blue when she'd needed them most. And she hadn't even realized how much she craved the kind of love he gave her. The sense of belonging she'd found here. The sense of safety.

Travis was just setting the plates on the table when Lila came out of the bedroom, freshly showered and dressed in her favorite aqua leggings, crop top, and running shoes. He gave her a wolf whistle, making her blush as she slid into her seat.

"Have you decided what you're going to say on your first video?"

She shook her head. "I've been thinking about it. I don't want to explain exactly why I shut down my account. It seems like that would be giving the creep too much power."

"I agree." He cut into his pancakes and took a big bite.

"So I was thinking I would just say how glad I am to be back."

"Sounds good. I'll be happy to watch you. In case you want any feedback or mansplaining."

Lila snorted. "Great."

After they cleared their plates and washed the dishes, he leaned in to kiss her. "I don't really have to watch you, you know. I totally understand if you want privacy."

"Honestly, I've never had anyone in the room while I'm filming. I used to think it was so weird when I saw people at the gym set up their phones and record their workouts."

"I've never been a big gym rat, but I've seen those videos from time to time and wondered how all the other gym goers felt about that one person filming."

"How'd you get such big muscles if you've never been a gym rat?"

"These?" Travis flexed a bicep and kissed it. "Good, old-fashioned elbow grease. Okay, I'll get out of your hair. I'll have my phone. Call me if you need me."

They kissed one more time and then he was gone, leaving Lila alone to sink into the world she'd left behind.

She set up her phone on the tripod and positioned it near the backdrop. When she opened the video camera app, a wave of excitement hit her. The backdrop looked absolutely perfect onscreen. She couldn't wait to tell Callie and June.

"This is the moment of truth." Lila took a deep breath, hit record, and took a seat on the barstool she'd set up.

For a few seconds, she sat frozen, uncertain of what to say even though she'd thought through the words so many times. She cleared her throat, grateful she could edit out that and the long silence preceding it.

"Hey, you guys." Suddenly, she smiled. *I'm back.* "I stepped away from my social channels for a bit, but I'm back, and I'm so happy to be here. I've got several new posts planned for you and I'm so looking forward to connecting with you again."

There. That was a good start. She stood up to turn off the recording, and then spent a few minutes editing the video. Doing her best to be objective, she told herself she looked pretty good—a little nervous, but not enough to redo anything.

Feeling confident, she checked that first video off her list and set up her dumbbells for the second one. It had been so long since she immersed herself in her passion, she was surprised when she finally checked the time and realized several hours had passed. Five videos were complete and edited, and the joy of feeling like herself again was pumping through her veins. She didn't even need champagne to celebrate; she was almost lightheaded with happiness.

Sitting at the table, notebook in front of her, she checked off *Filming.* Next up: editing all five videos, then typing up the text that would go with each post, and finally, scheduling them.

Her phone lit up with a text notification. It was from Travis: *I'm ready for lunch but wasn't sure whether to go home or come to your place. I didn't want to interrupt.*

Heart swelling, she wrote back: *You're so thoughtful. I'm ready for a break. Come on over.*

A few minutes later, he let himself in. "How's it going?" His expression was at once excited and concerned.

Delighted, she laughed and went up to kiss him. "It's going great."

"Whew. I've been thinking about you all morning."

Moving in a rhythm that had become their norm, they worked together to pull food out of the fridge for lunch.

Once they sat down Lila said, "Don't worry. I haven't forgotten my whole reason for being here is to get your paperwork organized."

She saw a flash of hurt in his eyes. "I wasn't worried."

Right away, she realized she'd chosen her words wrong. "Travis." She put a hand on his arm. He stilled momentarily, but then kept eating. "I didn't mean—"

He swallowed, wiped his mouth, smiled at her. "It's fine. I knew what you meant."

She hadn't imagined that flicker of pain and a desperation took hold of her to make it right. "I just didn't want you to worry that I get so wrapped up in my posts that I'd let the paperwork fall by the wayside."

Again, an overly bright smile. "I wasn't worried about it, Lila."

His curt tone smarted. She blinked. "Okay."

They finished eating in relative quiet, the tension hanging thick and wet and heavy in the air.

"I can do the cleanup." She cleared her throat. "If you want to get back to your work."

"Thanks." Standing, he took his plate to the sink before returning to bend down and kissed her on the temple. "Thank you for lunch."

And then he was gone. A literal ache expanded in her chest. They hadn't even fought, but she knew she'd misstepped. Her words, however unintentional, had gone straight to his core.

How could she fix things? She started cleaning, and the process felt slow and laborious, her limbs heavy. The only way to repair the damage was to show him, with actions, how much she cared for him.

Dishes loaded in the dishwasher, the kitchen counter and table wiped down, Lila returned to the ranch paperwork. She'd sorted almost everything; only two boxes remained. The first contained more of the same types of documents: invoices, receipts, unopened junk mail. As she sorted, she was distinctly aware of the path of the sun as it arced across the western sky. Soon, evening would come, and Travis would return. Hopefully.

As she sorted the final papers from the first box, a flare of excitement ignited in her chest. Just one more box. Immediately on the heels of the excitement, a realization struck: her work at Sweet Springs Ranch was nearly complete. Once she had everything sorted and filed, she would spend a couple of days getting all the numbers into the computer. And then she could work remotely.

A tiny voice piped up in the back of her mind. *Your stalker is still out there.*

She brushed away the thought, reminding herself that she'd recaptured her confidence and didn't need to be afraid. The police were handling things.

A glance at the clock told her Travis would be done for the day soon. Making him a special dinner could be her first step toward fixing things. Before she even made it to the kitchen though, she heard a notification for a text message.

Travis: *Going to dinner with the boys.*

That was it. No promise to catch up with her afterwards or see her that evening. Dread swirled in her stomach. What if she'd made a fatal mistake? What if her words had served as a reminder she was leaving soon, and Travis decided to cut his losses right then? Her fingers hovered over her phone's keyboard. She had to talk herself down from begging him to come back immediately and settled on, *Have a great time.* Then, because cooking for one was infinitely less satisfying than cooking for two, she heated up some leftovers and sat down at the table with her plate and her laptop. If she was going to be alone that evening, she may as well schedule some of the posts she'd created.

Thanks to the fact that she'd scheduled thousands of posts over the course of the past several years, she made quick work of the task, delighted to find herself running on autopilot as she added music, selected the times she knew her followers were most likely to interact with her, and typed in hashtags she knew would draw people interested in fitness and confidence.

Her first post—the I'm-back video—would go out first thing in the morning, just as the sun rose.

She promised herself she wouldn't look at the posts or any comments on them for at least a week ... she didn't think she could bear it if no one responded, welcoming her back.

Forcing herself to focus only on the task at hand did help to distract her from thinking about Travis, but when he still hadn't called or texted or stopped by the house by the time she was done, she felt another wave of dread washing over her, encapsulating her, making it hard to breathe.

"I need to keep busy."

The last box of ranch documents waited for her on the work table. Although she could hardly bear to go through yet another box, she also could see the light at the end of the tunnel.

Filled with renewed determination, she fortified herself with a glass of wine and lifted off the lid. The sound of her own gasp surprised her.

Hand-addressed envelopes made up the entire top layer. The cursive handwriting was slightly slanted, neat and tidy. Every return address was the same: *Sophia Stewart, 4894 E. Stardust Lane, Los Angeles, CA.* From what she could see, at least one letter was addressed to each Wilder boy—Sterling, Hayes, Travis, Cash. And many—the majority—were addressed to Levi Wilder.

At first, Lila thought she'd stumbled upon a sweet discovery. Levi must have saved these letters for his sons. Special words from someone who loved them. Whoever Sophia Stewart was, Lila thought as she lifted the first layer of envelopes and discovered even more beneath them, she wrote a lot.

But then she realized every single envelope was still sealed. She started taking them out in stacks of four or five, quickly checking for any that were open. But no. As she dug deeper and deeper, lifted out more and more letters, she found that none of them were. Which meant chances were good Travis and his brothers didn't even know about the letters. But why would Levi keep them a secret?

Chapter Twenty-Four

"So when are you going to tell us why you're fighting with Lila?"

Cash pinned Travis with what was becoming an all-too-common expression: *You may as well tell us what's going on—we already know there's something.*

"I can't remember." It was a lie, and Cash, the rascal, caught on to that too.

"You can't remember, or you don't want to say?"

"I don't think we're even fighting." Because he practically buried his face in his beer, he couldn't see his brothers exchanging a three-way glance. But he could sure as hell feel it.

Out of the corner of his eye, Travis saw Hayes shrug before he spoke. "What's going on then?"

"Can we talk about something else?"

Another three-way glance. How could he tell his brothers the truth—that one tiny, offhand comment had practically torn him in two? It was stupid. Childish.

But it's also true. He picked up his beer, grateful for the cold glass against his fingertips. Then he started drinking, swallow after swallow. Lila was only being honest. She *had* come to Sweet Springs Ranch to take care of paperwork. Of *course* she hadn't come for him.

But hearing her say as much, especially on the heels of him declaring his love for her, sent him into a downward spiral.

She hadn't come for him, and she didn't plan to stay for him.

But getting all worked up about it was stupid. Had he thought she'd abandon her life in Alabama for good? The job here was a short-term agreement. She wasn't bound to him ... no matter how bound he felt to her.

His beer empty, he put his glass down with a *thunk* and wiped his mouth with the back of his hand. "Really. Let's talk about something else."

"You sure?" Sterling said. "If you really don't want to, we can move on to Cash's hair. Because dude could use a haircut."

The corners of Travis's mouth twitched upward into a half-smile. "Truer words were never spoken."

While giving them all the middle finger, Cash said, "Seriously though. Not to sound like a girl, but if you change your mind, you know we're here for you. We'll at least pretend to listen while thinking about the next Cardinals game."

Travis rolled his eyes. "Thanks."

They didn't talk about it, but after they'd finished dinner Sterling suggested they head to A Cold One to play pool.

Hayes broke, and while they watched the balls scatter across the surface of the pool table, Travis asked Sterling for an update on the big house.

"It's coming along. I can tell Hayes is going to have a rough night —he didn't get a single pocket. Why don't you be on his team?" After taking a shot and getting in three stripes, he went on. "If we weren't going to use it for events and stuff, it'd be done. But we've got all these commercial requirements to meet. Which is why I usually work on houses. You're up."

Travis took a turn, sinking one solid, and then Cash was up.

"Get 'em, baby," Hayes hollered just as he positioned his cue. Laughing, Cash went for it but didn't make solid contact with the cue ball, which spun off wildly.

The rest of the game unfolded in much the same way, as did the second game.

"I vote we switch to darts," Sterling said after it took about a dozen rounds for them to sink all the balls.

By the time they finished two rounds of pool and three rounds of darts, and the others started talking about closing time and getting home, Travis felt like he'd lifted a thousand-pound burden off his shoulders and set it on the floor. But he still didn't want to talk to Lila. "Lila who's leaving. Hey, I like the sound of that."

His brothers gave him yet another look, obviously questioning his sanity as he repeated the three-word phrase. Hayes offered to drive him home in his truck and when he checked the time and saw it was well past midnight, he hissed through his teeth.

Then he noticed he had a text from her. *I need to talk to you.*

"Whatever it is, it's gonna have to wait." His words were soft around the edges, which meant he had crossed the line between sober and drunk. Maybe he was standing on it, but still. "Probably better if we don't talk tonight anyway."

Chapter Twenty-Five

S leep was elusive for Lila that night. Restless, she checked her phone for a response from Travis whenever she was lucid enough to pick it up off her nightstand. She never received one, and slept for an hour or two before waking up groggy at six a.m. Travis's face was the first image to appear in her mind, an apparition since he wasn't beside her as he had been for the past couple of weeks.

Why had she spoken so carelessly? The fact that she'd hurt his feelings tore at her. But surely he knew she cared about him.

And if he cared about her, then why the hell would he just run off like that? Why wouldn't he fight for her? Why wouldn't he tell her that her being at the ranch just for paperwork wasn't enough?

The thoughts, circling around themselves on repeat, made her want to scream. She got out of bed instead.

For the first time since her arrival in Prescott, the air that hit her skin when she threw back the covers felt chilly and made her shiver even as she hurried to the window, pulling aside the curtain and lifting one slat in the blinds so she could see if Travis's truck was in the driveway. She exhaled when she saw it, relieved he'd come home. Only then did she realize she had worried he might run into the arms of another woman. Lila might be new to town, but she hadn't missed out on the fact that the Wilder brothers were a hot commodity. Two of them officially spoken for, the ladies in town wanted to snap up the others. Another thought hit her with full force then: he could have brought a woman home. But no, no matter how much she'd hurt him, he wouldn't do that—not when he lived just a few steps from where she was staying. She let go of the blinds, shut the curtains, and went into the kitchen.

In solitude, the fear came sneaking back in. She jumped at every sound. A tree branch brushing against the window sounded like a door opening. The creaking of the stove vent in the ceiling sounded like a footstep on a loose floorboard. The heater clicking on and revving up sounded like a car pulling into the bunkhouse's tiny parking area. Still, knowing the power of ritual, Lila forced herself through each step of her morning routine.

Just as she sat down with her breakfast, she heard Travis's truck rumble to life. Through the narrow window next to the front door, she saw him drive toward the ranch's main driveway. She could hear the engine quiet as he stopped at the main road, and then roar as he accelerated onto it.

Where would he be going this early in the morning?

Lila spent the day steeped in the kind of misery that made her feel sick. Nauseated, joints aching with tension, she sat at the computer, organizing the Sweet Springs Ranch's finances into online accounting software. Yes, she'd chosen the program she'd always used in her business with intentions of continuing to manage the accounts.

But now anyone would be able to take over. Sadness lodged in her throat.

As much as she tried, she couldn't stop rehashing the last conversation she'd had with Travis—the one that made him run away—literally, apparently.

I haven't forgotten my whole reason for being here is to get your paperwork organized.

The hurt that flashed in his eyes revealed a deeper pain ... one she'd unknowingly triggered.

By lunchtime, he hadn't come back. Lila fixed herself some

food and then decided to go for a walk. Fresh air always did a body good, and maybe she'd come across someone with some information about Travis. She couldn't even decide which was her primary motive.

The breeze was warm, carrying the final reminders of summer. Birds chirped. The leaves on the cottonwoods and sycamores were starting to change. If she'd taken this walk twenty-four hours earlier, she would have felt and heard and seen all this and felt contentment, joy, and confidence.

But it seemed that when Travis walked out of the bunkhouse the day before, he took all of those things with him.

She walked slowly, the sun on her face and her feet crunching on the gravel that covered the little roadways all over the ranch. A sudden sound coming from somewhere on the property made her jump. Then she realized it was just a car door shutting. For an instant, hope swirled in. Maybe it was Travis, coming home from wherever he'd gone. But when she turned around, she saw it was Cash who had parked next to the big house and was getting something out of the bed of his truck. Her heart sank. He lifted an arm in greeting, but didn't make to come over to her.

And that made her sixth sense tingle.

Out of all the Wilder brothers, Cash was the most social, the one always up for a chat, unable to resist a chance to interact. At that very moment he was tucking a box under his arm and walking away from her.

The old Lila would have let him go. She would have stood there, shoulders slumped, and watched him walk away from her, his broad shoulders and trim waist so similar to those of the man she was in love with.

The new Lila?

"Cash!" He didn't turn around, so she called his name again and started jogging toward him.

Eventually he did hear her—either her voice or the fall of her feet as she ran—and swiveled slowly.

"Lila. Hi." His expression said, "I'm caught," or, "Oh, no," or "What am I going to say to her?" and Lila would have laughed if she didn't think that expression was directly related to whatever was going on with Travis.

"Any idea where your brother is?"

"Which one?" He laughed, an awkward bark, and he looked anywhere but at her.

"Travis." She imagined she looked crazy, her eyes sparkling with determination and her glare direct.

"Right." He shifted the box in his arms. "He may or may not be in Montana."

"Montana?" Every bit of the fury Lila had been feeling until that second drained out of her body. "What in the world is he doing there?"

"Ah." He shifted his weight again. "I'm not sure if I'm at liberty to say."

"Cash Wilder. You tell me right this very minute."

"He's gone to another auction. Didn't ask anyone's opinion, just registered as a bidder and took off. Drunken, brokenhearted, rash decision, if you ask me."

Brokenhearted? "How long will he be gone?"

Cash looked around, probably hoping someone would come to his rescue, save him from Lila's interrogation. When no one materialized, he said, "Three days."

"What did you mean when you said 'brokenhearted'?"

His eyes widened. He couldn't believe his own mistake. "Look. I've got to go. I'm delivering this—" he held up the box—"to Sterling. He needs it ASAP."

She nodded. She'd learned enough—she could let him walk away now.

Before he did, he said, "I'm sorry. He'll be back." Then he turned on his heel and practically scampered over to the big house, leaving Lila alone with the warm breeze and the birds and the changing leaves. And her thoughts of Travis.

As she walked back to the bunkhouse, she tried to sort through her emotions. Relief was probably at the forefront. He hadn't run off to see an old girlfriend. Or to become a hermit. He'd left to build his business.

But ... heartbreak? She knew it was Cash's choice of a word and not Travis's, but Travis must have said something to his brothers. Although to be fair, the four of them demonstrated an uncanny ability to read each other's thoughts. Even if Travis hadn't spoken about his heartbreak though, they'd been able to see it ... and that frustrated Lila. If it took just a single sentence to break Travis's heart, she didn't know if she could live with that kind of pressure.

Frustration brewing, she opened the door to the bunkhouse and stopped in her tracks. What was she thinking, she couldn't live with that kind of pressure? She wouldn't be living with it. For all Travis knew, she planned to head back to Alabama as soon as the coast was clear—as soon as the police reported they'd found her stalker.

So when she'd reminded him that she'd come to Arizona primarily to do paperwork, he'd thought about her leaving.

"You're a real jerk, Lila Sullivan."

For the next two days, she played music continuously so she wouldn't hear her own racing thoughts. She kept herself busy entering facts and figures and accounts into the software system. At one point she texted Travis, *I'm sorry. Can we talk?* He didn't respond, and she let herself stew in regret.

On the third day, she decided to risk a look at her online accounts. "You told yourself to wait a full week," she said, then added, "Never mind. You do you."

First, she opened the social app, grinning when she saw the notification count in the upper left corner. People were welcoming her back, expressing their excitement about seeing her, and dropping hearts and clapping hands and thumbs up in her comments. She knew then that she'd made the right choice when she decided to get back to posting. Her chest filled with excitement and gratitude and Travis was the first person she wanted to share those with.

She groaned, did her best to shake off the icky, uncomfortable feelings that went along with that line of thinking, and opened her social media inbox, which showed an astounding twenty-three messages.

The first several were cheerful greetings, followers surprised and happy to see her back online. She responded to those with equal excitement. A couple of the messages were from those who purported to be influence experts, offering their services, promising they could help Lila expand her follower base by thousands or tens of thousands. She deleted those.

About a dozen messages down, there was one from an anonymous user.

The standard profile icon, gray with a white torso cutout, gave her the creeps right away—it was what the stalker had used when she was in Alabama.

When she opened the message, she got more than just the creeps. She got a full-blown wave of fear, the kind of chills that instantly made her freezing. The hairs on her arms and the back of her neck stood up—she could feel them—and her heart picked up speed until it was galloping.

First, she saw a photo of herself there, in Prescott, at the hardware store. She was pushing the cart as she came out of the double doors. She looked happy, carefree, confident.

Nice to see you again.

Every ounce of the sense of security she'd developed since coming to Arizona evaporated then and there. Her entire being, body and mind, went into fight or flight. Her spine went rigid. Her senses went on alert. Her head swiveled, eyes and ears open for any sign of whoever had taken the picture. The bunkhouse was quiet. So much so that she could literally hear her heartbeat.

Someone could be standing outside right this very minute and she wouldn't even know. Travis wasn't home to hear her if she called for him, and Sterling and June were too far away in their RV next to the big house.

Moving slowly despite the speed at which the adrenaline-spiked blood rushed through her veins, she crept to the linen closet and retrieved a flat sheet, then into the kitchen where she found a box of push pins in the junk drawer. She then tiptoed to the tall, narrow window next to the front door and praying no one was outside it, she pinned the sheet over the window.

Because Travis wasn't there, and because she still hadn't developed full comfort in being alone, she'd already closed the blinds and curtains as dark fell. She thanked her past self for that and then stole around the house checking to make sure both doors and all the windows were locked.

They were—again, thanks to her past self—but she didn't feel any safer.

With light, quiet steps, she made her way into her bedroom, because at least there she could climb into bed in the corner with her back to the wall and see all the room's entry points. She closed and locked the bedroom door before climbing onto the bed, clutching her phone so hard, her fingers hurt where they wrapped around it. There was no way she'd sleep now.

She should call or text someone.

Again, Travis was the first person who came to mind. No matter how much she'd upset him, she knew he'd help. But he was in Montana, of all places. She had no idea how far he was from Sweet Springs Ranch, but she knew several states lay between them. Rebecca. She could call Rebecca.

Sure enough, Rebecca picked up right away.

Hearing the grogginess in her voice, Lila said, "Shit. I forgot about the time difference."

"It's fine. It's fine." Which usually meant it wasn't fine. "Is everything okay?"

Lila huffed out her breath. "Not exactly."

She explained what had happened and heard Rebecca's quick intake of breath. "What are you doing? Hang up with me right now and call the police, Lila."

Chapter Twenty-Six

Travis told himself time and space away from Lila would allow him to clear his head. But the farther he got from Sweet Springs Ranch, from Prescott, from Arizona, the more he wanted to turn around and go back ... the more he wished he could return to the bunkhouse, sweep her up in his arms, and declare his undying love for her.

He was now a full day gone and halfway through Wyoming, country music blasting on his truck's speakers, and every song gave him a bones-deep ache for her. Only, declaring his undying love wasn't enough to convince her they were meant to be together.

Hadn't he declared his love only the day before she reminded him their time together was only temporary?

The thought put a bitter taste in the back of his throat just as another sappy song came on. Movements jerky, he changed his streaming station to hard rock and began head banging.

Mid-song, his phone rang, cutting off the music and halting his movements.

"Cash."

"Wow. You sound decidedly unhappy to hear from me."

Travis sighed. "Sorry, man. I was just rocking out. You interrupted a serious head-banging session."

"I can call back." His brother sounded unusually terse.

Travis softened his own tone. "No, it's fine. I'm sorry. What's up?"

"What's up is that I just ran into Lila on the property."

"Yeah? She does live there. At least, *temporarily*." He hated himself for sounding like such an asshole. She'd never promised to stay any longer than was necessary. In fact, he'd been the one to say she could continue working for the ranch—from home. From two-thirds of the way across the country.

Cash cleared his throat. "Listen, bro. Are you okay? I mean, we thought it was weird when you decided, last minute, to drive all the way up to Montana. Without Lila. Since you've been spending every spare moment together. We thought it was even weirder that you asked us not to tell her where you were going. Which, by the way, I told her." Before Travis could respond, Cash plowed on. "I had to, man. She pinned me with those eyes and asked me where you were and I couldn't help but answer. It was like she hypnotized me or something."

He could tell Cash was trying to be funny, but an irrational fear that Cash would seduce Lila took hold of him and wrapped its bony fingers around his throat. "Why are you calling, Cash?"

Silence.

"You know what, you dick? I was calling to check on you, make sure you're okay, let you know I told Lila where you're going so you'd have a heads up. But now it seems like I'm under fire, too, for no damn reason. So you can drive your happy ass to Montana, buy some more damn cattle, and come back, and none of it is going to make you feel any better. And I don't even care."

He disconnected and quite unexpectedly, Travis felt his lips twitching. It was probably a combination of Cash's "I don't care," and Travis's borderline hysteria.

Cash answered right away when Travis called him back. He didn't say anything, forcing Travis to speak. "I'm sorry."

"Apology accepted. What happened?"

Travis *could* play dumb, pretend he didn't know what Cash was really asking. But he couldn't keep it to himself any longer. The situation was eating him alive and he knew he needed perspective.

"I know how stupid it's going to sound when I say it out loud."

Cash's laugh, more of a hoot than anything else, came through the earpiece. "Since when has that ever stopped any of us?"

While he took a moment to compose his thoughts, Travis admired the grassy fields around him, and the mountains off in the distance. This part of the country was so different from Arizona. Alabama was probably different still. And Lila lived in the city. Travis could never live in a cement jungle, but surely her home state had some country spots... not that she'd asked him to move out east.

"You still there?"

"Yeah, man. Sorry. What happened is Lila was getting ready to film some new videos for her social media. You know she's like a famous fitness influencer, right?"

"I heard, yeah."

"Well, we were having breakfast and she told me not to worry, that she knows she came here for the paperwork."

Travis waited for Cash's reaction, indignation, anger, spluttering. But none of that came. "I'm hearing crickets."

"Wait. That was it?"

"Yeah, that was it! She said she came for the paperwork."

"Yeah." Cash drew out the word. "But didn't she?"

It was Travis who started spluttering then. "Yeah. She did. Well, I mean, she *did*. But then we, you know."

"You *what*?"

Travis growled. He could picture his brother, his eyes twinkling with mischief.

"We were together."

"*Together* together?"

Now Cash was just egging him on. He sucked in a breath, held it, exhaled through his teeth. "Yes. If you must know, we were *together* together. I told her I loved her, for God's sake."

Silence. Then a long, low whistle. "Man. So when she said she was just here for the paperwork, you felt rejected. You'd just declared your love for her and she reminded you she's here to work and she's leaving when she's done."

There was something soothing about hearing his feelings summarized so succinctly. His body relaxed and he leaned forward and draped his arms over the steering wheel to stretch his back. "Exactly."

"I mean, couldn't you just say that to her?"

How could Travis possibly explain that he couldn't? That fear paralyzed him, because he just knew that no matter what he said, she would end up going back to Alabama, and he would end up losing the only woman he'd ever loved?

"I don't know, bro. I don't think I can."

"Let me ask you this."

A giant bison stepped out of the trees at the edge of the road, startling Travis and causing him to slam on the brakes and curse.

"Are you afraid of what I'm going to say?"

"No! A damn bison just stepped onto the shoulder. I thought I was going to hit it. Proceed."

If Lila were here, she'd be talking about what a bison represented or symbolized. Travis realized he'd missed what Cash said. "What?"

"You didn't hit the bison, did you? Those things travel in herds."

"No. It froze when it saw me. But I missed your question making sure to avoid it."

"What would it take to make you feel better?"

"What do you mean?" He glanced in his rearview mirror and could swear the bison was watching him drive away.

"I mean, what would have to happen? What would she have to say or do to make you feel better about your situation?"

"There's nothing." Travis scoffed and hated the way that sounded.

"Nothing?"

"Okay, fine. I'll play. Ideally? She'd have to say she wants to be with me. And that she's willing to move to Arizona."

Imagining Lila saying those words gave Travis a rush unlike anything he'd ever experienced. But the rational side of his brain shut down his fantasy. She'd never say that. She loved her hometown and hadn't she made it perfectly clear she planned to go back?

"Have you guys talked about that?"

Hell, no.

"No, we haven't. I mean, it's been, like, a few weeks. Nobody can have that kind of conversation after only a few weeks."

"Can't they?"

"Oh, listen to you. The expert on all things romance."

"Hey, man. I'm just trying to help. You getting prickly should serve as a sign your emotions are all twisted up."

Huh. When had Cash gotten so mature? The GPS on his phone started talking into his ear, giving him instructions about taking a different highway.

"I'd better go. I've got to make an exit and I don't want to end up in Timbuktu."

"Fine, man. But will you just think about what I said?"

"Sure."

"You're an ass."

"No, I mean it! I will. I appreciate your advice, bro."

They hung up and Travis turned up his music, then switched it back to country and let himself fantasize about having that conversation with Lila. What if he asked her to stay? What if she said she would?

And ... what if she left?

The thought of having her and then losing her was almost more than he could bear, and that's why the conversation would never happen beyond the fantasy he allowed himself right now.

He could hear Cash's voice: "If you don't ask her, you'll never know." Was regret worse than the pain of rejection?

That night when he got to his motel room, he showered and then sat on the bed and turned on the TV. While the evening news played, he opened the Internet browser on his phone and typed in, *What does a bison symbolize?*

The first search result made his breath catch. *The bison symbolizes strength and resilience.* The answer was obvious, wasn't it?

He knew what he had to do when he got back to Prescott, to Sweet Springs, to Lila. But first, he had an auction to attend.

Chapter Twenty-Seven

Lila didn't call the police. She already knew they couldn't do anything.

While curled into the smallest possible amount of space in the very corner of her bed after receiving the latest picture, she ran through what Huntsville Police Officer Mauricio Gomez told her the first night they met: sending her a photo of herself definitely crossed the line into the creep zone, but wasn't actually a crime.

Teeth chattering thanks to her fear, she attempted to calm herself with some deep breathing and rational thought. For a second, she considered lighting a candle to calm herself—lavender, maybe—but she couldn't quite bring herself to move from her spot on the bed.

She probably *should* report the message, so she had a paper trail ... but obviously a paper trail wasn't going to keep her safe. She was the only person who could do that.

Her mind flashed an image of Travis. She'd trusted him, felt safe with him ... but he left. He hadn't even bothered to *try*. A flicker of anger snapped to life in her core, but she tamped it down. He hadn't known this would happen. And anger wouldn't help now. Besides, didn't everyone know anger was a secondary emotion? She was *hurt*.

Hurt that he'd been mad enough to leave, but not mature enough to talk to her about what was bothering him.

How many times would she wish she could take back the words she'd said about coming to Prescott for the paperwork? Countless times. And each time, she kicked herself for being so thoughtless.

Her deep breaths finally calming her, she vowed to do what she needed to do—to prove to herself that she wouldn't let anyone bully her, especially as an adult who had an important message to share with the world.

A plan began to form in her mind and as she considered each step, her body began to relax. Calm settled over her. She knew what she had to to.

First, she would put everything in order at Sweet Springs, without letting on that she was afraid. She didn't want to pull the Wilder brothers, Callie, or June into her mess.

Then, she would tidy up the bunkhouse so it looked like she'd never been there.

Then, she would write Travis a letter.

If she holed up inside the bunkhouse, everyone would probably think she was hiding because she and Travis weren't getting along. They'd assume she was embarrassed that he'd taken off and kept his destination a secret.

Determination took hold, almost replacing the fear. Figuring she wasn't going to sleep anyway, she slid off the bed and retrieved her computer, then returned to her bedroom, tiptoeing and checking the entrances all the way.

For the next two full days, she did exactly as she planned and stayed inside the bunkhouse. Callie and June texted a couple of times, inviting her to eat with them and checking to make sure she was okay. Although their messages filled her with gratitude, she couldn't leave the safety of her little cocoon. She missed seeing the leaves flutter through the windows, hearing the birds chirp outside, and feeling the fall sun on her skin. But for her own safety, she'd forego all that and remain indoors until the last possible moment.

Despite her intense focus on preparing for her next steps, she ached for Travis. During meals, tasks, and activities, she noticed his absence as if she were missing part of herself.

Living alone had never fazed her in all the years she'd done it. But now, the loneliness was almost paralyzing. If she wasn't working toward an ultimate goal, she probably would have climbed into bed and stayed there until he returned.

Cash said he'd gone to Montana for an auction, and Lila couldn't help but picture him driving, rocking out to country music, his windows rolled down. Remembering how proud he'd looked when he brought home that first group of bulls, she imagined him perusing the cattle at this new auction, wondered if he was still looking for the ugliest stock he could find. Her lips quirked, quite involuntarily, at that thought. Although she'd developed deeply affectionate feelings for that first batch of ugly bulls, they weren't nice to look at.

None of that mattered, because she wouldn't be at Sweet Springs to watch Travis's story unfold.

Rebecca had been texting her constantly: *Did you call the police? Have the police come by? Have you heard anything? Has the creep sent you any more texts?*

Lila kept her responses short: *No, not yet, no, and no.*

Apparently those answers weren't enough for Rebecca, who called her the second evening as Lila was folding towels. She was tempted to let the call go to voicemail. She didn't want to let on that she was going to go rogue (at least, according to Rebecca's standards). But she knew that if she didn't answer, Rebecca would keep calling—and maybe even come all the way to Prescott.

"Hey."

"Are you okay?"

The worry in Rebecca's voice made Lila feel like she should be even more afraid than she was. She folded faster, making sure the corners matched up and the final products were neat and tight. Breathing deep, she said, "Yes. I'm fine."

"Why haven't you called the police?"

"You know they can't do anything, Beck. This creepy stalker guy hasn't broken any actual laws. But don't worry. I have a plan."

Phone wedged between her ear and her shoulder, she hefted a pile of towels and headed for the linen closet.

"What are you planning, Lila?"

"Nothing. I've got to keep it under wraps."

"You sound crazy."

She sighed, stuffed the towels into the closet, and returned to the couch where she'd placed the laundry hamper full of sheets. "I'm not. I promise."

"Do I need to come out there?"

"No!" She rushed to soften her tone as she shook out a flat sheet and started folding it. "No, but thank you. I appreciate the offer. I'm fine. And I'll be home before you know it. We can go for drinks at Sparky's the second I get back."

Rebecca's sigh came through the earpiece and Lila could picture her expression, exasperated and—hopefully—a little amused.

"Fine. But if you don't improve the quality of your text messages going forward, you're going to force my hand and I'm going to come out there and see what's really going on, before you get yourself into serious trouble with this crazy plan of yours."

"Who said it was crazy?"

"Well, no one said it wasn't."

Chapter Twenty-Eight

Someone who didn't know Travis would think he made it through the entire two and a half days without thinking about her. Sure, he put on a good show. He drove the fifteen hours up to Montana with the music blasting and—except for the time he'd spent talking to Cash on the phone—he'd probably appeared perfectly happy dancing to his favorite tunes.

He'd checked into his motel, enjoyed an overcooked steak dinner at the small town's nicest dining establishment, and lay in bed all night, absolutely still.

But Travis knew himself ... and he knew he was completely miserable. Every song reminded him of how he'd walked out on Lila. Sitting alone in the booth at the diner reminded him that he'd eaten almost every meal with Lila for the past several weeks. And laying in bed—awake—reminded him that she wasn't there next to him.

He wished with fervor that he could punch himself right in the nose. He imagined it about a million times.

The auction went well. Yes, maybe he'd chugged a few beers in the half-hour leading up to the first bull on the block. And yes, maybe he'd bid recklessly thanks to that. But dammit if he hadn't enjoyed himself and almost forgotten to think about Lila.

There was the moment when he almost saved her a seat, as

accustomed as he'd come to having her by his side. There was the moment when he won his first bull—an uglier than ugly blue guy, Bluebonnet, with horns as wide as a Volkswagen—and looked over at Lila to gauge her reaction, only to remember he was sitting next to a stranger who gave him a thumbs up and a grin, as if to say, "Whatever you think is great, man, is great. Good for you." There was another moment, when came time to go, that he offered her his arm and she didn't take it.

He cursed himself for reacting to her comment like he had. But he also couldn't shake the idea that no matter how oversensitive he'd been, she was *leaving*. His sensitivity didn't matter if the end result was the same. He headed to his truck fifteen thousand dollars more broke and three bulls richer ... and still alone.

Although he hadn't planned on it, he decided he'd stay one more night in Montana. He couldn't bear to face Lila or his brothers or June or Callie just yet. He knew he'd acted like a fool and yet his feelings hadn't changed.

Lila might not be with him in Montana, but he could find company in a six-pack of beer, and that's exactly what he did.

So when his phone rang at six a.m. the following day, he woke to a pounding headache, a dry mouth, and a certain kind of self-hatred resulting from overdoing it the night before.

"Sterling."

"You sound like hell, bro."

"What's up?" He certainly wasn't going to admit he'd been drinking half the night.

"Lila's gone."

That woke him up. A jolt of energy zapped every nerve ending in his body. He sat bolt straight and scrubbed a hand over his face to make himself feel more alert. "What do you mean?"

"She's gone, man. We woke up this morning and noticed her car wasn't there. Thought it was a bit early for that, so we went over to the bunkhouse and knocked. She didn't answer—obviously, but we thought it would be weird to bust in. So we got the emergency key and went inside and it's all cleared out."

Travis's stomach swirled dangerously. His throat worked. He might throw up. "All cleared out?"

"Yeah. Spotless. Like she was never there."

He couldn't breathe.

"Trav?"

"I'm here." The sheet felt scratchy against his skin as he tossed it off his legs. He stood up. "I'm on my way. Thanks for letting me know."

"Sure. But, Trav?"

"Yeah?"

"I mean, I hate to say it, but I wouldn't rush back. She's not here. And we have no idea where she is."

Travis nodded, even though Sterling couldn't see him. He couldn't speak around the lump in his throat. He headed for the bathroom, his head throbbing with every beat of his heart.

"You there?"

"Yeah. I'll head home anyway. I don't know what else to do."

"Okay, bro. Drive carefully. And there's one other thing I feel like you should know."

He didn't know if he could handle one other thing, but he said, "Okay, shoot."

"Lila found something in one of the boxes. She left it for us."

Puzzled, Travis braced himself. "And?"

"It's a bunch of letters from Mom."

The world tilted dangerously. "Letters?"

"They're all sealed still. Seems like Dad received them but never told us. There are some addressed to Dad, but most of them are for the four of us."

He couldn't say why this news pushed the threat of tears even closer, but it did. He had to hang up. Voice gruff, he said, "Okay. Thank you for the heads up. I've got to pee like you wouldn't believe. I'm heading straight home after that."

Because he could still taste the beer on his breath, he decided he'd better shower, brush his teeth, and use mouthwash before he left the motel room. Those things done, he got a scalding coffee from the motel lobby, then made a few calls and arranged for the delivery of his three new, ugly bulls. Finally, to soak up the alcohol that still sloshed around in his stomach, he drove through the first fast food place he saw and grabbed a breakfast sandwich.

Then he hit the road. And although Lila had occupied most of his mental space for the past two and a half days, he found she dropped away and his mom replaced her. She'd written them letters? Why hadn't their dad ever told them? If she'd written, why hadn't she called or come back?

A fresh round of emotions swirling around in his veins, he turned up his music to drown out his own thoughts. Part of him—a part born when he was just a little boy—begged him to wait to judge her until he read what she had to say.

The speedometer reached ninety and he set the cruise control.

Chapter Twenty-Nine

Lila recognized her own recklessness, but she wasn't going to let it stop her. She cleared the bunkhouse of all her safety measures: the crystals, the salt barrier, and the lucky bamboo plant.

For the first time in three days, she walked out of the bunkhouse. She wasn't afraid. Head high, she carried her suitcase to the car and put it in the trunk.

"And that's it."

She almost couldn't believe that when so much had shifted inside her over the past few weeks, she was leaving with the same belongings she'd brought. It somehow seemed like her car should be packed full. That thought made her eyes prickle with tears, and the image before her shimmered. She was going to miss the sweet little bunkhouse, which she'd come to think of as home in such a short time.

The birds chirped happily in the trees, the sun warmed her skin, and the cattle grazed in the pasture, tails flicking and ears twitching. She was going to miss the whole ranch.

And most of all, she was going to miss Travis. Would things be different if he hadn't left? Maybe ... for a short time. But who knew which carelessly chosen words would send him running in the future?

Tears were streaming down her face by the time she got into the car. Eyes on the rearview mirror, she drove down the driveway of the Sweet Springs Ranch. Her throat was tight and she swore she could feel her heart breaking.

She wished she could call Rebecca, share her sorrow with a friend. But she couldn't—if she told Rebecca why she was leaving and what she was doing, her friend would try to stop her. Or worse, come to Arizona.

With one last glance at Sweet Springs Ranch, Lila pulled onto the main road and headed toward downtown Prescott. Hoping for good luck, she'd chosen the hotel where Sterling and June stayed when they both came to town over the summer. Conscious of her confidence as she parked and walked into the lobby, she held her head high and kept her shoulders back. If her stalker was watching, he'd know she wasn't afraid of him. And if he wasn't, *she* knew she was projecting that she wasn't afraid of anyone.

The room was cozy and cute, with a view of the courthouse plaza. Just a few weeks before, Lila would have snugged the curtains closed and refused to stand near the window. But today she threw them open and spent a few minutes watching the buzz of activity down on the grassy plaza. Some kind of fair was going on, and shade tents lined the grass along the wide sidewalk. People strolled along, sipping fresh lemonade from the lemonade stand, eating ice cream, and carrying purchases in trendy paper gift bags.

It was only natural, because of what she was about to do, that her thoughts drifted to her childhood, to Dane Jackson, who'd bullied her so ruthlessly. One morning when she'd opened her locker before first period, about a hundred wrapped Twinkies fell out. It was a waterfall of Twinkies, a deluge of baked goods.

Of course, because *everyone* was in the hallway, waiting for the bell to ring, *everyone* saw what happened. Lila's face burned as she scrambled to pick up the Twinkies.

"Oh, my God." Rebecca rushed to her rescue, kneeling down to help. "Dane is such an asshole."

Because she couldn't speak, Lila simply nodded, pressing her lips together.

"I'm so sorry, Lila. We're going to have to figure out a way to get him back."

She nodded again.

Rebecca dragged a trash can over, and they finally managed to gather up the dozens and dozens of packages and dump them in.

"Are you okay?" Rebecca threw her arms around Lila before she could respond. "We're going to get revenge. I promise."

Lila just nodded into Rebecca's neck, squeezing her back.

They never did get revenge. Dane walked the halls throughout the rest of their high school career, stalking through the campus with his hunched shoulders and prominent brow and permanent scowl.

But maybe *this* was Lila's time for revenge. She brought herself back to the present moment and watched the people milling around below. Maybe her confidence, her growth, her happiness and success were revenge in and of themselves.

But could she be happy, without Travis?

A heavy sigh escaped of its own accord. Of course she could ... eventually. Did she want to? No. Another round of tears filled her eyes. She didn't want to. But the fact that he'd left so easily proved she was worthless and unlovable, just as Dane had always implied.

Didn't it? She didn't know what to believe, but she knew that she felt lost, despondent, brokenhearted without him.

Wouldn't a strong woman believe she didn't need a man?

But Lila didn't need Travis. She wanted him.

Forcing herself to clear her mind, she put those thoughts in a box, locked it, and shoved it to the back of her mental space. She'd think about Travis later.

Right now, she had a plan to put into motion. All the pieces were in place. Fear gripped her then, but she reminded herself that courage meant moving forward even in the face of fear. Could she really do it? Could she tempt fate, rely on herself and her strength, and take control of the situation that had scared her into hiding?

She nodded at her reflection in the window, envisioning the young, insecure version of herself. "You can do it, Lila."

Whatever happened next, she knew her past self would thank her for standing up to a bully.

And then she was doing it. She pulled her phone out of her pocket, opened her social media app, and clicked on her inbox. She opened the text string from the anonymous stalker and felt her heart pick up speed when she saw that picture of herself at the hardware store.

The message shone up at her: *Nice to see you again.*

Fingers shaking, she typed back: *Nice to hear from you again. I'd love to meet in person. How about tomorrow?*

Chapter Thirty

Sterling told Travis not to rush home, but he couldn't help it. He was compelled. Was it because he felt like home was the place to start tracking down Lila? Or because his mom's letters waited for him? Either way, he knew he had to get there as soon as he could.

So he made the fifteen-hour drive in thirteen, fueling himself with caffeine and misery. By the time he finally arrived back at the ranch, it was after midnight. Someone (probably June or Callie) had thought to turn on his porch lights, and he blamed exhaustion when that made his throat constrict. He'd assumed he'd fall into bed and deal with his brothers in the morning, but it seemed they were waiting for him. As soon as he turned off his truck, they came out of the shadows and met him at the front door. Again, his throat tightened (or maybe it had simply remained that way after he saw the porch lights).

Hayes wrapped him in a long hug, and then Cash and Sterling did the same. He tried, halfheartedly, to come up with a wisecrack about the greeting, but he was way too tired.

Inside the house, someone grabbed beers from the fridge and Sterling produced a packet of envelopes, a rubber band around the middle.

His heart stuttered when he saw the familiar handwriting. He remembered all the school papers his mom had signed, all the notes she'd written to his teachers, the cards she'd signed on holidays. He could picture the exact shape of her fingernails and her knuckles, and he could see the scar on the back of her left hand from the time she'd caught it on a barbed-wire fence.

He licked his lips. "Have you guys read yours?"

"We were waiting for you." Cash pulled his own bundle out of his back pocket and dropped it on the counter.

The others did the same and Travis looked at each of them in turn before tossing his down, too.

"So Dad had these all along?"

"Must have." Sterling shrugged, his eyes going icy.

Hayes nodded. "They were in a box, along with all the other ranch paperwork."

"All the ranch paperwork he neglected for years," Sterling said. "Running this place into the ground."

"I guess he was neglecting us for all those years, too." Cash's voice sounded scratchy and Travis had the urge to wrap an arm around his brother and comfort him.

"And probably Mom," Travis said. "Although he'd probably argue she deserved it."

"Who's gonna read the letters she wrote to Dad?" Cash wanted to know.

Sterling shook his head. "I'm sure as hell not. I almost feel like we should burn those. Whatever's in them was between Mom and Dad."

"You guys are going to kill me for this. But I'm in no state to read these letters tonight. I've been driving for thirteen hours and I can barely keep my eyes open."

"We figured." Hayes picked up all four bundles and stacked them together, then set them back on the counter. "We're actually here for moral support due to the Lila situation. We were worried about how you were going to be when you showed up here, after hearing she's gone."

The reminder of Lila's absence hit Travis like a punch to the jaw. He hadn't forgotten, but the letters had served as a decent distraction. He swore, rubbed his forehead, and started to drain his beer before his stomach lurched, reminding him he'd had too much the night before.

"Do you want to try to find her?" Arms crossed, Cash hitched a hip onto the kitchen counter.

He did, with an urgency that made his chest ache. "Yes. But it feels impossible. I've been texting her ever since I left Ennis this morning, and she hasn't responded. I have no idea where she'd go, other than all the way back to Alabama."

"Do we need to take a road trip?" Cash grinned, and Sterling elbowed him. "Not if you think you're riding shotgun."

Travis could cry. "Maybe we do. But I'm going to have to sleep, first. I've been awake since this guy woke me up at six a.m." He elbowed Sterling, who looked around at them all as if to say, *What else was I supposed to do?*

They all drained their beers, and Hayes suggested they reconvene in the morning.

Travis managed to remove his boots before he fell into bed in his jeans and flannel shirt. It wasn't any wonder he dreamed of Lila, the images flickering in his subconscious, a parade of reminders of how much fun they'd had together, how much her presence changed his life, how much he loved her. How he couldn't live without her. There they were, laughing in the kitchen when he forgot he'd left the coffeepot filling under the spigot because he got carried away kissing her and it overfilled, running off the counter onto the floor. Another image shimmered to life: the two of them sitting on the floor in front of the fire, playing cards, the heat of competition in her eyes just as hot as the flames in the fireplace. Then his mind started playing tricks on him, showing him scenes that hadn't even occurred yet. Scenes that would have scared the shit out of him before he'd met Lila. In the golden light just before the sunset at Sweet Springs, he knelt on one knee and offered up a sparkling ring, asking her to commit to him for life, to stay with him, to be his partner forever.

One spring day, he waited at the altar while she walked down the aisle toward him, their gazes locked. They stood facing each other, vowing to love each other forever.

This is forever.

He woke up bitterly disappointed, feeling like his brain had played a cruel trick on him.

Chapter Thirty-One

Lila didn't question the wisdom of her plan until she received a message back from her admirer.

I'm just a few blocks away from where you are. I'd love to meet up.

The words made her blood run cold and she almost considered pulling out of the whole thing.

"You can't. You can't let him win."

This guy knew where she was and he was nearby. Until now, she'd had full confidence in her plan. But hearing back from him so quickly—like he was waiting, and somehow knew what she was going to do—made her question herself. What if the situation didn't go like she anticipated it would? What if he acted faster than she did?

Although he'd never hinted at wanting to hurt her, the way he'd behaved all along screamed crazy. Bonkers. Deranged. He could be capable of anything.

Her armpits prickled with sweat and her breath quickened. She could write, *Never mind. I'm not coming.* Just giving herself that option calmed her. She could, but she wouldn't.

Thumbs shaking, she typed, *Great!* She replaced the exclamation point with a period and went on, *How about the fountain on the courthouse plaza tomorrow?*

Her anonymous follower responded with a thumbs up and then a grinning smiley face emoji, and Lila's stomach roiled ... all night long.

The next morning, she dressed and spent a full ten minutes with her eyes closed, focusing on deep breathing and visualizing a successful outcome.

With five minutes remaining before the planned meet-up time, she gathered her things and walked out of her hotel room. The finality of the door clicking closed sent another shiver over her skin.

The hotel carpet felt thick under her feet as she walked to the elevator, which stood open as if to expedite this terrifying thing she was about to do. She'd chosen a public place because she felt safer surrounded by all those people enjoying the warm fall day.

The elevator doors slid shut and she pressed the button for the lobby.

Was being in public, surrounded by others, actually safe? It was impossible not to think of those darkest days of junior high. Her schoolmates were all around. They saw and heard what happened and no one stepped in to help her. She couldn't really blame them for not standing up to Dane. Weren't kids that age notoriously afraid of standing out? And didn't every pre-teen know that if you stood up to a bully, you became his next target?

The elevator's crawling descent was painful.

When the bell dinged to let her know she'd reached the first floor, she felt like she might pass out. But by the time the doors opened, she'd squared her shoulders and lifted her chin, and she hoped she conveyed confidence as she emerged from the hotel lobby and onto the sidewalk.

Because her senses were on high alert, all the colors and sounds and smells overwhelmed her. But she forced herself to put one foot in front of the other, to keep moving forward. Her eyes focused on the fountain from the second she could see it. A few kids stood at its edge, looking into the water. One of them said something to the woman with them, who Lila assumed was their mom, and she nodded and pulled her wallet out of her purse. She handed out coins and the kids tossed them in, leaning over to watch them fall.

The closer she moved, the heavier her legs became. She didn't dare look around; she forced herself to focus on the area around the fountain.

Before she knew it, she was standing across from the coin-throwing kids. If she turned just a tiny bit, she could sit on the edge of the fountain and dip her fingers into the cool water. A breeze swirled in, blowing the water from its cascade and sending sprays over Lila's skin. Goosebumps rose and she shivered again.

"Hi, Lila."

Despite the fact that she'd been expecting him, despite the fact that his voice was as light as cotton candy, she jumped, then turned around to face him. He was handsome in the traditional sense—he had a strong jawline and a tiny spot in his cheek where she imagined a dimple would flash. He put a hand on her arm as if his touch could calm her. "It's okay."

She didn't recognize him until she looked into his eyes. They weren't cold or lifeless like she would have imagined. They actually looked friendly. Which terrified her even more.

"You're PRSteve." She'd seen his accounts all over the online fitness space.

Sure enough, a dimple appeared when he smiled. He nodded and his hand remained on her arm. "I knew you'd recognize me."

"It's nice to meet you." She swallowed, hoping he wouldn't recognize the lie.

"Can I hug you?"

Again, she had to force herself to keep still, to avoid looking around. Doing her best to act nonchalant, she shrugged. "Sure."

He lifted his arms, revealing sweat stains underneath. So he was nervous, too. That was strange. Then his arms were around her and her body felt rigid and uncompromising as he melted against her. He smelled like cigarette smoke and the kind of cheap cologne a person would buy at a big box department store. It was everything she could do to prevent herself from crying or throwing up.

"Aren't you going to hug me back?"

A sob rose up from her core, into her chest, her throat. She stifled it, gulped, nodded. And wrapped her arms around his shoulders as if he were a friend. He exhaled and she counted to ten before releasing him. When he stepped back, he held onto her hands and looked into her eyes.

Smile. She obeyed herself, stretching her lips over her teeth in what was undoubtedly a grimace.

"I've been dreaming of this moment, Lila."

Her name coming out of his mouth invoked a bone-deep fear. She stretched her smile even wider.

"Me, too."

"Don't lie." His eyes went cold, then, and she knew he was a sociopath.

She licked her lips. "I'm not. I'm—nervous. I've never met one of my followers in person—"

"Wouldn't you say we're friends, Lila?"

Chapter Thirty-Two

Travis woke up the next morning to the sound of birds chirping, their cheerful tunes in direct contrast to his mood. The wood floor felt cold against the soles of his feet. In the kitchen, he grunted at the stack of envelopes they'd all left on the counter the night before.

Only then did he check the time and realize it was early—only five a.m.—and the others weren't coming over until eight.

Which gave him three hours to torture himself over the shit decisions he'd made when it came to Lila. Back in his bedroom, he tried texting her again, then crawled back in bed and closed his eyes.

He woke two hours later with only an infinitesimal improvement in his attitude.

In what had become his new normal, he would have sought Lila's warmth while the coffee brewed. But as it was, he was alone and chose instead to wander the house.

She may have cleaned out the bunkhouse, but she'd left traces here, at his house. One of her sweaters, the light green one that made her eyes look like actual emeralds, was draped over the back of a dining room chair. The slippers he'd bought her to wear at his place stood next to the couch. Sometimes her feet overheated while they sat there in the evenings. Her water glass, still half-full (he chuckled when he realized he was probably in the place where he should consider it half-empty), sat on the end table.

He picked it up, ran a thumb over the mark her lipgloss had left, and then carried it to the kitchen and hurled it into the sink, where it shattered into a million sparkling pieces. Adrenaline spiking his blood, he stalked to the front door, pulled it open with way too much force, and continued over to the bunkhouse. He flung that door open. The fact that it wasn't held shut by several deadbolts drained all his anger as if someone had pulled stoppers out of the bottoms of his feet.

Finally, the tears started to fall, hot against his face, cool when they plopped onto his forearms. God, he missed her. How could he have been so stupid?

Fueled by a desperate need to make things right, to get her back, to keep her, forever, he rushed over to her workstation.

He had to figure out where she'd gone.

He had to find her.

He had to get her back.

At first, he didn't see anything remotely helpful. The boxes and boxes of documents were organized and labeled and color coded. He pulled a file folder out of one box and touched the label that contained her handwriting. Then he replaced it, on the move to search for something else; a clue that would lead him to her.

Nothing.

He couldn't believe she'd so cleanly scrubbed her own existence from this place—aside from the perfectly systemized paperwork.

Then he spotted something out of place: an envelope, with his name written on the front in her small, tidy handwriting.

She, too, had left him a letter? A groan escaped; he couldn't handle a letter from her unless it was accompanied by her actual presence.

Still, the envelope shaking in his hands, he used his thumb to break the seal and pulled out two sheets of paper. To his colossal disappointment, he could tell right away that the words on the page related to Sweet Springs Ranch—and not to him.

This was no love letter in which Lila proclaimed her undying feelings for him.

But what was it?

As he started to read, his eyes prickled anew with tears. It was a spreadsheet entitled, *Sweet Springs Ranch Business Plan*.

Beneath that title, she'd written a comprehensive list of money-making ideas and estimates for just how much each idea could bring in. They'd discussed some of them; the dude ranch, breeding cattle, leasing land for grazing. Others were new to him: tours, trail rides, barn dances. She'd included the sources where she'd found the information, and on a second page, she'd typed out various scenarios and estimates of how much the ranch could make in different scenarios.

He couldn't believe it: even though he'd run off and acted like a fool, she'd spent tons of time creating this spreadsheet.

"You're a damn idiot, Travis Wilder."

"I feel like arguing with you is the right thing to do here, but you know I agree with you through and through."

Travis whirled around at Callie's voice. "What are you doing here?"

"That's not a very nice greeting for your sister-in-law."

Pressing his lips together, he exhaled through what were surely flared nostrils. "Sorry. To what do I owe the pleasure?"

Her eyes had been twinkling with humor, but they went serious. "I think I know where Lila is."

His stomach leapt and he took a step forward. "Where?"

She held up a hand. "Throttle back. I should have said, 'I know where she'll be later today.'"

He shook his head. "Where?"

Suddenly, his tougher-than-nails-attorney sister-in-law looked pensive, nervous. Clasping her hands together in front of her, she looked at the floor. "You know how that guy was stalking her before she came here?"

Alarm bells were blaring and Travis could barely contain his preemptive rage. He clenched his fists. "Yes."

She looked at him then. "Well, she's going to meet him."

"What?" His blood boiled. "She's going to meet him? Is she crazy? Or stupid?"

Now Callie held up both hands. "Neither. She's determined to put an end to this, once and for all. She's tired of being bullied, tired of being scared, and ready to live her life without him in it."

"She said all that?"

"Not to me." Her gaze hit the floor then, and he realized she was sad Lila hadn't shared this with her.

"Who the hell did she say it to, then?"

"Officer Rowland."

His eyebrows shot upward. "Tommy Rowland?"

"None other."

"Tell me everything."

By the time Callie was done, Travis was on fire, literally unable to stand still. He had no idea how he'd wait until later that day to get back to Lila, but he had no other choice.

Chapter Thirty-Three

"Wouldn't you say we're friends, Lila?" His hands in hers had gone clammy.

Friends? She wouldn't say they were friends. Online acquaintances, maybe. "Definitely."

"How would you like to go out for drinks? Happy hour?"

Lila's gaze flicked to the right and to the left, and PRSteve's head followed, whipping in both directions, his eyes wide.

"Um, sure. But I'll do something non-alcoholic. Just because—you know..." She was saying too much.

"No, I don't know, actually. It's late afternoon. I think a drink would be acceptable."

Again, she licked her lips, nodding so fast, she could practically feel her eyeballs rattling around in her skull. "Yeah. Sure. Sounds great. Do you have a place in mind?"

"Of course I do." As if he were waiting for her to ask. He dropped her hands, but fear quickly replaced relief when he pulled a set of keys out of his pocket. "I'll drive."

Turning a quick one-eighty, he offered his elbow. She had no choice but to take it, tucking her hand into his elbow.

It felt so different from Travis's—more sinew and skin, less muscle. And PRSteve smelled different, too. Stress wafted off his body, pushing her gag reflex to the limit. Her mouth watered and her throat worked and she had to remind herself to relax, to walk like a human and not a jointed wooden puppet.

"Isn't this nice?" PRSteve looked down at her and she attempted another smile.

The same sunny sky, chirping birds, and shady trees that had warmed her heart in the days leading up to this moment seemed garish and creepy in this new light. "It is." She dreaded what she had to do next, but she knew it was necessary if she was going to get the results she wanted. "You know, I don't feel comfortable going in your car. It's just—we only just met."

He froze. "Lila, Lila, Lila. We didn't just meet. We've known each other for ages. Months, at least."

Her high-pitch laugh was perfectly maniacal and she wondered if he could tell. She gave his arm a playful swat and tugged him forward. "You know what I mean, silly. I mean, in person." She raised the volume of her voice. "Is there somewhere we could walk?"

He used his left hand to cover hers, which was still tucked into his right elbow. Cover wasn't exactly the right word; he trapped it. She couldn't get away if she wanted to. *Good.*

"I'd like to drive us somewhere. I know a really special spot."

This is all going according to plan. Lila repeated the mantra even as her heart hammered and the blood roared in her veins.

Again, she increased her volume. "I don't want to go in your car." She softened her tone. "I mean, if that's okay. I'd really prefer to walk somewhere."

"It's not okay, actually."

If she could see the knuckles on the hand that was gripping hers, she knew they'd be white. How was she supposed to respond?

"I'm a cautious person and don't want to get in the car with someone I've just met for the first time today."

"But we haven't met for the first time today, Lila." His tone was at once insistent, pleading, and slow, like he was talking to a toddler. "We've been friends for a while now. Seven months, three weeks, and four days. Which is why you should feel perfectly safe coming with me."

"It's not you."

"'It's not you, it's me'?" He smiled but his eyes remained cold.

She tried for another laugh. "Exactly! I just don't feel comfortable getting in the car with anyone, really."

Before her mind caught up with what was happening to her body, he was sweeping her away, his head tilted at a strange angle as he laughed an unnatural laugh, towing her along, forcing her to move her feet at an unnatural walking pace.

This scenario was exactly what she'd planned, exactly what she'd hoped for, but she felt out of control and scared and she wanted it to be over. Which meant she had to get him to get her to the car—while continuing to resist.

"But—" She couldn't quite string together a coherent sentence. "Can't we walk somewhere?"

"No, no, *no*, Lila! There's somewhere special I want to take you."

The soles of her feet were starting to smart from slapping against the sidewalk. And then they reached his car, a small black SUV parked along the sidewalk surrounding the courthouse plaza. He released his grip with his left hand, but somehow had managed to hold her hand in his elbow crook like a vise grip.

Using his free hand, he pulled out his keys and unlocked the car before yanking open the door and forcefully shoving her into the passenger seat. Before he shut the door, he leaned in so they were eye to eye and his lips were just an inch from hers. "I can't wait to enjoy happy hour with you. Buckle up."

He leaned in as if he planned on kissing her, but she pulled back and turned her head away from him. "I'll get you eventually."

Then he shut the door and clicked the lock button on his key fob. While he walked around the hood to get in the driver's seat, Lila glanced around outside the car. Still no sign. But they had to be nearby, didn't they?

PRSteve threw the car into reverse, did the quickest glance over his shoulder, and slammed on the gas. The tires squealed as the car backed up, and then again after he put it in gear and accelerated.

Chapter Thirty-Four

Travis's brothers had to literally hold him back from going after Lila when her stalker—puny little wart that he was—dragged her toward his car.

"You've got to let it happen, man," Sterling told him, his voice quiet but insistent.

"Tommy's a good cop." Hayes released his grip on Travis's upper arm. "This is all going to plan. Don't mess it up by running in there and being the hero."

Seething, Travis nodded. He clenched his molars so hard, he wouldn't be surprised if they cracked. Lila and that asshole had made it to his car, a small black SUV parked along the curb. The guy "helped" her into the passenger seat and paused to say something to her before shutting the door.

"He looks shifty as hell," Cash said. "Look how he keeps looking around, checking to see if anyone's watching."

And then the guy was in the car and Lila was trapped in there with him, and Travis was positive he'd never wanted to kill someone so much in his entire life.

"Pull away from the curb, bro," Sterling said, and Travis's rage took aim at him.

"What? Don't look at me like that. We want him to commit a crime, so the police can actually arrest him and throw his ass in jail."

Travis exhaled through his nose. "I know. You're right. There's just something about hearing my brother encourage a guy to kidnap my girl."

The black SUV backed away from the curb, stopped, and then headed south. Lila's posture was rigid. Travis could tell she was doing everything in her power to remain calm.

"Come on, Tommy." Cash drummed his fingers on his thigh.

"He has to wait for him to do something he can pull him over for," Hayes reminded them.

"There he is." Sterling lifted his chin. Sure enough, a police cruiser pulled out from one of the side streets and headed south behind the stalker's car. Within a few seconds, both vehicles were out of sight. This time, when Travis's body went into motion, heading south as well, his brothers didn't try to stop him. They fell into step beside him, and the four of them moved as one, all but running along the sidewalk in pursuit.

The single *whoop* of a siren sounded. Still in motion, Travis said, "Yes. There it is."

The police cruiser had stopped and its lights flashed. The SUV must've pulled over immediately. Tommy was still in his police car, probably running the stalker's license plate. The Wilder brothers stopped short, waiting. Finally, Tommy's door opened and he extended a lanky leg before pulling himself to standing. Although he didn't look their way, Travis was sure he knew they were there.

He walked up to the driver's window and said something to the stalker, who was prepared: he handed out what Travis assumed were his license and registration. Tommy looked them over and returned to the patrol car, where he spent several agonizing minutes.

Finally, he returned to the SUV and handed back the license and registration. Then he put his hands on the door, at the bottom of the window frame, and leaned down. He was talking to Lila.

His body language changed; he went from friendly and relaxed to alert. He must have asked the stalker to get out of the vehicle, because he stood back as if he was waiting for the door to open.

Only, it didn't. The brake lights came on, the reverse lights flashed on and then off, and the car lurched forward with a screech of its tires.

"Shit!" All four Wilder brothers swore, and Tommy Rowland ran back to his patrol car, his hand on the radio attached to his shirt collar.

"We've got to follow them." Travis was already running back across the plaza toward his truck, and for one no one argued with him. They were in the truck and whipping around the square within a minute.

It was easy to find the stalker's car. He'd continued straight and another couple of police cruisers joined in the chase and managed to sort of herd him into a dead end. This time, they hadn't left the choice up to the driver—Tommy and another cop were yanking him out of his seat when Travis flew up on the scene.

Without wasting another second, Travis threw his own truck into park and jumped down, running up to the car where Lila sat paralyzed in the passenger seat. He threw open the door and she startled, putting her hands up and leaning back to get as far away from him as possible ... until she realized it was him.

Then she threw herself forward and into his arms and she was crying or laughing, he couldn't tell. He was crying *and* laughing, and she was kissing his neck and whispering about how glad she was to see him and how stupid he'd been.

And then his mouth was on hers and he could taste her tears.

He finally managed to speak, between kisses. "Where have you *been?*" He kept his arms wrapped around her waist, and her upper arms rested on his shoulders.

"Where have *I* been? Where have *you* been?" Her eyes were fire, born in courage and grit and maybe anger. At him.

"I've been in Montana. But then I came back and you were gone."

"I had a thing to do."

"I guess so. And just for the record, that might have been the craziest thing I've ever heard of."

"I had to do it. I had to show him that he couldn't go around scaring people. That he couldn't go around scaring me."

"I get it. I hated it when I heard what you were up to, but I understand. And I'm proud of you for standing up to him."

"Thank you." Finally, she was smiling at him. As if they hadn't just spent the past three days apart. As if he hadn't run off when he overreacted to one thoughtless comment. As if he hadn't just been in danger of losing her forever. He smiled back, and then, without a care in the world about who was watching, brought his lips to hers again.

When she kissed him back, he knew he'd never walk away from her again—and he'd never let her go.

Chapter Thirty-Five

Back in her hotel room, Lila paced the floor while she talked to Rebecca on the phone.

"I'm so glad you're safe, but promise me you'll never do something like that again! Ever!"

Laughing—as much from relief as she was from being chastised in such a loving way—Lila promised she wouldn't. "But only if you promise you'll come visit Sweet Springs Ranch."

"I will. I'll do anything."

They hung up and Lila set her phone on the table. She turned to face Travis, who hadn't left her side and had insisted on accompanying her to the room to pack and then back to the ranch.

For about the hundredth time since he'd come running up to the car when the police arrested PRSteve, he opened his arms and she stepped into them. "I'm so sorry I left."

"I'm so sorry I wasn't more careful with my word choice."

"It's not your fault. I did a lot of soul searching while I was driving to Montana. I tried not to. I tried to drown out my inner voice with rock music, but it broke through."

She chuckled.

After a brief smile, he asked, "Have any of the others told you much about my mom?"

When Lila shook her head, Travis led her over to the room's small table and pulled out a chair for her. She sat and he retrieved bottles of water from the mini fridge. After handing her one, he sat down. "For the first ten years of my life, my mom was a wonderful mom. She cooked most of the meals, helped us with homework, listened to our stories, tucked us in at night, you name it. She loved us. I remember catching her watching us when we were playing, this smile on her face that said, 'I helped create those guys.' She came to all the school functions, taught us how to ride horses, comforted us when we were sick."

"Sounds lovely."

"It was. And then she left." His expression was so sad, so pained, that Lila reached out and took his hand.

"We had no idea why. Sterling was always stoic, and figured her reasons were adult and mysterious. Hayes took a harder approach and acted like he didn't care. And Cash was so little, he almost didn't seem to realize the weight of it. That leaves me. Her leaving hit me hard. I assumed something was wrong with us—with me."

Lila's throat tightened at that thought. She opened her mouth to object, to insist that nothing was wrong with him, but he held up a hand. "I know now that it wasn't us. I mean, I believe it wasn't. I have to, don't I? Something else was at play. But those feelings go deep. Those feelings of being unlovable."

"So when I said I'd come to Sweet Springs for the paperwork, I reinforced that little-boy fear."

He nodded and the tears brimming in his eyes made her heart ache. "I know it's stupid."

"It's not." She stood up and went to stand next to him.

He wrapped his arms around her and rested his head on her chest. "I should have told you."

"It sounds like you didn't even realize what was happening until you had some time to think. Even the least obvious comments or situations can trigger those deep, deep wounds and you don't even realize it's happening."

He nodded and his stubble scraped her chest. The intimacy of that contact made her cry. When he felt her tears landing in his hair, he pulled away from her and stood up so they were face to face. Taking her hands in his he said, "I'll never leave you again."

"You'd better not."

They kissed, and although she could taste tears—his or hers, she didn't know—she felt as though her joy would allow her to fly if she wanted to.

"Now that we've got my apology out of the way, tell me again why you made your crazy plan without telling me. Or my brothers. Or Callie and June, for God's sake."

Laughing now, because she couldn't believe the audacity of it herself, she returned to her seat, sat down, twisted the top off her water bottle, and drank. "Well, my reason was twofold. One—" she held up a finger—"I didn't want anyone to talk me out of it. That would have been easy to do, as terrified as I was, but I knew I had to do it."

"And two?"

"Two—" she held up a second finger—"I didn't want to put anyone else in danger. I was fairly confident I'd survive, since I created the plan with Tommy Rowland's help. But PRSteve—the creepy stalker—he was kind of a loose cannon, wasn't he? If he'd hurt anyone else, or put anyone else in danger, I couldn't have lived with myself."

"If he'd hurt you, I couldn't have lived with *myself*."

"Well then it's a good thing he didn't hurt anyone. For a minute though, I thought he was going to put me in danger when he tried to drive away from Tommy."

"Me, too. Remembering that moment makes me sick to my stomach."

"Then let's not remember it any more." She stood and held out her hand. "In fact, I propose that we create a brand-new memory, right here, right now. To take our minds off the experiences we just suffered through."

"Mmm." He slipped his hand into hers and stood up. "I like the sound of that."

Feeling every ounce of feminine power she'd earned over the

course of the past hour, she towed him to the bed, hips swaying, and then turned around to face him. She put her hands on her hips, turned him so his back was facing the bed, and gently pushed him down before climbing on top of him. "We'd better get started."

Chapter Thirty-Six

After spending two luxuriously sensual hours in Lila's hotel room, Travis asked her to come home with him. Not to the bunkhouse, but to his house. He wanted to ask her to stay —permanently—but thought it was only fair to wait until she had a clear head. So he settled on being present. Enjoying this one night, because wasn't that all they were guaranteed?

As high as he was riding on the emotion of their reunion, he'd allowed himself to leave his mom's letters in the back of his mind. When he and Lila walked inside and he saw them sitting on the counter, he swore.

"Oh, good. You found those letters. But also, you don't seem happy to see them."

He took a shaky breath. "It's not that I'm not happy to see them. I'm just nervous about what they might say."

She tucked her arm into his, which was becoming a routine and comforting gesture. "Who are they from?"

She had no idea. Of course she didn't. "My mom."

"Oh." She sank down onto one of the barstools. "I didn't realize. I should have. There were so many of them, mostly addressed to you boys. But her last name—"

Travis sat next to her and closed his eyes. "She never took my dad's name. She thought her maiden name had a better ring to it. For Hollywood."

Lila picked up the stack of letters. "These are all of them. I figured you would have given your brothers theirs."

"I did. We were going to read them together this morning, actually. But then we found out about your crazy plan, and no one mentioned it again."

She set down the bundle. "Are you dying to know what they say?"

He considered. Was he? He'd wanted to hear from her for so long. And now, after all this time, he had a chance. But what would her letters say? When he was a kid, angry at her, he imagined her writing beautiful travelogues, telling him how much fun she was having, wherever she was. But she wouldn't do that, right? He didn't know. After all, she'd left them, hadn't she?

"You *are* dying to know. But you're also scared." Her hand found his.

Once again amazed and perplexed by her ability to read his thoughts, he nodded.

"Do you think everyone still wants to read them together?"

Travis nodded. "I reckon."

"Then you know what I'm going to do? I'm going to get together with the girls, and leave you boys to it."

How he had gotten so lucky, he would never know. But after a handful of text messages and a few minutes, she and the girls had a date in June and Sterling's RV, and the guys had a date at Travis's.

Before she left, Lila kissed his mouth and gave his hand a squeeze. "Just so you know, no matter what's in those letters, I love you."

That made him want to cry again, and his brothers came through the door as he was fighting that urge. Relief had made them downright jovial after the police arrested Lila's stalker. But now, the nerve-racking task ahead of them, they came in subdued, greeted Travis with quick handshakes, and headed straight for the kitchen.

Sterling separated the letters and handed them out. "Some of them have clear postmarks, with dates. Others wore off. I was thinking about reading the oldest one first. What do you guys think?"

Cash shrugged. "I'm going to choose one at random."

Hayes chuckled. "Of course you are. I'm taking Sterling's tactic. I'm going to find the oldest one I can." He'd had already started rifling through his, looking at the postmarks.

"Then I'm going to choose the most recent." As Travis checked his postmarks, he felt a sense of reverie, knowing his mom had held these very envelopes in her hands, thought of him while writing the letters. He wondered what emotions she felt as she wrote out his name and address. "Here's the most recent." He held it up for his brothers to see. "Looks like she wrote it just before I turned sixteen."

Sterling held up one of his. "Here's the oldest. I was eight."

Hayes went next. "I was seven."

Grinning, Cash said, "I was thirteen. Do you think Mom had any idea I would hide in Old Man Hendrickson's apple tree and drop apples on his head when he walked by?"

They all snickered. Travis went to the fridge, pulled out four beers, and set them on the counter. Each Wilder brother picked one up, twisted off the cap, and took a swig.

"To Mom. For better or for worse." Travis held up his bottle and the others did the same. "To Mom."

Travis waited while his brothers opened their letters. Sterling used his knife to slice the seal neatly. Hayes held out his hand and Sterling flipped the knife around and put the handle in Hayes's palm. Cash tapped his envelope on the counter and tore open one end. They all looked at him. He used his thumb to open his, leaving the edges ragged.

Sterling smiled. "On your marks, get set, go."

His entire body vibrating with nerves, Travis unfolded the paper and let the familiarity of her handwriting wash over him.

* * *

Dear Travis,

My blue-eyed boy, I miss you so.

I'm sure by now you believe I've forgotten all about you. Your father promised me that if I wrote, he'd give you my letters, as long as I didn't try to contact you another way. But I have the feeling he didn't hold up his end of the bargain. If he had, at least one of you would have written back. Sterling's the most likely one, isn't he? I admit, I hoped all of you would write, but that hope has faded more and more with each day I check the mailbox and it contains nothing but bills and junk mail.

Years ago, your dad and I promised one another we wouldn't speak disparagingly of each other to you boys. But I can't stand the thought of you all believing that I left and never thought about you again.

I think about you every day. Every <u>hour</u> of every day.

* * *

Travis's eyes smarted with tears. She *had* thought of him. He'd always known that, but he'd started to doubt it. He kept his head down so his brothers wouldn't see him crying, and blinked, fast, to clear the liquid so he could keep reading.

* * *

And now you're going to be 16. I'm sure your brothers have taught you how to drive, haven't they? Which means you're probably a speed demon. I was a terrible driver when I first learned. Did I ever tell you that? I ran my daddy's pickup truck right into that big old oak tree in front of our house. That was just one time.

At this point, I know I won't get to see you again. I'm sick, Trav.

For all this time, I've dreamed of the day I'd come back to Sweet Springs Ranch. I'd waltz up the driveway, and your father would stand there with his mouth hanging open in disbelief that I'd defy his orders. That I would bow to his threats (and he did threaten me). He always ruled with an iron fist, didn't he?

But I'm not up to traveling anymore.

My biggest regret in life is waiting. Waiting for the "right time" to come back to you, to tell your father to buzz off and let me have my boys back.

I'll close with this advice to you: don't wait, son.

Do the things you want to do. Not just want to do, but need to do. When that quiet voice in the back of your mind breaks through all the other noise in this universe, listen to it.

I know my leaving and my continued absence have caused you and your brothers unspeakable pain. And I am so, so sorry for that. Only as I've gotten older have I finally achieved the courage I wish I'd had all those years ago. But it's wasted, because my body is failing me.

So I hope this one lesson will spare you even more pain; will give you the courage now to do what you need to do.

No regrets, right?

All my love,

Mom

* * *

Now the tears fell freely, running down his cheeks and plopping onto his thighs. She loved him. She loved him all along. She thought about him every hour of every day. No, she hadn't been brave enough to come back. But who knew what threats Levi Wilder had made? Travis had spent so long being angry at her. He could be angry at their dad, but hadn't he spent enough time on that when he found out the bastard had all but gambled away the ranch?

He looked up from the letter to see his brothers all sitting there stunned, tears in their eyes, too.

"Not what you expected?" Travis's voice was gravely.

The others shook their heads.

Cash spoke, and it came out in a whisper. "I'm so relieved. I didn't realize how much it meant to me that she cared about me."

"Same," Hayes and Sterling said.

"I realized," Travis said. "And it feels so good to read it in her words."

Cash stood up and held out his arms. "Bring it in, guys. Bring it in."

As they stood there, arms around each other in a big group hug, Travis knew: the time for anger had passed. Now, he would do what he needed to do.

Chapter Thirty-Seven

"So did the police say how that guy tracked you down?" Callie, having claimed the RV couch, stretched out her legs.

June nodded. "Yeah. I guess he had some sort of hacking software. He used it to get my IP address. So when I came to Arizona and went online with my laptop, he had a good starting point."

"What a jerk." June sat across from Lila at the RV dinette. "He *belongs* in jail. I'm so glad you were able to finally get him arrested."

"Me, too," Lila said. "Now I can get back to making my posts without worrying someone's going to kidnap me, tie me up, and throw me in the trunk of his car before taking me out to bury me in the desert."

Callie laughed. "And now you've got more backup than you ever imagined."

"It's a good feeling."

"Speaking of backup." Callie sat up and put her elbows on her knees, her glass dangling from her hands. "I can finally tell you more about that case I've been working on."

"Do tell," June said, rubbing her hands together. "This is going to be juicy."

"I wish it was juicy in a different way." Callie sighed and took a sip of her wine. "I have this friend, Opal. She grew up here, and we were in the same class from kindergarten to sixth grade. We had almost all our classes together in junior high and high school. We were on the rodeo team together and everything." She made a dismissive gesture. "I digress. Long story short, she's getting divorced —and it's a doozy. I never liked the guy she married. Boone." She sneered. "I chalked it up to my cynicism and protectiveness. A few years ago, he convinced her to move across the country with him. Now it appears he's been planning this divorce for a while and he's taking her for everything she's got."

"So that's why you've been so stressed." June said.

Callie nodded. "Yep. This guy moved a bunch of his assets before asking for a divorce. And in the state where they lived, he's not obligated to give her any of it." She shook her head. "That's probably why he moved there in the first place. I'm sure this was his plan all along. And they were *so in love.*" She scowled.

June scowled, too. "I take it you can talk about the case because the divorce is final?"

"Yes. Although he managed to take almost everything, I was able to get her enough to buy a new place, cash, and start a new life."

"You're the best, Cal," June said, and Lila added, "That's impressive."

Still, Lila, who'd been seeing all floating hearts and rainbows since reuniting with Travis, felt a prickle of unease. "What do you think went wrong between them?"

Again, Callie flung out her arm. "What went wrong is that he was a first class, grade-A asshole. She misread his character."

"Oh."

June's hand shot across the table and grabbed the Lila's. "But don't worry! That's not going to happen with you and Travis. He sees the error of his ways. He would never run off like he did again."

"I sure hope not."

Callie, obviously still fired up, grinned. "If he does, I'll track him down and kill him myself."

All three of their phones dinged then.

"Looks they're done and ready to head home." Callie stood up and stretched. "I hope it wasn't too brutal, reading those letters."

"Me, too," Lila and June said.

"I feel bad that Cash has to go home alone."

"Do you think he minds?" June asked.

"You know," Callie said. "I think he's the sweetest of the bunch. I think he minds more than he lets on. He loves to flirt and all the girls think he's a ladies' man, but I have a feeling he'd just as soon fall in love and settle down. I suspect he's gonna be feeling real lonely tonight."

Lila passed Sterling, Hayes, and Cash on her way back to Travis's house. Each of them nodded at her and offered a quick, "Goodnight," but none of them stopped to chat.

Her need to see Travis growing more urgent, she walked faster and was almost jogging by the time she reached his door and pushed it open.

He was waiting for her, arms outstretched. She flew into his embrace.

"How was it?" she asked when he finally set her down.

"Good." His half smile belied deeper feelings. "Hard. Sad. But good."

"Want to tell me about it?" Curiosity tugged at her.

"I do. I want to tell you everything. But first, I need to ask you something."

She nodded. "Okay. You can ask me anything."

He was on his knee in front of her, his big, warm hands wrapped around hers, his eyes staring into hers. "I've spent all this time wondering if my mom just stopped loving me—loving us. And now I know—she didn't."

"Of course she didn't." In speaking the truth—it was impossible a mother could stop loving these four—her throat clogged with emotion because she so badly wanted him to believe it.

"Reading her words—it healed something I'd held onto for a long time. And because of that, when she gave me advice at the end of the letter, I was able to take it in. You know what she told me?"

Lila shook her head. "I don't. What did she tell you?"

He sighed, and his expression softened. "She told me not to wait to do the things I need to do. And ever since I left Sweet Springs Ranch to go to Montana, I knew I needed to do this."

Excited, joyful energy buzzed through Lila's body, bouncing off her nerve endings.

"I have to ask you. Lila, will you marry me?" She gasped, and her heart leapt into her throat. He went on, "I promise, I'll screw up. I promise, I'll get my feelings hurt and probably hurt yours. But I also promise that no matter what, I'll keep trying, working to be the man you deserve. I'll give you everything I've got."

Her heart soaring, she tugged on his hands, bringing him to standing. Looking into his eyes, she said, "Travis Wilder, I'd love to marry you. I promise that I, too, will screw up and probably hurt your feelings. But I also promise that I'll do everything in my power to earn your love."

"Don't you see? You already have it." His mouth came down on hers then, rough and urgent. She leaned into the kiss, breathing in the scent of him, making a silent promise to do whatever she could to heal every single hurt he'd ever experienced.

Travis ended the kiss and hands still on her waist said, "What do you say we elope? Drive to Las Vegas and get married tomorrow?"

"Travis Wilder. I love that idea. But you have a new sister-in-law who is a professional event planner. We can't just *elope*."

"Why not? We'll let June plan a party for us when we get back. A huge reception, if she wants to."

"Okay."

"Okay?" His giant grin and raised eyebrows made keeping a straight face impossible.

"Yes. Okay. Let's do it. Let's elope to Las Vegas tomorrow."

Chapter Thirty-Eight

As always, word traveled fast amongst the Wilder brothers.

The next morning when Travis and Lila came out of his house, bags packed, Sterling, June, Hayes, Callie, and Cash waited for them, bags in hand.

Travis was only half-surprised, but pretended he hadn't expected this at all.

When Lila looked at him, he shrugged. "What can I say? I may have mentioned we'd be gone for forty-eight hours, and that no one should worry."

"So I'm driving the party bus!" Cash hooked a thumb over his shoulder at a ten-passenger van. On its windows, someone had painted, *We're going to Vegas to get married! Travis + Lila = Love! Vegas, Baby! She said, "Yes"!*

"Not exactly what I was expecting when you suggested we elope," Lila stage whispered, a huge smile on her face.

"It's even better, right?" Callie drew out the last word, making everyone laugh before they started whooping and hollering and cheering and made their way to the van.

During the four-hour drive they received lots of honks and waves, and by the time they arrived in Las Vegas, Travis was riding high on excitement.

"Two hours 'til the main event," Cash hollered back to the rest of them as he put the van in park. "The countdown is on."

Everybody cheered, and Travis figured if they hadn't already booked an officiant, he'd be just as happy hanging out with his family and the woman he loved. But then he looked across the seat at Lila, who was grinning over at him, her gaze soft, and he wanted to propose to her all over again.

"Let's get this party started!" Callie raised her arm and gave another cheer, and everyone else cheered, too.

"This is getting ridiculous," Travis said.

Lila gave him a gentle punch on the arm. "They're excited for you. That's not ridiculous."

They split up into two suites, the women in one and the men in the other.

Travis wasn't surprised when Hayes pulled a fancy bottle of bourbon out of his suitcase.

"You got the good stuff, huh?" Travis accepted a tumbler and inhaled the spicy scent of the golden liquid.

"Only the best for you, my man." He poured three more shots and when everyone held a glass, Sterling lifted his. "To true love, and finding it in the most unexpected places."

"To true love."

The twenty-second-floor suite had a view of the strip, and Travis stood at the window with his brothers, sipping bourbon and watching the buzz of activity below.

"What do you think the girls are doing?" Travis wondered out loud.

"Oh, you know what they're doing." Cash grinned. "They're getting Lila all prepped for the wedding—and the wedding *night*." He wiggled his eyebrows.

Travis elbowed him halfheartedly. "You talking about my woman's wedding night?"

Sterling grunted. "Me caveman. You talkin' 'bout my woman?"

"Seriously, man," Hayes said. "Women love this stuff. You know they're next door primping. Maybe *you* should be primping, bro."

He pulled out his phone and after a few minutes several taps on the screen, they were headed down to a barber shop to get hot shaves.

When Travis leaned back in the chair and closed his eyes, Cash said to the barber, "Careful, man. It's that guy's wedding day."

"Wedding day, huh?" The guy sounded like he'd come straight there from Boston.

"Yep."

"I remember mine." He lathered up Travis's face, his hands sure and moving quickly. "Forty-two years ago."

"You still married?"

"Of course we are. I married the love of my life, didn't I?"

Travis had to force himself not to smile as the barber started moving the razor across his face.

"How'd you know she was the love of your life?" Cash's voice came from his spot, two chairs down, surprising Travis.

"Ah. You just know, don't you? You just know. And when you find her, you fight for her. And once you marry her, son, you fight for your marriage. Some days feel like the most glorious, golden hours you've ever experienced. And others feel like a goddamn slog. But you fight for your woman, for your marriage. You hear me?"

"I hear you," Travis said.

"Young people these days, they expect things to come easy. You know what comes easy? Falling in love. But life is hard. You've got bills, schedules, your kids doing stupid shit."

While he talked, Travis imagined daily life with Lila, over the years. A feeling of deep contentment settled over him.

"You've got family dynamics, broken dishwashers, broken-down cars. Those things come and go, but you know who's the compass in every storm? Your wife. So my advice to you today, on your wedding day, is, do everything you can to make her happy. You hear me?"

"I hear you."

"You're all done. Sit up." Travis did, and the barber, dark brown eyes serious under bushy gray eyebrows, said, "Congratulations, young man. *Possano l'amore e la gioia che provate oggi accompagnarvi per sempre.* May the love and the happiness you feel today be with you forever."

Travis's throat tightened as the barber shook his hand.

"You look handsome, man." Sterling came up and put a hand on his shoulder. "*Now* you're ready to get married."

The guys went back to the hotel to change and an hour after his hot shave, Travis stood at the altar waiting for his bride. His brothers, Callie, and June sat in the first row.

Music filled the space.

And there she was at the back of the room, her gaze locked on his, her smile confident like she knew this was exactly where she was supposed to be ... and her hair the most beautiful shimmering copper color.

His mouth dropped open and he snapped it shut as tears threatened. *She is so, so beautiful.* Their gazes remained locked and he was certain he'd never smiled any bigger.

All five of their audience numbers saw his reaction and turned around in their seats—and he swore he could hear every one of them gasp when Lila came out.

Travis had no idea how the girls had managed to bring back her natural hair color, or where they had procured such a nice dress, a magical combination of lace and silk that showed off every perfect curve and made her look like an angel.

She walked up the aisle in time to the music and he could feel their hearts falling into the same rhythm. Then she was in front of him, her hands in his.

The officiant welcomed everyone and then asked Travis to repeat after him. Although Travis did, he barely knew what he was saying.

This moment mattered, of course. But all of a sudden he was becoming aware of how many moments they'd get to spend together after this one. He couldn't stop imagining everything they would do —vacations, trips to cattle auctions, quiet nights at home in front of the fire. Children one day (maybe even one or two with that fiery hair), and dogs.

He was so lucky.

"Mr. Wilder, would you like to say your vows?"

Travis nodded, excited to get through the vows so they could start their life together. "Lila. I fell in love with you sight unseen. Literally. It was the moment I heard your voice on the phone."

His brothers snickered. Lila's smile grew just a little.

"When I finally was lucky enough to see you in person, I knew you were it for me. There was something special about you. Something that tugged at my heart like no one ever had before. And then I got to know you. I was a goner. Like I said, I know things won't be perfect all the time. But they will be perfect for *us*. You are perfect for me, and I'm so grateful that I get to spend the rest of my life proving that to you."

The officiant nodded and turned to Lila.

She cleared her throat. "Travis, when I first met you, I thought you were a surly country boy." Everyone snickered at that, too. "The more I got to know you, the more I realized my first impression was right. But under that surly exterior, there is a kind, dedicated man who cares more about his family than anything else. Every day since I met you, I thank my lucky stars that our paths crossed like they did. I cannot wait to start our married life together."

The officiant beamed at Lila, then Travis, then their small audience. "With the power vested in me by the state of Nevada, I pronounce you husband and wife."

The kiss started off sweet and gentle, but when Lila made a tiny whimpering sound and relaxed into his embrace, Travis couldn't help it; he took the kiss deeper while everyone else in the room whistled and hollered. They ended the kiss and he tilted her back, then turned to face their family, hand in hand.

"May I present to you, Mr. Travis Wilder and Mrs. Lila Wilder."

Hearing his last name attached to hers and gave him a rush of joy and he gave her one more kiss before they walked back up the aisle.

The others met them in the back of the room, giving hugs all around.

"Should we go celebrate?" Cash held up a flask he'd stowed in his coat jacket, and while Hayes, Sterling, Callie, and June agreed, Travis wrapped his arms around Lila's waist.

"You guys go ahead. I can't wait another moment to be alone with my wife. The missus and I are going to retire to our honeymoon suite."

To a chorus of catcalls, the two of the two of them took their leave and headed for the hotel.

The elevator was unbearably crowded, and Travis was certain Lila could read his thoughts as he let his gaze roam over her hair and collarbone and cleavage and the curve of her waist. She flashed him a devilish smile, and by the time they got out of the elevator and made their way down the long hall to their suite, he couldn't resist tearing that dress off her, then pulling the pins out of her hair so it tumbled down her bare back. "I think I'd like to have my way with you now, Mrs. Wilder."

"Oh, please do, Mr. Wilder."

Chapter Thirty-Nine

Lila stood just outside the front door of Travis's house—*their* house—and surveyed the scene before her.

Party prep was in full swing under June's expert command. Lila and Travis's wedding reception would take place in just three days, exactly three months after they'd tied the knot.

Winter's crisp air had put a dazzling frost on the bare tree branches and the whole property sparkled in the late-morning sunlight. June had suggested an indoor reception—the first event in the big house now that construction was complete.

Still, she'd hired crews to come out and tidy up the ranch, trimming trees and shrubs, installing landscaping rock to keep the dust down, and moving construction debris and farm equipment out of the way. Another team was decorating, stringing lights and putting up signs.

The ranch felt like a buzzing hive of activity, and Lila almost couldn't believe it was all for them.

"Pretty big event, huh?" Travis came to stand next.

She leaned against him and rested her head on his shoulder. "Pretty big."

"You want to go over the list one more time?"

Lila laughed. "You're just giving me a hard time."

"No. I really think a tenth time today will ensure we've got everything covered."

"Thank you, but I'm pretty sure we're ready."

"Extra bedrooms prepped for Rebecca and your family?"

"Check."

"Dinner reservations for the night before the reception?"

"Check."

"Pre-reception blow job for your husband?"

She turned toward him and smacked his arm. "Ask me again the night before."

"You just told me you're pretty sure we're ready. I thought that meant I wasn't supposed to ask you any more questions."

"You're not. Are you ready? Have you checked off all your items?"

"I assigned them to Cash." He gave her a side eye.

"No you didn't."

"You're right. Yes, I've checked off my items. I just have to report for duty on the morning of the reception."

"Perfect." She gave him a perfunctory kiss. "Now can we go enjoy the rest of the day?"

"We can." As they walked, he said, "I'm just so excited to see the ranch coming back to life."

"Me, too."

Together, they turned toward the pasture where all the cows grazed. Beyond that, the new stables were nearly finished, and would be filled with horses within the month. To the west, crews were building a giant bunk house for the Sweet Springs Dude Ranch Experience, and they'd welcome their first batch of visitors in less than two months.

"You know," Travis said. "I spent so long being mad at my parents. At my mom for leaving and at my dad for gambling away all his savings. But the truth is, I wouldn't have met you if it wasn't for all of that."

"I hope it was worth it." She tried to keep her tone light, but she really did hope, that after all was said and done, he had begun to heal from the past and could embrace their future.

"It was. So, so worth it."

Chapter Forty

The reception was in full swing. Music played, people danced, and glasses clinked. The big house shone, a renewed and gorgeous homage to its former life as a home. Travis stood with his brothers at the edge of the dance floor. Each of them held a champagne flute and although they all claimed not to like the bubbly stuff, Travis was fairly certain they'd all picked up second or third flutes off the passing trays.

"This is an awesome evening, man." Cash lifted his glass and downed its contents.

"We should all take a drink any time anyone uses the word 'awesome,'" Hayes said.

"I mean, I think we're gonna be drinking a lot." Sterling grinned. "This is an awesome party."

"Drink."

Travis thought he may as well join in. "Lila's an awesome woman."

"Drink."

Hayes took a deep breath, held it, and let it out.

"What, man?" Sterling pointed at him.

"I'm going to be an awesome dad!" Hayes's smile was so big, it illustrated where the phrase "smiling ear to ear" had come from.

Travis wondered if his own eyes were as big as Sterling's and Cash's. And since Hayes had made the declaration, he wasn't telling them all to drink. So Travis stepped up on that front: "Yeah! Drink up, fellas!"

"You're going to be a *dad*?" Sterling grabbed Hayes by the shoulders and shook him. "That's! So! Awesome!"

Hayes held up his glass. "Drink."

The song—rock with a fast, heavy beat—ended and the DJ called Travis and Lila to the dance floor for their first dance as a married couple.

Everyone else cleared out, standing at the edge of the parquet to watch. The first strains of the music played. Travis took Lila's hand and twirled her into his embrace. They started to sway.

"I can't believe my brother's having a baby." Travis laughed, both in disbelief and at the wonder in his own voice.

"That's so wonderful. You're going to be a great uncle."

"I know I am. You know what else?"

"What?"

"Maybe we should start making babies."

Lila laughed, held onto him a little tighter. "I'm not against it, but maybe we should spend a little time being married, first."

"You're right. But we can practice, right?"

"Right. I mean, I know our marriage was legal before, but I guess this dance makes it official." Lila's breath tickled his ear and neck and made him shiver.

"Does that mean I get a post-reception blow job?"

"You're terrible."

"Is that a yes?"

"Incorrigible."

"I take it that's a yes, then."

"Irredeemable."

"I knew it."

They swayed some more.

"You know," he said. "The way everything worked out—luck, wasn't it?—I feel like we are meant to be."

"I agree." She rested her head on his chest and he rested his cheek on her head and he knew without a doubt that the words he'd spoken were true.

Lila was his just as he was hers, and they were beyond lucky to have found each other.

"I love you, Lila Wilder."

"And I love you, Travis Wilder."

"What about now?"

Chapter Forty-One

The whole group gathered the next day for tear-down and cleanup. While the men were particularly subdued—Lila had heard something about them overdoing it on champagne—the women were giddy with the news of Callie's pregnancy.

"I can't wait to find out if it's a boy or a girl." Lila hoisted a stack of folded tablecloths and started walking toward the laundry room just off the big house's main reception hall.

"Me, neither," June said as she lifted a trash bag out of the can. "I've got to start buying baby clothes now. Keep our new little niece or nephew properly outfitted."

"This baby is going to be so spoiled," Callie said, her eyes glistening with tears. "You guys are going to be the best aunties."

"We know," the other two chorused, making her laugh.

"Where did the guys get to?" June wanted to know.

"Oh, I suppose they're outside having a celebratory cigar." Callie wrinkled her nose.

Because the giant main doors were open to let in the fresh air, the sound of tires on gravel carried into the reception hall.

"Are you guys expecting anyone?" That old fear, smaller than it once was but still present, made the hairs stand up on Lila's neck.

Callie waved a hand. "It's probably a pizza delivery or something. Let's go see."

Despite her casual attitude, Lila didn't miss how her friend came to walk right beside her, slipping an arm around her waist, or how June went out first to see who'd pulled in.

A giant moving van came trundling down the driveway. In Lila's estimation the driver was going way too fast, but only for a few seconds. He or she slammed on the brakes, making the tires skid and the truck lurch. She—Lila could tell it was a woman thanks to her slim fingers and toned arms—waved apologetically before rolling down her window.

Lila hung back while Callie and June walked over there and then there was an explosion of shouting and laughter and the door was flying open and the driver was jumping down and throwing herself into Callie's arms.

"That must be Callie's friend, Opal." Travis had materialized next to her. "She's buying the place next door. Looks like she took a wrong turn."

"She seems happy to see Callie, that's for sure." Lila forced herself to breathe slow and deep, filling her lungs with oxygen and expelling it with force.

"You okay?"

"Yeah. Just had a little scare when I didn't know who was coming up the driveway."

"I get that. But look. It's a friend. You're safe."

"I am."

Callie and June were coming back, and the moving van was backing down the driveway.

"I told her she could drive around the loop, but she insisted on backing out." Callie hooked a thumb at the truck. Lila thought Opal was doing an impressive job of backing it up and she said so.

"She's a pretty independent woman," Callie said, pride filling her voice.

They watched as Opal drove the truck down the main road to the next driveway and pulled in.

Within seconds, she'd rolled open the cargo door on the back of the truck and slammed down the ramp.

"Well, if this is any indication, I don't think she's going to be the quietest neighbor." Sterling had materialized too. He took a puff on his cigar.

Their new neighbor rolled something heavy down the ramp—they could hear the wheels turning and the ramp groaning. Lila was curious. She was half-tempted to go talk to Opal, to make friends right away.

But then the music started blaring.

Travis covered his ears and Callie threw her head back and laughed. "Hasn't changed a bit."

Cash came out of nowhere, stalking down the driveway like an angry bull. Lila glanced at Travis, whose eyes went round as Cash marched all the way to the main road, took a right, and turned into what was now Opal's driveway.

If she craned her neck, Lila could just see him stalking toward the moving truck. He stopped short just even with the back of it and she assumed he'd encountered Opal. His arms waved frantically, like he was trying to convey an urgent and important message.

Then they dropped to his sides.

"I don't think this is going the way he expected." Lila leaned against Travis, who'd come to stand behind her.

"I don't, either."

Cash, his posture droopy and defeated, turned around. He straightened his back almost right away and strode with purpose back toward the main road. "But I do think this is going to be interesting."

The End

Want more from the Sweet Springs Ranch? Read Cash's story, Terrific Luck, now.

About the Author

Hilary Dartt loves great adventures, whether she's writing, reading, or living them. The author of twelve novels, Hilary lives in Arizona's high desert with her husband, their three children, and her Weimaraner, Leia. She loves camping, exploring in the Jeep, and dance parties with her kids. Learn more and sign up for her newsletter at www.hilarydartt.com.

www.ingramcontent.com/pod-product-compliance
Lightning Source LLC
Chambersburg PA
CBHW061754190726
48289CB00007B/1943